ANIMAL ARK

Where animals come first

Ben M. Baglio's

ANIMAL
Where animals come first
ARK®

Dog Days Collection

SCHOLASTIC INC.

New York Toronto London Auckland Sydney
Mexico City New Delhi Hong Kong Buenos Aires

Special thanks to C. J. Hall, B.Vet.Med., M.R.C.V.S., for reviewing
the veterinary information contained in this book.

Puppies in the Pantry, 0-590-18751-1, Copyright © 1994 by Ben M. Baglio.
Illustrations copyright © 1994 by Shelagh McNicholas.

Dog at the Door, 0-439-34386-0, Text copyright © 1997 by Working Partners Limited.
Original series created by Ben M. Baglio.
Illustrations copyright © 1997 by Jenny Gregory.

Sheepdog in the Snow, 0-590-18757-0, Copyright © 1995 by Ben M. Baglio.
Illustrations copyright © 1995 by Shelagh McNicholas.

12 11 10 9 8 7 6 5 4 3 2 1   6 7 8 9/0 1

Printed in the U.S.A.   23

ISBN 0-439-84684-6

First compilation printing, April 2006

Contents

ANIMAL ARK®

Puppies in the Pantry

Ben M. Baglio

Illustrations by Shelagh McNicholas

To Sue Welford

One

"How exciting!" said Mandy's mom, Emily Hope. "They're going to make a film at Bleakfell Hall."

Dr. Emily was busily reading the morning's mail over breakfast. She stuffed the letter back in its envelope. Breakfast at the Hopes' busy veterinary practice, Animal Ark, was always a hurried affair. Fruit juice, cereal, low-fat yogurt lately as Dr. Adam was on a diet . . . toast if you were lucky. All eaten at a huge old pine table in their oak-beamed cottage kitchen.

Mandy dragged her eyes away from her last-minute studying for a biology test that morning.

Dr. Emily took a final mouthful of juice and rose from the table. "We've been asked to check out the animals they're using," she said.

Mandy's father looked up from his newspaper. "Bleakfell Hall, huh? That'll be interesting." He stroked his dark beard thoughtfully. "Socializing with movie stars. Don't let it go to your head, Emily!"

Mandy felt a flutter of excitement in her stomach. That would be a real event for the sleepy village of Welford. Famous movie stars in their midst! Her friend James Hunter would be excited too, although she knew he really preferred soccer to movies.

"What kind of movie are they making, Mom?" Mandy tucked a strand of blond hair behind her ear. Her blue eyes sparkled. "One about animals?"

Emily Hope smiled. "Trust you to think of that, Mandy." She stood in front of the mirror, ran a comb hurriedly through her long red hair, then tied it back with a green silk scarf. "Apparently it's a Victorian murder mystery."

"Wow! Bleakfell Hall's just the place then. I've always thought it was kind of spooky. Hear that, Jess?"

Jess, a small Jack Russell terrier, sat at Mandy's feet. Mandy fed her a piece of toast secretly. One huge gulp and it was gone. The terrier gave a little woof.

"Don't think I didn't see that, Mandy." Dr. Adam had a twinkle in his eye. "She's getting quite pudgy. What's Auntie Mary going to say if she comes back from Australia and Jess has put on ten pounds?"

Mandy giggled. She had been so excited when her Aunt Mary had asked the Hopes to look after Jess for a couple of months while she went to Australia for a university course.

"You know I can't resist those brown eyes, Dad." Mandy bent to give the little dog an affectionate hug.

"You can't resist any animal that crosses your path," Dr. Adam said.

Mandy grinned. She scratched Jess behind the ear. "You love toast, don't you, Jess?" Having the terrier stay at Animal Ark was like heaven to Mandy.

Since turning twelve, Mandy Hope had been allowed to help out at her parents' veterinary practice, Animal Ark, in the pretty Yorkshire village of Welford. Mandy cleaned out cages, helped comfort sick animals . . . nothing was too much trouble. Mandy just couldn't wait to grow up and become a vet herself!

"Well?" Adam Hope looked expectantly at his wife. "Come on, spill the beans. What animals are they using for the movie? Chimps, elephants . . . ?"

"That would be *really* great!" Mandy swallowed her last mouthful of toast and rose from the table.

Dad was teasing, of course. Even if it was only cats and dogs, Mandy thought it would be fabulous to go and see them. She might even get to see a real movie star in the process!

Dr. Emily laughed. "I don't know exactly. The letter didn't say very much. Just that the animals are being supplied by an agency called Animal Stars and that the company will hire horses from the local stables. They all have to be examined by the vet before they can use them. And . . . oh, yes . . . they mention a dog. Apparently it's one of the stars of the film."

"What kind of a dog?" Mandy asked.

Her mother shook her head. "I don't know. Sorry, Mandy."

"Perhaps it's a mystery dog?" Mandy's imagination began to run away with her. "Like in that Sherlock Holmes story, *The Hound of the Baskervilles.*"

Dr. Emily gave her daughter a quick hug. "You'll just have to be patient, Mandy. They're not coming until Monday." She planted a kiss on top of her head. "Since you will be on midterm vacation, you can come up with me if you like."

"Mom, that would be great!" Mandy exclaimed.

Dr. Emily glanced at the clock. "Got to rush," she said. "Time I opened the office."

Mandy could hear a puppy's excited yelp from the waiting room of the vet's clinic attached to the back of the old stone cottage. She would have loved to go and see the puppy but there was no time. School and the dreaded biology test beckoned.

Dr. Adam folded up his newspaper with a sigh. "Yup, I'd better get going, too. I have to inspect a consignment of beef cattle arriving at Walton market."

"Time for me to go, too." Mandy gave Jess a last hug. She hated leaving the little terrier shut up in the kitchen while she was at school. If Mandy had had her way she would have tucked Jess into her backpack and carried her off to class. She grabbed her backpack. "I guess James is waiting."

"No racing to school on that bike of yours," Dr. Adam warned.

"I won't Dad . . . bye, Jess," Mandy said. "See you later."

"And don't slam the door as you go out," Dr. Adam shouted from the sink.

The front door banged loudly as Mandy went out.

The following Monday morning there was a ring at the back door.

"I'll go," Mandy called from the front room where she had been playing with Jess.

The terrier was ahead of her, hurtling down the corridor like a bullet.

"If it's anyone for me . . ." Dr. Adam dodged away from the speeding terrier. He donned his green jacket and tweed cap. ". . . I'm off to Baildon Farm. One of Jack Mabson's cows has mastitis. I should be back in about an hour."

"Poor thing," Mandy muttered. She knew the inflammation of a cow's udder was very painful. "You'd better hurry up then, Dad."

Dr. Adam was checking his bag. "If it's anything urgent, Mom can go after surgery. Or better still, get them to make an appointment with Jean."

"Yes, Dad." Mandy almost pushed her father out of the front door. The sooner he got to Baildon and treated that poor cow, the happier Mandy would be.

By now Jess was hurling herself at the back door with the ferocity of a tiger, and barking furiously.

Mandy ran to grab her collar. "Jess, for goodness sake, we're not being invaded by aliens." Mandy swooped the noisy little dog up in her arms.

The antics of the Jack Russell always amused her. She would miss Jess so much when Aunt Mary came back. Mandy had three pet rabbits and she loved them dearly. But they weren't quite as much fun as the little terrier.

Mandy's best friend, James Hunter, stood on the doorstep.

"Oh . . . hi, James."

James looked cold. The wind ruffled his straight brown hair. Mandy thought he looked a little like a Shetland pony but didn't say so. She knew James was sensitive and she wouldn't have hurt his feelings for all the world.

Blackie, the Hunters' black Labrador, sat at James's feet. As soon as he saw Jess, Blackie wagged his tail like mad. Jess barked and wriggled furiously. Mandy put her down. The two dogs tore off around the garden, jumping and barking.

Mandy winced. Her dad wouldn't be at all pleased if they crashed through the flower beds. The two dogs had been great friends from the first moment Jess had come to stay at Animal Ark.

"Blackie!" James called. "Come here!" The Labrador ignored him, dashing around the garden after the agile terrier. James sighed. "That dog never listens. Blackie!" Blackie gave one last excited bark and ran to sit at James's feet. He looked up at James as if to say "sorry."

James adjusted his glasses on the bridge of his nose. "I thought you might want to go for a walk, Mandy," he said.

"Oh, James, I'm sorry," said Mandy. "I'm going out with Mom when the office closes."

James raised his eyebrows. "Anywhere nice?"

"To Bleakfell Hall. Remember, I told you last Friday, James. The movie."

James clapped his hand to his forehead. "Of course you did . . . how stupid. Sorry, Mandy, I forgot."

"We'll be back later. I'll give you a call. We could go out then."

"Okay," James said. "Come on, Blackie. We'll have to go on our own this morning." He made a face. "Looks like I'll have to do that shopping for Mom after all."

Mandy smiled. She knew James hated going shopping. He would rather be playing with his computer or helping Mandy at Animal Ark.

"If we have to go to Bleakfell Hall again, James, I'll ask Mom if you could come, if you want."

James grinned. "That would be great. I'd love to." He waved. "See you later, Mandy."

Jess was digging a hole in the flower bed. Blackie had run off and stood watching.

Mandy whistled. "Jess, Dad'll go bonkers if you dig up any more of his plants!"

James waved again as he clipped on Blackie's leash and headed off toward the village green.

Mandy felt guilty. James had looked a little down-hearted. She sighed. She'd buy him an ice cream later to make up for it. And, if they were lucky, next time they had to go, James could come, too.

Half an hour later Dr. Emily's four-wheel drive wound its way up the narrow road to Bleakfell Hall. The sun was warm on the windshield. Crossing the river bridge, Mandy could see its rays hitting the water in a shower of silver sparks. She stared out of the window. The jigsaw pattern of green fields and dry-stone walls flashed past. Mandy opened the window and took a deep breath of fresh country air. Her heart drummed with excitement. Visiting movie stars was definitely a great way to spend the first day of midterm vacation!

They turned a corner, and hundred-year-old Bleakfell Hall loomed at the end of its long gravel

drive. Its towers and turrets really did look like something out of a murder mystery story.

"I said it looked spooky." Mandy peered up at the gray stone house.

Several cars and two huge trailers were parked by the stables. One of the trailers had "Curtis-Smith Films Limited" written on the side in black letters.

They drew up outside the dark, oak-paneled front door.

"Doesn't Mrs. Ponsonby live here anymore?" Mandy asked. Mrs. Ponsonby was one of the bossiest women in town, and definitely a force to be reckoned with.

"Yes, I saw her in the post office on Saturday

morning," Mandy's mom confirmed. "But she's gone to stay with her sister while they're using the house. The film company pays tons of money, apparently."

Mandy's eyes lit up. "Hey," she said thoughtfully. "How about offering them an old stone cottage with a vet's office attached? Then we could get lots of money, too!"

"Mandy!" Her mother laughed. "You should be ashamed."

"Not at all," Mandy said. "We could give it to the animal sanctuary." Mandy's heart lurched with pity when she thought about all the pathetic and abandoned animals the sanctuary took in.

Dr. Emily smiled at her daughter. "Mrs. Ponsonby really needs the money, too. Apparently some of the old house is almost falling down."

"Oh. I hope it doesn't collapse while they're filming." Mandy took a wary look at the massive chimneys.

"I don't think it will, Mandy. Come on. We'd better find out who's in charge."

"It'll be great having movie stars staying near the village," Mandy said as she got out. "I might get their autographs. The girls at school would be really jealous." She looked around. "I wonder where the animals are?"

"Let's find out." Dr. Emily took her vet's bag from the car.

They went up the flight of elegant stone steps that led to the front door. Dr. Emily pressed the old-fashioned doorbell.

Mandy's heart pounded with excitement as she heard light footsteps coming toward the door. It swung open. A blond-haired young man in jeans and a college sweatshirt stood in the doorway. He held a clipboard in his hand.

"Good morning," said Dr. Emily. "I'm Emily Hope, the vet. I've been asked to take a look at the animals. I hope it's convenient."

The young man grinned. Behind him, Mandy could see three or four people with ladders. They seemed to be setting up huge lights in the hallway.

"Hi," the young man said. "I'm Ben Burton, Mr. Curtis's personal assistant. Mr. Curtis is the director."

"This is my daughter, Mandy."

Mandy smiled, feeling shy. It wasn't every day she got to meet a movie director's assistant!

"You'll find Mr. Baggins and the others in the kitchen," Ben explained, stepping back for them to enter.

Mandy gulped. "Mr. Baggins. Who's he?"

Ben's eyes twinkled. "You'd better go and see."

Inside, the house seemed to echo with hammering and banging. From the top of the wide, winding staircase Mandy heard a woman shouting something. The whole place was buzzing.

Suddenly a head appeared over the first floor banister. "Ben, Mr. Curtis wants you — now!" a young woman with a white scarf tied around her head and red dangly earrings shouted down.

"Oh, dear." Ben looked slightly flustered. "He'll go ape if I don't go right away. Go through into the kitchen, Dr. Hope, Mandy. Someone there will help you." He ran his hand through his hair. "To be honest, I'm not sure about anything at the moment. Got to go!" He ran up the staircase two steps at a time.

"But . . ." Dr. Emily looked at her daughter and shrugged. "Oh, well," she said. "Let's see if we can find the kitchen and Mr. Baggins, whoever he might be!"

"Maybe he's the man in charge of the animals. Funny name, though," Mandy added.

Crossing the hall seemed sort of dangerous. There were thick cables absolutely everywhere on the floor. Ladders trembled overhead. Workmen with hammers in their belts scurried around like ants.

"It's like that obstacle course at the adventure

center," Mandy remarked, hopping over a thick cable that snaked across the floor.

"I think this is it." Dr. Emily pushed open a large oak door. "I was here once before, when Mrs. Ponsonby's Pekingese was sick."

The door led them into a dark, oak-paneled corridor. Another door at the end was ajar. From inside a voice screeched.

"She loves you yeah, yeah, yeah! She loves you yeah, yeah, yeah! A cup of tea with two sugars, cup of tea with two sugars!"

Mandy's mom turned to look at her. They both giggled.

"I bet I know who that is!" Mandy skipped on ahead. She couldn't wait to see the owner of that strange voice.

Two

Mandy pushed open the door. She had guessed the voice came from a parrot. And there he was, sitting on the edge of the table in the huge Victorian kitchen. Beady, black eyes stared at her.

"Oh!" Mandy breathed. "Mom, he's gorgeous!"

She stepped forward and stretched out her hand to stroke the bright red and green feathers.

"This has to be Mr. Baggins," Mandy said. The bird arched its neck in response to Mandy's gentle caress.

"Two cups of tea and a sugar," it murmured in a funny, soft voice. Mandy loved the feel of his feath-

ers against her fingertips. Scratchy, yet soft at the same time.

"Who's a pretty boy, then?" she said softly.

A thump, thump came from over by the fire. Curled up on a chair was a beautiful black Labrador. Her long, silky tail beat a welcome to Mandy and Dr. Emily.

"Hello, old girl." Dr. Emily crouched down to pet the dog. "Her name's Charley," she said, examining the tag on the dog's red collar.

"She's beautiful," Mandy said, stroking behind Charley's ears. "I bet she's the star of the movie."

There was more. Three sleek cats were curled up on the fireside rug. One purred gently, its pink nose turned upwards. All had soft, red collars with silver tags.

"This one's Snowy . . ." Mandy looked at the tag, ". . . and this one's Echo. What lovely names." Echo, a small tabby cat, stirred and stretched lazily under Mandy's loving fingers.

"What's the gray one called?" Dr. Emily asked.

"Sky. These must be the 'others' Ben told us about."

"I guess so." Dr. Emily looked around. "I wonder who's in charge of them."

Just then a tall, burly man came in through the back door. He wiped his boots on the mat. Mandy

heard him sniff, then snort. He was wearing a green quilted jacket and a flat cap. His ears stuck out like jug handles and he had a rough, red face.

Charley jumped off the chair. She eyed the man suspiciously and sat down on the floor beside Mandy, pressing herself against Mandy's legs. Mandy had a strange feeling. It was as if Charley had suddenly decided Mandy was her owner — as if she wanted Mandy to look after and protect her. Mandy put her hand down and let it rest softly on Charley's sleek head. A small whine came from the Labrador's throat.

"It's okay, Charley," Mandy whispered. "I'll look after you, don't worry. There's no need to be nervous." But it was clear at once to Mandy that Charley wasn't at all fond of the man who had just come into the kitchen.

"Good morning," the man said in a deep, gravelly voice.

"Good morning." Dr. Emily held out her hand.

"I'm Emily Hope, the vet. This is my daughter, Mandy."

The man shook Dr. Emily's hand and nodded to Mandy. "George Sims," he said gruffly.

"Perhaps you can help, George," Dr. Emily went on. "We're looking for the person in charge of these animals."

Mr. Sims tipped his cap to the back of his head. "It looks like I am," he muttered.

Dr. Emily frowned. "I don't understand."

He pulled out a chair and sat down. Charley was still sitting against Mandy's legs. She felt the dog jump nervously at the sound of the chair legs scraping on the flagstone floor.

"There's been a bit of a problem," Mr. Sims explained. "I do work for Animal Stars but I'm really only the driver. The girl who's supposed to supervise the animals hasn't turned up."

"What's happened to her?" Dr. Emily asked.

Mr. Sims shrugged. "Not really sure — some mix-up about locations. She's gone off to France to do a commercial for pet food when she should be here with this movie."

"Oh, dear," said Dr. Emily.

"They've asked me to stay until she turns up," Mr. Sims went on grumpily. "I mean, what do I know about looking after a parrot?"

Mr. Baggins squawked, *"Mr. Sugar, cup of bags."*

Mandy giggled, then put her hand over her mouth.

"Well," Dr. Emily said, "I'm sure we could give you any advice you need. Especially if it's only for a day or so. I'm sure the agency will send someone as soon as possible."

"I certainly hope so," Mr. Sims said, still looking grumpy.

Snowy, the white cat, got up from his place by the fire. Purring, he rubbed himself against Mr. Sims's corduroy trousers, arching his back and waving his tail like a flag.

Mr. Sims moved his legs away. Mandy stepped forward and picked Snowy up, cradling him in her arms.

"Can't stand cats," George Sims muttered. He glared at Mr. Baggins. "Nor parrots."

Mr. Baggins stared back at him with beady eyes.

"Left, right, left, right, quick march!" Mr. Baggins suddenly screeched.

Mandy put her hand over her mouth to stop herself from bursting into laughter.

"Bah!" said Mr. Sims.

Mandy bit her lip, suddenly feeling serious. How on earth could anyone dislike either Snowy or Mr. Baggins? Both of them were beautiful and perfectly harmless.

"Right," Dr. Emily went on in a businesslike way. "My job is to examine the animals. Should I do it here?"

George Sims shrugged. "If you like."

Charley suddenly got up and ran through a door beside the old pine dresser.

"Charley!" Mandy called. "Where's she going?" she asked Mr. Sims.

"She's made her bed in the pantry," Mr. Sims said. "Best place for her. Keeps her out of the way until she's needed."

Mandy felt sorry for the Labrador, hiding away in a cold pantry when a cozy fire burned in the hearth.

"Who shall I give the certificate to?" Dr. Emily was asking.

"Certificate?" Mr. Sims looked blank.

"Yes, I have to pass the animals as fit before the film company can use them."

"Leave it on the table if you want. I'll pick it up after my break."

Mandy was trying to persuade Charley to come out of the pantry.

"Come on, Charley. Mom wants to have a look at you."

"I would leave her," Mr. Sims said, opening the back door. "She's a bit moody, if you ask me."

"Well, she is an actor," Mandy said. She thought George Sims might feel moody, too, if he was being looked after by someone who didn't like him.

Mr. Sims snorted. He went out and slammed the door behind him.

"He's not too crazy about animals, is he, Mom?" Mandy said. She coaxed the Labrador out of the pantry. "Come on, Charley, Mom won't hurt you."

"I think Mr. Sims is just worried," Dr. Emily replied. "He's had the job just thrust upon him, by the looks of it. Let's hope the real trainer arrives soon."

Mandy sat on the floor with her arms around the Labrador's neck. She rubbed her cheek against the shining coat. Her heart stirred. If George Sims just took time to get to know Charley, he'd soon find out how gorgeous she was.

"Come on, Charley." Dr. Emily lifted the big dog onto the table. "Let's have a look at you."

She examined the dog gently. Ears . . . eyes . . . teeth. All looked fine. She felt Charley's sleek, muscled back and ran her hands over her legs. She held Charley's head between her hands and looked at her muzzle. Then she ruffled the hair on the back of Charley's head and lifted her down.

"She's great," Dr. Emily said. "The picture of health."

"Are you going to look at Mr. Baggins?" Mandy asked when her mom had finished examining the three cats.

"Mr. Baggins . . . Mr. Baggins!" the parrot suddenly screeched. *"A cup of tea and two Baggins."*

Mandy burst out laughing. Dr. Emily laughed, too. "Yes, but I'm almost certain there's nothing wrong with him," she said.

Dr. Emily carefully wrapped the bird in a dish towel and gently examined him. She stroked the parrot's feathers and put him back on the table. "His claws look a little long but nothing to worry about."

Suddenly Mr. Baggins took off, flying up and landing on one of the high oak beams of the ceiling.

"I wonder what part he plays in the film?" Mandy asked.

"A naughty part, I would think." Dr. Emily took a book from her bag. She sat at the table and wrote something on one of the pages. "I think I'd better wait to explain these certificates to George."

"Do you think it's okay if I take a look around the house?" Mandy asked. "I'd love to see the movie set."

"I think so. Don't get in anyone's way, though. It looked pretty chaotic out there."

"I'll take Charley." Mandy saw a dog leash hanging from a hook on the back door.

"And don't be too long," Dr. Emily added. "I have to go by Mrs. Platt's on the way back."

Mandy's heart skipped a beat. She knew Mrs. Platt's poodle had been ill for a long time. "Not Brandy again?" she said anxiously.

Dr. Emily looked grim. "Yes, I'm afraid so. Mrs. Platt called this morning and asked me to stop in to look at him."

"Oh, dear." Mandy's heart sank. Brandy, Mrs. Platt's poodle, was very old and had trouble with his kidneys. Mandy had a horrible feeling that this time there wouldn't be any pills that would make him better.

Dr. Emily patted Mandy's arm. "Cheer up, Mandy. It may not be as bad as you think."

"I hope not," Mandy said. "I don't know what Mrs. Platt will do without a dog. She'll be really lonely."

Mrs. Platt's husband had died over a year ago. Since then Brandy had been her only companion. She had a son, but he lived miles away in London and couldn't visit very often.

Mandy pulled herself together There was no use worrying about it. Whatever happened, neither Mrs. Platt nor her mom would want poor Brandy to suffer.

"Come on, Charley," she said. "Let's see if we can spot any movie stars out there."

In the hall, a single huge spotlight was being erected in the corner. A short, balding man with an extremely large stomach and a loud voice to match was shouting instructions. He wore an out-of-shape gray T-shirt that announced he was "The Boss."

"No, point it this way!" he yelled. "We want it to look as if the light's coming through the window, not from a hole in the ceiling!"

"Hello, young lady." The man had spotted Mandy. "Are you the animal trainer?"

"Er — no," Mandy stammered. "I'm Mandy Hope, the vet's daughter. I'm just taking Charley for a little look around."

The man bent down to pat Charley affectionately. Mandy could see he liked dogs. She always knew when people were good with animals. And, as far as Mandy was concerned, anyone who liked animals had to be a nice person.

"Is Charley the star?" Mandy asked.

"She sure is." The man looked over his shoulder. "But don't tell Antonia that."

"Antonia?"

"Miss Antonia Kent. Our *human* star."

Mandy giggled.

"The dog sees it all happen."

"Gosh!" Mandy's eyes were wide. "Sees what . . . not the murder?"

The man looked somber. "Yes, the dirty deed itself. The lady of the manor stabs her husband in a fit of jealousy in this very hallway. Her pet dog — she's called Black Rose in the story — witnesses the terrible crime."

Mandy was staring at him, wide-eyed. "Wow!" She felt quite breathless.

"Why don't you stay to watch the filming?" the man said. "Maybe Charley will give a truly great performance if you're here. You two certainly look as if you're great friends already."

"We are." Mandy grinned. She felt pleased the man had noticed how well she and Charley were getting along. She patted Charley's head affectionately. "I'd love to stay and watch." Then she re-membered something important she had to do. Her face fell. "Oh . . . but I can't. I'm sorry. I have to go back with my mom."

Mandy would have loved to have stayed with Charley. But she had to see Mrs. Platt's dear little Brandy. And if he was so ill that nothing could be done to cure him, then Mrs. Platt might need a shoulder to cry on.

Just then, Ben came running down the stairs.

"There you are, Mr. Curtis!"

"Mr. Curtis!" Mandy gasped. She hadn't realized the man really was "The Boss"!

"I've been looking all over for you," Ben went on. "Miss Kent's throwing a tantrum again."

The sound of crashing china came from one of the upstairs rooms. *Oh dear*, Mandy thought. *That's not all she's throwing.*

Mr. Curtis sighed heavily. "What now, Ben?"

"She says she won't work with a parrot. She says she's allergic to birds and that it might have fleas or something."

"Fleas!" Mandy couldn't help blurting out. "Mr. Baggins has nothing of the sort."

Mr. Curtis sighed again. He turned to Mandy. "These actresses are so temperamental. I'd better go and calm her down. Ben, look after this young lady, will you?"

Just then Dr. Emily came through from the kitchen. Charley wagged her tail in greeting.

"Mom," Mandy said. "This is Mr. Curtis, the director."

Dr. Emily shook his hand. "The animals are all fine," she said. "You can begin using them whenever you're ready." She handed him the certificate. "I was going to give this to George Sims but I can't wait any longer."

Mandy saw Ben and Mr. Curtis exchange worried glances.

"I'm afraid he's not turning out to be very reliable," Ben said with a frown. "Let's hope the real trainer turns up soon."

"Yes," Dr. Emily agreed. "Let's hope so."

Mr. Curtis strode off up the stairs.

Ben took Charley's leash from Mandy's hand and ushered them to the front door.

"Could I bring my friend James next time?" asked Mandy. "He's crazy about animals."

"I don't see why not," Ben replied. "And since George doesn't seem to have much idea what to do with them, it looks as if we might be very glad to have your help!"

Three

"I'm a little worried about Charley," Mandy said as they drove back down into Welford. They went along the main street, past the church, past the Old School House adult education center that used to be the village school until a few years ago. They soon reached the section of modern homes where Mrs. Platt lived with Brandy.

"Why?" Mandy's mother glanced in her direction.

"She just doesn't seem very happy." Mandy had been worrying about Charley ever since they left the hall. "A dog needs love and affection, not a smelly old blanket on the floor of a cold pantry."

Dr. Emily patted her daughter's knee. "She's

okay, Mandy. She's just taking a little time to settle down. Remember how Jess was when she first came to stay with us?"

Mandy managed a small smile. "Yes," she said. "I think she missed her boyfriend."

"Who, Tad?" Tad was the Jack Russell that lived next door to Aunt Mary. Dr. Emily laughed. "Yes, I think you're right, Mandy. And don't worry about Charley. We'll keep a good eye on her."

Mandy felt reassured. Her mother was always right.

They drew up outside a semidetached home with a large back garden at the end of the block. They got out and went around past rows of neatly planted vegetables to the back door.

Mrs. Platt hurried to answer their knock.

"Thank goodness you're here," she said anxiously. "I was afraid I'd missed you. I just had to run over to the church to change the water in the vases." Mrs. Platt was well known in the village for her floral arrangements. "Come in, come in."

The kitchen was warm and cozy. Pots and pans shone on the shelves and bright red-and-blue curtains adorned the windows.

"I've kept the radiator on for poor Brandy," Mrs. Platt explained. "I thought he might feel better if he was tucked up nice and warm." Her voice trembled a little. Mandy felt sorry for Mrs. Platt.

Brandy, a miniature champagne poodle, lay in his basket. Mandy felt her throat swell and her eyes began to fill with tears. The little dog's eyes were red and weepy, and his coat looked dull. "Poor Brandy," she whispered. She remembered Brandy when he was bright and active, a darling, friendly little animal. She crouched down beside the basket.

Dr. Emily gently probed the dog's swollen stomach. Her fingers touched a tender spot and the poodle gave a little whine. Mandy winced. She wished she could take the dog's pain away.

Dr. Emily rose. Her face looked sad. "I'm sorry, Mrs. Platt. If those tablets I gave him last week haven't worked . . ."

Mrs. Platt shook her head. "He did seem a bit better. We even went for a little walk yesterday when I got in from church. But this morning he wouldn't even get out of his basket. I had to carry him out to do his business."

Mandy stroked Brandy's curly coat. The little dog felt hot, and his nose was dry. She felt a tear creep from beneath her eyelid and trickle down her cheek. It fell on Brandy's fur.

"He's in a good deal of pain, I'm afraid," Dr. Emily

was saying. "I really think the kindest thing would be to put him to sleep."

Mandy looked up through a mist of tears. Her mom had her arm around Mrs. Platt's shoulders.

"Yes," Mrs. Platt nodded. "You're right, of course. We can't let him suffer. If you're absolutely sure . . . ?"

Dr. Emily nodded sadly. "I can give him an injection now, or you could bring him along to the office."

"No . . . no." Mrs. Platt took a hanky from her pants' pocket and blew her nose loudly. "Brandy would want to go to sleep in his own basket."

Dr. Emily opened her bag and took out a syringe.

Mandy wiped her eyes with the back of her hand. She drew in a deep breath. It really was no good crying. All the tears in the world wouldn't make Brandy better. She tried to pull herself together. "Would you like me to help you, Mom?"

"No, it's all right, thanks. Why don't you take Mrs. Platt into the garden? Take a look at those beautiful roses. Unless you want to stay?"

Mrs. Platt shook her head. "No. I'm not very good at this sort of thing." She knelt down by Brandy's basket. The little dog lifted his head at the sight of his mistress. Mrs. Platt stroked his head gently. Mandy could see she was crying.

Mrs. Platt bent and touched Brandy's head with

her lips. Mandy put a hand out to steady her as she rose to her feet.

"Come on, Mrs. Platt. Let's see those roses."

Mandy shut the door gently behind them. She swallowed the tears that threatened to spill over once again. There seemed to be a hard lump in her throat.

She linked her arm through Mrs. Platt's as they walked slowly up the garden path. Mrs. Platt blew her nose once, then seemed to recover.

"There's no use crying," she said in a determined voice. "Brandy has had a wonderful life. He's been treated like a little prince. It's wrong to let him suffer."

Mandy managed a sad little smile. "Yes." Mrs.

Platt was right, of course, but it was still horrible to think they would never see Brandy alive again.

"See this . . ." Mrs. Platt pointed to a pink climbing rose just coming into flower. "I brought this with me from my old house. My husband gave it to me for my birthday — the same birthday my son gave Brandy to me." She sighed. "What a gorgeous little puppy Brandy was. Nothing but a bundle of fluff with two huge black eyes —" Her voice broke. "He's thirteen years old, you know, Mandy."

"Same age as me," Mandy said softly. They looked at each other and smiled. There was a bond of understanding between them. Brandy wouldn't be running in the garden anymore, but at least Mrs. Platt had this beautiful rose to remember him by.

"Will you get another dog?" Mandy asked as they reached the end of the garden and looked out toward the high meadows. She felt a bit better. It was time to think about the future and not the past.

Mrs. Platt shook her head. "I'm afraid I can't afford one. I don't earn much with my little job at the grocer's shop."

Mandy turned to see her mother standing by the back door drying her hands on a towel. They walked back toward her.

"How . . . ?" Mrs. Platt began. Mandy heard a tremble in her voice.

"He just went to sleep peacefully," Dr. Emily assured her.

Mandy squeezed Mrs. Platt's arm.

"What would you like me to do with Brandy, now, Mrs. Platt?" Dr. Emily asked gently. "I've wrapped him in his blanket."

Mandy looked past her mom and Mrs. Platt. She could just see a pathetic little bundle wrapped in a blue blanket lying in Brandy's basket. She felt the tears coming again but managed to hold them back.

"I'll see to him, don't worry," replied Mrs. Platt. "I'll bury him beneath the roses. He'll like it there. It was his favorite place on a hot summer's day. Nice and shady."

Mandy could just imagine Brandy as he used to be, and she knew they had done the right thing.

"How much do I owe you, Emily?" Mrs. Platt said in a practical voice. She squared her shoulders. Mandy admired her bravery. She didn't think she would ever get used to animals having to die this way.

"Don't worry about that. I'll get Jean to send the bill at the end of the month."

Mandy gave Mrs. Platt a hug. "I hope you won't be too lonely."

Mrs. Platt managed a wan smile. "Maybe I'll get a parrot. They're not so expensive to keep."

"No, but you can't take a parrot for a walk," Mandy said sadly.

Mrs. Platt watched from the window as they drove away. Mandy thought she looked so lonely with no little dog to cuddle in her arms.

They headed straight back to Animal Ark. The main street of the village was quiet.

Dr. Emily patted her daughter's knee. "Cheer up, Mandy."

"I'm trying to," Mandy said. "I just know how Mrs. Platt will miss poor Brandy."

"I know darling."

Mandy looked thoughtful. "You know, Mom, Mrs. Platt would really love another poodle. She just can't afford one."

"They are pretty expensive." Dr. Emily changed gears to go around the sharp curve.

"I know. That's what she said. I've been thinking."

"What?" Dr. Emily glanced knowingly at her daughter. "What scheme are you cooking up now, Mandy?"

"I just thought maybe they'd have one at the animal sanctuary."

"Yes, they might." Dr. Emily raised her eyebrows.

Mandy fidgeted in her seat. "Could we go up there now?"

"Hang on a minute, Mandy. Give Mrs. Platt time to get over poor old Brandy."

"But having a new pet will help her," Mandy insisted. Once Mandy had an idea in her head, wild horses wouldn't drag it away.

"We'll go as soon as your dad or I have a spare minute. Does that suit you?"

Mandy sighed. "Yes, okay, but you won't forget, will you?"

"I don't suppose you'll let me!"

They pulled up under the wooden sign that said "Animal Ark, Veterinary Clinic."

Mandy jumped out, anxious to see Jess. She felt better now. The thought of finding a new dog for Mrs. Platt had cheered her up.

"I'll just check with Jean to see if there have been any calls." Dr. Emily headed for the office door.

Mandy hurried through into the kitchen. Jess was curled up in her basket, fast asleep. She hadn't even heard the door open.

"Jess!"

The little dog opened her eyes sleepily as Mandy bent to cuddle her.

"Jess," Mandy said again. "You lazy old thing. You

didn't even hear me come in. You're getting to be a real lazybones."

Jess licked her face. Mandy picked her up and gave her a quick cuddle.

Mandy went to the phone and dialed James's number. He answered after a dozen rings.

"Oh . . ." Mandy said. "I was just about to give up."

"Sorry," James said. "I was playing with my new computer game."

Mandy screwed up her nose. She hated computer games. "Do you still want to come over later?" she asked.

"You bet. How did it go at Bleakfell Hall?"

"It was great. I'll tell you all about it when you get here."

After lunch, Mandy helped Simon, Animal Ark's nurse, with his jobs at the back of the office. Simon was laying newspapers on the bottom of one of the animal cages. Mandy was washing and drying the feed bowls.

"Simon?" Mandy said. "Any idea if the animal sanctuary would have a poodle for Mrs. Platt?"

Simon, a young man in his twenties, tall and thin with fair hair, shrugged his shoulders. "I don't know, Mandy. I know they get all sorts of dogs turned in."

Mandy breathed a sigh. "Aren't people horrible?" she said, suddenly feeling angry as she always did at the thought of all the abandoned and unwanted animals at the sanctuary.

Simon gave a little smile. "*Some* people are, Mandy. Not everyone."

"You know what I mean." Mandy thought of Simon as a good friend. Someone to talk things over with if her mom and dad were too busy to listen right away.

"I mean people who abandon animals," Mandy went on, still feeling angry. "Remember that cat I found? Walton. We thought someone had abandoned her because she was pregnant. I was so angry. Why don't people realize a pet is for life, not something you can throw away like . . . like . . ." Mandy felt so indignant all of a sudden she couldn't think of the right word.

"Like an empty cereal box?" Simon suggested.

"Exactly," Mandy said.

"You know it's not always people's own fault." Simon tried to calm her down. "Sometimes people move and can't take their pet . . . sometimes they just can't cope with them any longer."

"Yes, I suppose so," Mandy agreed. "But people *should* be more responsible."

"Can't argue with that," Simon said with a grin.

Mandy stacked the feed bowls inside one another and put the damp towel in the dirty linen basket. She looked at her watch. "Is there anything else I can do to help, Simon? James should be here in a minute. We're taking the dogs for a walk."

"No, thanks, Mandy." Simon was washing his hands. "That's great."

Just then James arrived. He handed Mandy a container of sherbet. "I got you this at the store," he said, grinning. "I know it's your favorite."

Mandy was going to hug him, then thought he might be embarrassed in front of Simon. "Thanks, James," she said. "Come on. I'll tell you all about Charley, the movie star dog."

Four

The next morning Mandy jumped out of bed. The garden sparkled in the morning sun. There had been a storm in the night. Mandy had woken once to a tremendous crack of thunder.

She had a tight knot of excitement in her stomach. If she was lucky George Sims would call from Bleakfell Hall today to say the horses had arrived. She would get to see Charley and Mr. Baggins again!

But when the telephone rang, it was Grandpa.

"Will you be coming to see us during vacation, Mandy?" he asked as she picked up the receiver.

Mandy smiled. She loved visiting her grandparents at Lilac Cottage, just up the lane from Animal Ark.

"Yes, of course, Grandpa. I'm hoping to go out with Mom this morning, but James and I could come over later if you like."

"Oh, good. Your Grandma's trying out this new recipe for chocolate orange cake and she thought you might like to try it," Grandpa said.

"Yum," said Mandy. "We'll definitely be over later, Grandpa."

Mandy felt restless. She had her chores to do in the office but couldn't seem to settle down to anything. Luckily, the call from Bleakfell Hall came just a few minutes later.

"The horses have arrived," Dr. Emily said, popping her head around the door.

"Great!" Mandy said excitedly, full of energy all of a sudden. "I'll call James."

James arrived on his bike just as they were getting in the car. Mandy could see he had rushed. His sweatshirt was on backwards, but she figured she'd wait to tell him.

Jess climbed onto James's lap, curled up, and fell asleep right away.

When they arrived at Bleakfell Hall they could hear a lot of shouting from inside.

They left Jess curled up in the back of the car, making sure to leave the windows open.

"Maybe we'd better go around to the yard," Dr. Emily suggested. "It sounds as if they're pretty busy in there. I know where the stables are."

"Let's go and find Charley," Mandy said to James.

There was no answer to their knock on the back door. Cautiously, Mandy opened it and poked her head around.

"Hello . . . anybody here?" She turned to James. "Come on, I'm sure they won't mind if we go in."

The vast kitchen was empty. No Charley, no Mr. Baggins, no cats, no George Sims. Where on earth was everyone?

The sound of Mr. Curtis's voice came echoing along the passage that led to the great hallway.

Mandy pulled James's sleeve. "Come on, let's take a look. Maybe all the animals are on the set."

They crept along the corridor and peered around the half-open door.

The place was in an uproar.

Mandy stifled a giggle. "I told you it was chaotic," she whispered to James.

Ben sat on top of a stepladder, waving his arms about. The ladder wobbled. Someone rushed forward to steady it. Mandy put her hand over her mouth to stop the laughter coming out.

"No!" Mr. Curtis was shouting. "Not there, for goodness sake, someone get hold of that parrot!"

A woman in an ankle-length white dress was sitting by the fireplace. There was a blanket over her head. The cats were asleep on the sofa as if nothing was going on.

"That must be Antonia Kent," Mandy whispered in James's ear. "She's the human star."

"I'm not acting with that horrible bird!" a voice came from under the blanket. "I'm not, I'm not, I'm not!"

"Look!" Mandy said, suddenly spying the parrot. "There's Mr. Baggins!"

Sure enough, high up on the elegant crystal chandelier, Mr. Baggins preened his feathers. Beneath, an assistant held up a cup of sunflower seeds.

"Come down, Mr. Baggins," she was shouting. "Nice dinner."

"Two sugars!" the parrot screeched. *"A cup of Baggins if you please."*

Mandy was laughing so hard she felt sure someone would hear.

"Where's George Sims?" Mr. Curtis yelled suddenly. "He's supposed to be supervising these wretched creatures."

"What a mess," James whispered.

"We'd better get out of here before we get in trouble," Mandy said.

But it was too late. They had been spotted.

"Ah, young lady," Mr. Curtis called. "Come in, come in. Any hope of you getting that bird to come down?"

Mandy and James sidled into the hall. Mandy looked up. "I'll try," she said. She felt a bit shy in front of all the crew. "But I can't promise."

Across the hall, Antonia Kent peeped out from under her blanket. Mandy almost laughed again. The actress looked like a nun in a cocktail dress with the white blanket around her face. But when she took the blanket off, Mandy drew in her breath. She recognized her right away. Antonia Kent was the heroine of one of Mandy's favorite soap operas! She just couldn't help staring.

"Mandy . . ." James nudged her in the ribs.

"Oh!" Mandy shook herself. She stood under the chandelier. "Mr. Baggins," she called softly. "Come on down, Mr. Baggins. You're being very naughty."

"She loves, you, yeah, yeah, yeah," Mr. Baggins said.

"Yes," Mandy couldn't help grinning. "I know, but please come down, huh?"

Mandy heard laughter echoing around the set.

She glanced at Mr. Curtis. He had a face like thunder. He definitely didn't think it was funny, even if everyone else did.

Mandy pursed her lips. She pretended to frown. "Now come on, Mr. Baggins, stop fooling around." Someone passed her the cup of sunflowers seeds and she held them out. "Come on . . . please."

To Mandy's relief, Mr. Baggins cocked his head on one side, spread his bright wings, and fluttered down toward her. He landed on her head. Mandy tottered. Then she caught sight of herself in a big, gold-framed wall mirror. She looked as if she was wearing a gaily colored hat in an Easter parade. She put her hand up. "Come on, you rotten thing. You're holding everyone up."

Mr. Baggins stepped daintily onto her fingers. A sigh of relief washed around the room.

"Well *done*, darling." Antonia Kent swept toward Mandy in a wave of pale silk and strong perfume. She had black hair tied up in curls on top of her head, and a pale complexion with a dark beauty spot on her rouged cheek. The actress eyed the parrot warily as she put her arm around Mandy's shoulders. "This girl has a magic touch." She turned to the crew. "Is she the new animal trainer? Has that hopeless man gone at last?"

Mr. Curtis walked over. "No," he said. "She's the

vet's daughter. That was terrific, Mandy. Maybe you could stay and help out? We need Charley next. Could you get her?"

"Oh, yes." Mandy's heart leaped with excitement. "I'd love to."

Just then the front door opened and George Sims came through into the hall. He looked upset. His green boots were covered with mud. His face was red, as if he had been running.

"Sims," Mr. Curtis said, "I was just sending Mandy to get the dog."

George Sims bit his lip. "The dog's gone," he said gruffly, looking down at the toes of his boots. "She ran off."

"What!" Mr. Curtis groaned.

Mandy's stomach turned icy with fear. "Oh, no!" she cried. "When?"

George Sims looked at her. His face was full of remorse. "I put her out last night and she didn't come back in. The thunder — it must have scared her."

A tide of anger and fear washed over Mandy. How could anyone be so crazy? "You put her out during a storm? Don't you know dogs hate thunder?" she exploded.

Mr. Sims pursed his lips. "I didn't know. I told you

I'm only the driver. Anyway, she seemed to have settled down. I thought she'd be okay."

Mandy whirled around. "Come on, James, we'd better go and look for her."

"If the dog's been gone all night," Ben said, "she could be anywhere."

"I've been out there looking." George Sims took off his cap and scratched his head. "She's gone, that's for sure."

"Well, we're going to look anyway." Mandy's eyes blazed. She and James dashed from the hall.

"Where shall we start?" James panted behind her.

"We'll get Jess. She's good at sniffing scents."

"But she's never met Charley."

Mandy was already opening the back of the car. "Come on, Jess." She clipped on the terrier's leash. "We'll let her sniff Charley's blanket. That might do the trick."

They ran around the back and into the kitchen. "Look, Jess." Mandy thrust open the pantry door. Jess ran inside. She sniffed Charley's blanket and made a little whine in her throat. She began scratching it up to make a bed.

"No, Jess!" Mandy pulled the leash gently. "No time to sleep now. Charley is missing and we have to find her!"

"We'd better tell your mom," James said.

They dashed out into the yard. In the stable, Dr. Emily was examining a beautiful bay gelding. "What on earth's happened?" Dr. Emily asked in surprise.

"It's Charley," Mandy blurted. "She's run off."

"Run off . . . oh, dear. When?"

"Last night." Mandy's voice broke. The thought of the beautiful Labrador lost in the fields was awful.

"Mr. Sims let her out during the storm," James explained. "She must have been really scared. He's been looking for her all morning."

"We're taking Jess to look for her," Mandy said.

"It might be a good idea to search the outbuildings," Dr. Emily said. "She could be hiding."

"Good thinking," Mandy said. "Come on, James. Let's go."

"Mandy, don't go far. I have to get back to the office and don't forget you promised to visit Grandma and Grandpa."

"But we can't just leave . . ."

"I'm sorry, Mandy. Look, there's all the crew to look for her." Dr. Emily put her arm around Mandy's shoulders. "I'm sure they'll find her. Just do what you can while you're here. Okay?"

Mandy sniffed, then nodded. "Okay, Mom. Come on, James. Let's go."

*   *   *

By the time Dr. Emily was ready to leave, the outbuildings had been thoroughly combed for signs of the missing dog.

"Charley! Charley!" They had looked all over. The stables, the hayloft, the old dairy. Mandy and James and Jess had run around the grounds, peering in the shrubbery, the old walled kitchen garden, the toolshed. They had even gone up into the attic of Bleakfell Hall. But Charley was nowhere to be seen. Eventually it was time to get back.

As they drove down the road, Mandy felt miserable. What had promised to be such a great day had turned out to be just rotten.

"Cheer up, Mandy." Her mother put a reassuring hand on Mandy's knee. "You've done all you can to find Charley. The dog is really the film company's responsibility, not ours."

"I know," said Mandy. "But *I told* Charley I'd look after her. I can't let her down."

In the back of the car James sat silently hugging the tired terrier. It seemed as if they had run for miles in their hunt for the missing dog, and they were both exhausted.

"We haven't really done *anything.*" Mandy suddenly felt angry. She looked at her mother. "All we've done is searched some silly old buildings and the garden. Charley could be miles away by now, and we're doing nothing to help."

"You'll have to be content with that for now, Mandy," Dr. Emily said firmly. "We're going up to Syke Farm. I called Jean from Bleakfell Hall to see if there were any messages. Mr. Janeki wants me to look at a ewe that's been injured. If you keep a lookout, you might see Charley."

Mandy sighed. She gazed out of the window. She just wished they hadn't had to leave when they did.

Ahead, the hills and valleys seemed to stretch endlessly into the distance. The thought of Charley out there somewhere, lonely and lost, was almost too much to bear. Charley could be lying injured at the bottom of a ditch, shivering with wet and cold . . . hungry. Mandy couldn't stop the rush of terrible thoughts.

"We could ask around the village when we get back," James said in a small voice. "Someone might have seen Charley."

"Yes, you're right, James," Mandy said, her head clearing. She realized there was lots they could do. "We could put posters up," she said, brightening.

"You see," Dr. Emily said, changing gears to turn into Syke Farm. "You've only just begun to help."

Mandy felt a lot better as the car pulled into the farmyard. It was certainly no use moping. She had to think positive. And thinking positive meant doing everything they could to find Charley!

In the farmyard, Mr. Janeki stood in the doorway of the barn. He wore brown overalls and black, muddy rubber boots. His round face looked grim.

"Better stay in the car, you two," Dr. Emily said, getting out, "I won't be long."

Mandy saw the farmer greet Dr. Emily. They stood talking. Mr. Janeki pointed his finger toward the field that bordered the farmyard. Then he and Dr. Emily disappeared into the barn.

Mandy turned to James. "We'll tell Grandma and Grandpa about Charley," she said. "They'll have some ideas. Grandma's always helpful if you're in trouble. And Grandpa might take us out in his camper to search the valleys."

"Great idea." James brightened up. "And I'll do all I can to help."

"Thanks, James," Mandy said with a sigh. It was great to have such a good friend, she thought.

Dr. Emily came out of the barn with Mr. Janeki. Her face was grave as she came toward the car and got in.

"What's up, Mom?" Mandy asked.

"One of Mr. Janeki's sheep has been attacked by a dog," Dr. Emily said with a worried frown.

Mandy's hand flew to her mouth. "You don't think . . ."

Her mother's face was serious. "Yes, I'm afraid so, Mandy. It could well have been Charley!"

Five

"But how do you know it could be Charley?" Mandy insisted. "Surely she wouldn't do a thing like that?"

"Well, it was a black dog. It could have been her," Dr. Emily said as the four-wheel drive headed for the village and Lilac Cottage. "And you know, Mandy, if it *was* Charley, she could be shot."

"I know." Mandy's heart lurched with fear. "That's why we have to find her, Mom," she said determinedly. "As soon as possible."

As they pulled up outside the house, Mandy could see her grandfather mowing the lawn beneath the huge lilac tree that gave the cottage its name. Mandy loved the smell of new-cut grass. It reminded her of summery days and Grandma's homemade lemonade on the lawn.

Mandy, James, and Jess climbed out of the car and went through the front gate.

"This grass seems to grow as fast as I cut it," Grandpa said, stopping the mower's engine and giving Mandy a hug. "Hiya, James," he added with a grin.

"Hello, Mr. Hope," James said cheerfully.

Grandpa bent to stroke Jess. "Hello, Jack Russell. She's getting fat, Mandy."

"I know. Dad says I'm feeding her too much, but she always seems to be hungry."

Grandpa waved good-bye to Dr. Emily as she pulled away from the curb. "Come on, you two. Let's go and find your grandmother. The smell of that chocolate cake's been driving me crazy all morning." He ushered them past his bicycle leaning up against the wall, past the fragrant herb garden, and into the warm and cozy cottage kitchen. "The camper's in for servicing," he explained, "so I've been using my bike to go into Walton."

"They're here, Dorothy!" Grandpa called. Mandy could hear the sound of music and someone giving some kind of instructions. "She's doing her aerobics," Grandpa said with a wink. "Dorothy!" He disappeared into the back room. Mandy heard the

VCR being switched off. A moment later Grandma appeared in her green sweat suit, looking red in the face.

She gave Mandy a hug. "Mandy! It's great to see you. And you, James. Now, how about a slice of cake?"

She went to the pantry and brought out a huge chocolate cake with orange icing on the top. "Want some milk, too?" asked Grandma.

"Yes, please," they chorused. Mandy tried her best to look cheerful but she saw her grandmother glance knowingly at her worried face.

"What's up, Mandy?" Grandma cut four slices of cake and put them on pretty porcelain plates. "Tell us what's wrong."

Suddenly it all poured out: the visit to Bleakfell Hall; how George Sims had let poor Charley out in the thunderstorm; how she was missing; how they had searched in vain.

"And Mr. Janeki's sheep have been attacked," Mandy added, close to tears. "We're really scared it might be Charley, aren't we, James?"

James nodded, his mouth full of cake.

". . . and now we're going to ask around the village and make some posters saying Charley's missing," Mandy added. "Can you think of anything else we can do, Grandma?"

"I'd have taken you out in the camper to look for her if it were here," Grandpa said.

"Never mind, Grandpa," Mandy said with a sigh. "It can't be helped."

Mandy's grandmother looked thoughtful. "You know they have a program on local radio where you can phone in. Maybe you could do that, Mandy, put out a message about Charley?" She rose and went to her desk. "I have their number written down in my address book."

Grandfather rose and wiped his mouth. "That was really yummy, Dorothy. Oh, well, better finish that lawn before it rains."

Mandy took Grandma's address book and went into the back room where the phone was. She dialed quickly. She felt a little nervous. She had never spoken to anyone at a radio station before.

"Radio Yorkshire." They answered right away.

"Umm . . ." Mandy said. "Could you put me through to the afternoon show, please."

There were several clicks, then a man's voice answered. "Yes. Can I help you?"

Mandy quickly explained about Charley. ". . . so if anyone sees a black Labrador with a red collar would they please call Welford 703267." Mandy felt quite breathless after rushing to tell the story.

"Yes, we'll put that out about three o'clock," the man said.

"Oh, thank you," Mandy breathed.

"Good luck," the man said. Mandy heard another click as he put the phone down.

She went back into the kitchen. "They're putting out a message on the afternoon show," she said. "That should help, shouldn't it?" She ran to hug her grandmother. "Thanks, Grandma, you're brilliant. Come on, James, let's go and ask if anyone's seen Charley around the village!"

Mandy's grandparents stood at the gate to wave good-bye.

"Where should we go first?" James said, racing to keep up.

"We'll try the post office," Mandy said.

The small bell clanged as Mandy went in. James stayed outside with Jess, as dogs weren't allowed in the shop.

The postmistress, Mrs. McFarlane, was behind the counter.

"Hello, Mandy."

"Mrs. McFarlane," Mandy said, "have you seen a black Labrador dog?"

"You mean Blackie, James Hunter's dog? Has he gotten lost?"

Mandy shook her head. "No . . . like Blackie, but a female dog. She's with the film company up at Bleakfell Hall but she's missing."

Mrs. McFarlane shook her head. She was a kindly lady and she knew everyone's business. If anyone had seen Charley, Mrs. McFarlane would know. "No, I'm sorry, Mandy, I haven't."

"If we make a poster about her, would you put it in the window?"

Mrs. McFarlane smiled. "Of course, Mandy. I'd be glad to."

"Thanks, Mrs. McFarlane." Mandy felt pleased. It was great to live in a place like Welford where everyone was willing to help out.

Outside, James waited. "Any luck?"

Mandy shook her head. "No, but they'll put a poster up for us."

"Let's try Mr. Oliver in the butcher shop," James suggested.

But they had no luck there either. They asked Ernie Bell, who lived in the cottages behind the Fox and Goose, but he hadn't seen Charley. Neither had Eileen Davy from the Old School House. Nor grumpy Mr. Simmons, clipping the hedge in the churchyard. In fact, no one had seen her. By the time they had asked almost everyone they knew, their task seemed hopeless.

"Come on, James," Mandy said, feeling miserable again. "Let's get back to Animal Ark and make those posters."

Back at the cottage, Mandy found some paper to make the posters. They sat down at the kitchen table.

"If we just do one," Mandy said, chewing the end of her pen thoughtfully, "Jean will let us make some photocopies to put up around the village. Any ideas, James?"

"How about this?" James wrote on a piece of scrap paper.

LOST THE FILM STAR DOG
"CHARLEY"
A female black Labrador dog
gone missing from Bleakfell Hall
If you see her please call
WELFORD 703267

"That looks great," Mandy said delightedly. "Good old James!"

James turned a bit red.

Just then Dr. Adam came into the kitchen. "What are you two up to?" he asked.

"We're making a poster about Charley to put up around the village," Mandy explained.

Dr. Adam peered over James's shoulder at the poster. "That's a good idea. Mom told me about Charley. I hope she turns up."

"So do we," they chorused.

"Do you have to do it right now?" Dr. Adam asked.

"Well, the sooner the better. Why?" Mandy asked curiously.

"Well, I have to go up to the animal sanctuary. I thought you might like to come."

"Mrs. Platt's poodle!" Mandy exclaimed. In her concern over Charley she had forgotten all about it.

Adam Hope held up his hand. "I don't know if they actually have a poodle, Mandy, but it would be a good chance to ask. Someone's turned in a fox that's been injured; that's why I'm going."

"Want to come, James?" Mandy said to her friend.

James shook his head. "I'd like to, but I'd better get back. My aunt's coming this afternoon. I could do the poster if you like. Then we could photocopy it when you get back."

"Oh, James, that would be great."

James rolled up the paper. "See you later," he said, going out.

"Want to come with us, Jess?" Mandy bent down to stroke Jess, curled up in her basket.

"Leave her," Dr. Adam said. "She looks tired out."

Mandy frowned. "I hope she's okay. She's been looking a bit droopy lately."

"Hmm." Dr. Adam stroked his beard thoughtfully. "Remind me, I'll take a look at her when we get back."

Twenty minutes later Mandy and her father were bumping and rattling their way up the dirt road that led to the animal rescue center. Mandy stared gloomily out of the window. All she could think of was Charley, running loose somewhere in the hills and valleys. In the distance she could see the faraway lumps of the Pennine Hills. White clouds had built up over their tops like ragged puffs of cotton in a clear blue sky.

"What happened to the fox?" Mandy asked, dragging her thoughts away from Charley.

"It was caught in one of those wire snares," Dr. Adam said with a grim look on his face.

Mandy's heart went out to the poor wild creature. "I hate snares," she announced angrily. "They should be banned! I don't know how people can set them."

They drove through the gate. The big sign said "Welford Animal Sanctuary" with a picture of a donkey painted in gray.

Betty Hilder, the woman who ran the sanctuary, came out of one of the sheds to greet them. She wore a long floral skirt with a man's tweed jacket over the top and heavy boots. Her face was brown and weathered. A couple of rather skinny cats wound themselves around her legs as she walked.

"Thanks for coming, Adam." She shook his hand. "The fox is in the barn. Come and see."

The injured fox lay in a wire cage in an old stone barn next to a row of kennels. It snarled in fear as they approached.

"I think he's got a broken leg," Betty said. "He won't let me near it."

Mandy bent to look into the cage. She felt angry and upset that the fox had been injured. Why couldn't people just leave wild creatures in peace?

"Here." As she stood up, Dr. Adam handed Mandy a strong pair of gloves from his bag. "Put these on. We'll take a look."

Mandy held the young fox's head firmly. His coat

was red and glossy with a beautiful white bib. Dr. Adam quickly examined his swollen front leg.

"He's been licking it by the looks of it, Dad." Mandy felt a surge of pity. The fox looked at her with fear in its black eyes.

"Yes. I'm afraid it needs more than just a lick to make it better," Dr. Adam said with a frown on his usually good-humored face.

"It's okay," Mandy said gently to the struggling fox. "We're not going to hurt you."

"It's broken, all right," Dr. Adam said. "I'll give him an injection to make him sleep while I wrap it up. Could we have a bowl of hot water, please, Betty?"

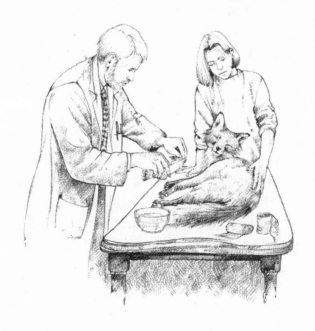

Mandy held on firmly as her father injected the scared creature with a mild anesthetic. Gradually she felt the fox go limp. His eyes closed as he fell asleep.

Betty came back with a bowl of steaming water.

"This won't take long." Dr. Adam took a roll of fine white mesh bandage from his bag.

"We soak this in the hot water," he explained. "It gets soft and we wrap it around the broken leg."

"Then when it dries," Mandy went on, "it sets hard, like plaster."

"How long will it have to be on there, do you think?" Betty asked, after they had finished.

"A few weeks," Dr. Adam said. "Then he should be as good as new."

"Thanks, Adam, Mandy." Betty smiled at them both.

"Keep him warm, plenty to drink." Dr. Adam stroked the glossy red fur while Mandy settled the fox back into its cage.

"How much do I owe you?" Betty asked.

Dr. Adam patted Betty's arm. "Nothing. I had to come up this way anyway." He winked at Mandy. Her dad never charged the sanctuary. *But don't tell your mom*, the wink seemed to say.

They all went inside.

"Betty," Mandy said, "I don't suppose you have a poodle to adopt? Mrs. Platt's just had to have hers put to sleep and she can't afford to buy a new one."

"I'm sorry, we don't, Mandy. Not at the moment," Betty said. "But I'll let you know if we get one."

"Thanks," Mandy said. "Oh, and by the way, if you see a black Labrador, or if anyone brings one in, the film company up at Bleakfell Hall has lost one."

"Oh, dear," Betty said. "Of course. I'll let you know if I hear of anything," she promised.

Mandy took a last glance back at the rows of kennels as they drove away. She felt sad and angry that there were so many homeless animals in the world.

A couple of miles from the village, the car phone rang.

"Yup," Mandy heard her dad say. "Where? I'll tell her. Thanks, Jean."

"Mr. Redpath's called Jean to say he's seen a black dog in one of his fields. Apparently it ran off toward the river," Dr. Adam explained.

"Oh, Dad!" Mandy's heart leaped with hope. "It could be Charley. Did Mr. Redpath say if it was wearing a collar?"

"Yes," Dr. Adam glanced at his daughter. "A red one."

"Yippee!" Mandy cried, clapping her hands together. "Oh, Dad, it really could be her."

Mandy's heart drummed all the way home. Charley was definitely still alive and in the area. It could only be a matter of time before they found her!

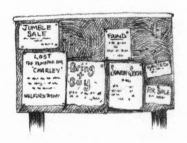

Six

"Can I turn the radio on, Dad?" Mandy asked as they neared the village.

"Yes, of course, Mandy."

"I phoned Radio Yorkshire. They're going to put out a message about Charley on the afternoon show," she explained. Mandy switched the radio on just as the show was ending.

"Oh," Mandy felt disappointed. "I would have loved to hear what they said."

The announcer was still talking.

"Shh," Dr. Adam turned up the volume. "Listen!"

"And just a reminder about that missing dog," the announcer said. "Her name's Charley and she's wearing a red collar. If you see her, phone Welford 703267. There's a very anxious girl waiting desperately for news."

Mandy looked at her father. "It sounded great, didn't it?" She felt a surge of hope.

"Yes." Dr. Adam patted Mandy's knee. "Let's hope it does the trick."

Back at Animal Ark James was waiting.

"I managed to escape from Mom and my aunt," he admitted. "I said this was really urgent."

"Well, it is." Mandy told James about Mr. Redpath seeing a dog with a red collar.

"It could be Charley!" James said excitedly.

"I know," Mandy said. "That's why we have to get these up quick, so if anyone sees her they'll know who she is."

James had written the poster in green marker pen with a drawing of a black Labrador on one side.

"Oh, James, it's wonderful! Come on, let's ask Jean if we can use the photocopier."

They went into the reception area.

Jean Knox was looking through the blue appointment book. She glanced up and smiled as Mandy and James entered.

"Can we use the photocopier please, Jean?" Mandy asked.

Jean took off her glasses. They swung on a silver

chain against her hand-knitted pink cardigan. "What is it, dear?" Jean was a bit fussy about the office machine.

"A poster," Mandy explained. "About Charley, the missing movie star dog."

"Yes, help yourselves."

They went into the back room. The photocopier whirred as Mandy made a dozen copies.

"Where to first?" James asked as they hurried outside.

"I'm going to ask the pastor if we can put one on the parish bulletin board," Mandy said. "It will be a great place. Everyone who comes to the village has to pass it."

They made their way across the village green and down the shortcut beside the Fox and Goose. Old Walter Pickard was in the front garden of his little stone cottage, pruning his roses. His fat tomcat was asleep on the front step in a pool of late afternoon sunshine. Walter was an old friend of Grandpa's. Both of them had been church bell ringers for years.

"Now then, you youngsters," Walter called. "Where are you off to?"

"Hello, Mr. Pickard. We're just going to ask the minister if he'll put one of these up." Mandy showed Walter the poster.

"What's that all about?"

Mandy quickly explained about Charley.

"Is she a star then? I haven't seen her."

"Well," Mandy said. "She's a star to us because she's such a beautiful dog."

"We thought it would make people pay attention," James added.

"Yes, it will. Well, good luck. I'll keep an eye out for her."

"Thanks, Mr. Pickard."

Outside the church, Pastor Hadcroft was just getting off his bicycle.

Mandy and James ran across.

"Well, hello, you two." The pastor took off his crash helmet. "You look like you're in a hurry."

"Yes, we are." Mandy had suddenly realized it was near closing time. In fifteen minutes or so the shops would be shut and the posters would have to wait until tomorrow. Her heart lurched to think Charley had been missing almost a whole day.

"Could you please put this poster up on the board," Mandy begged. "We'd be so grateful."

Pastor Hadcroft looked at the poster. "Sure," he said. He used several rusty thumbtacks to pin up the poster. He stood back. "That looks fine. Hope you have luck finding the dog."

"Thanks!" Mandy and James chorused. They sprinted across the green to the post office.

Mrs. McFarlane was counting the money in the cash register.

"Here's the poster about Charley," Mandy said breathlessly.

"Leave it on the counter, dear," Mrs. McFarlane said, putting a pile of dimes into a blue bag. "I'll put it up when I've finished doing the money."

Mandy and James dashed back to the grocer's, then to the butcher. Soon every shop in the village had the poster in its window. They even stuck one on the huge oak tree by the village pond.

"Just in time," James panted as the very last doorbell clanged behind them. "Now we'll just have to wait to see what happens."

"I'll phone Bleakfell Hall tonight and tell them what we've done," said Mandy. "I just have time to do my chores before dinner."

At Animal Ark, the evening clinic was just beginning. Mandy popped her head around the door.

"We're back," she said to her mom. Dr. Emily was sitting at the bench counting sterile-packed hypodermic needles. She looked up. "Where from?"

"We've been putting posters about Charley all around the village."

"Good job, Mandy." Dr. Emily replaced the box on the shelf. "Hope it does the trick."

As they passed the treatment room Mandy saw Jess up on the table. Dr. Adam was just finishing examining her.

"Is she okay, Dad?" Mandy went in to stroke the terrier.

Dr. Adam glanced at Mandy's anxious face. "She's fine, Mandy." He smiled. "She's absolutely fine."

"That's good." Mandy heaved a sigh of relief. A missing Labrador and a sick terrier would just be too much to cope with!

Later, after James had gone home for supper, Mandy called Bleakfell Hall. She was so anxious for news of Charley she had hardly been able to eat a thing.

Luckily, Ben Burton, Mr. Curtis's assistant, answered.

"Oh, hello, Mandy. I don't suppose you've heard anything about the dog, have you?"

"No," Mandy said. "That's why I'm calling. I hoped you had."

"No, nothing. And Animal Stars doesn't have another black Labrador available. I really don't know what we're going to do!"

Mandy's heart sank. In spite of the posters and the call to the local radio station, she had still been holding on to a desperate hope that Charley might find her way back to Bleakfell Hall on her own.

"One of the local farmers saw a black Labrador," she told Ben. "I hoped it was Charley, but we haven't heard anything since." She glanced at the clock over the fireplace. It was eight-thirty, almost twenty-four hours since Charley had run off!

"I know you're upset about her," Ben was saying, "but we have to get on with filming. I don't suppose you know of another dog we could use, Mandy?"

"Well," Mandy said, an idea occurring to her. "My friend James has a black Labrador."

"Great! Is he obedient?"

"Well . . ." Mandy hesitated. Should she tell a little white lie? James would be so proud if Blackie was in a movie. "Yes, he's not *too* bad." It wasn't a fib at all, really. Blackie wasn't too bad at doing as he was told. Just not too good, either.

"Could you bring him by? We could give it a try," Ben said, sounding pleased.

"I think that'll be okay. I'll ask."

"Mandy, you're wonderful. Mr. Curtis will be so happy." Ben sounded delighted. "Can you come tomorrow?"

"I guess so," Mandy said. "I'll call James now if you want. I'm sure my dad will bring us."

"Fine," said Ben. "See you in the morning."

James was very excited when she called to tell him what Ben Burton had said.

"I'll get up early and give Blackie a bath," James said. "He rolled in some manure this morning so he's not allowed indoors at the moment."

"That figures," Mandy said. She put the phone down with a sigh. It was all very well, Blackie being Charley's stand-in. But what they really needed was Charley herself!

Very early next morning, James and a super-clean Blackie were on the doorstep.

"Wow! You're early," Mandy said as she answered James's knock on the door.

"It's not every day Blackie gets his big chance," James said proudly.

Dr. Adam came through from the office. "I'm taking you up to Bleakfell Hall," he said. "Mom's busy with the clinic this morning. I just have to load the car. We have to stop by Sunrise Farm on the way. A cow's down with milk fever."

When they arrived at Sunrise Farm, Mr. Jones, the farmer, came out from the angular gray stone farmhouse to greet them. He had an empty tobacco pipe in his mouth. Mandy had never seen him without it. It hissed and bubbled like a kettle as he sucked.

"Make sure Blackie stays in the car," Dr. Adam warned. "We don't want the cow getting upset, especially since she has a new calf."

"Went down early this morning," Mr. Jones explained. *Suck, suck, hiss, bubble.* "We tried to get her up but it's no good."

In the barn, a cream-and-brown Jersey cow was lying in the straw. Her legs were folded up underneath her stomach. They had propped her up with a couple of straw bales to keep her from rolling over. By her side stood a soft-eyed calf barely more than a few hours old. It mooed softly and wobbled away on unsteady legs. There was a sweet smell of fresh milk and hay.

Dr. Adam knelt down beside the mother cow. He ran his hands over her flanks.

"Okay, old girl," he said. "We'll soon have you on your feet."

Mandy knew what was needed. "Shall I get the bottle of calcium from your bag, Dad?"

"Yes, please, Mandy. And a needle and a tube."

"Milk fever's caused by a sudden loss of calcium," Dr. Adam explained to a wide-eyed James. "It happens soon after a new calf is born. I'll inject some calcium into the cow and she'll soon be as good as new."

Dr. Adam took the needle from Mandy and attached it to a long, thin rubber tube. Then he fixed the other end to a bottle. He quickly stuck the needle into one of the cow's veins.

"Hold it up please, Mandy."

As the calcium flowed into the cow's blood, she began to stir. After a while Dr. Adam pulled out the needle. He wiped his hands on his overalls. "Okay, stand back, she's going to get up."

Mandy held her breath. The cow struggled to her feet. Mandy's heart pounded. Would the cow fall again? She had helped her father do this many times and knew it was always an anxious moment.

The mother cow was swaying about in the sun-yellow straw like a great ship on the sea. Then she seemed to get her balance. She moved forward as her calf came trotting. She mooed softly. A new sucking noise came as the calf greedily drank its mother's milk.

Mandy breathed a sigh of relief. It was times like this, knowing she could really help to save an animal's life, that made her more eager than ever to be a vet herself.

"Thanks, Adam." Mr. Jones looked relieved. *Suck, suck, bubble, bubble* went his empty pipe. "I can't afford to lose such a good milker. Nice work, Mandy. I can see you're going to make a great vet yourself one day." *Bubble . . . bubble.*

Mandy blushed with pride.

"We're on our way to Bleakfell Hall," Mandy heard her father say.

"Any sign of their missing dog? I heard about it when I went into the post office yesterday," Mr. Jones said.

"Not yet. We're keeping our fingers crossed. In the meantime James's dog is going to act as a stand-in."

The farmer grinned, then sucked even harder on his empty pipe. "Good luck!"

But things didn't quite go as Mandy expected. As they pulled up outside Bleakfell Hall, the front door suddenly flew open. Out surged a stream of people led by a woman in a white dress.

"That's Antonia Kent," Mandy whispered to her father. "What's happened now?"

Antonia Kent strode toward them in a swath of silk. After her ran Hammond Curtis, clipboard held aloft. Today a red bandanna replaced his usual baseball cap. After *him* ran Ben Burton, holding out what looked like a mug of tea. Next came one of the production assistants. Then Mandy gasped with surprise as a man in an old-fashioned frock coat and top hat came running out. His white shirt was covered in blood. Sticking out from his chest was a ruby-handled dagger, although he was striding along like a healthy athlete.

Last but not least, there was a flurry of red and green. Mr. Baggins the parrot!

"Mr. Baggins." Mandy climbed hastily from the car. She ran toward the parrot. "Mr. Baggins!"

With a screech the bright bird flew over Antonia's head. She crouched down on the driveway, hands waving like a windmill.

"Horrible thing! Take it away, someone!"

"Good morning!" Mr. Baggins screeched. *"Where's Charley?"* With that he promptly landed on Mandy's head.

"There you are," Miss Kent said dramatically. Her nose was up in the air, her wig falling over one eye. "If this girl's so good with animals, she can star in this dreadful movie. I'm leaving!"

Seven

"What on earth's going on?" Dr. Adam's mouth fell open when he saw the procession of people pour out of Bleakfell Hall.

"Come down, Mr. Baggins," Mandy commanded. The naughty parrot stepped onto her fingers. Then he hopped off onto her shoulder.

"Where's the cup tea. I wanna be a yeah, yeah," Mr. Baggins squawked in her ear.

The director, Hammond Curtis, was trying to soothe Antonia Kent with a mug of tea. They were sitting on the stone steps, talking earnestly.

"I'm sure the parrot will behave itself now that

Mandy's here," Mr. Curtis was saying. Mandy saw him wink at her over the actress's shoulder.

"He tried to peck my beauty spot," Antonia sniffed, wiping her eyes.

"He thought it was a sunflower seed. Now please calm down, Antonia." Mr. Curtis patted Antonia Kent's shaking shoulder.

Mandy tried not to laugh out loud. "We've brought Blackie," she managed to splutter.

Dr. Adam had gone around to the stables to look at one of the horses that had gone lame. Blackie was sitting, good as gold, at James's feet.

Suddenly Mr. Curtis stood up. He clapped his hands. "Okay, everyone, back inside. I've managed to persuade Miss Kent to continue, and it seems Charley's understudy has arrived. Let's get on with the job, shall we?"

They all filed back indoors. Mr. Curtis waited for Mandy and James.

"So this is Blackie?" He gave the dog a pat. "Thanks for bringing him, young man."

"That's okay," James mumbled shyly.

"I hope he's going to be obedient."

"Oh, no, yes, I mean." James went red.

"I expect he will," Mandy said hastily. "For the first time ever," she whispered under her breath.

"I've been training him," James said, looking up at Mr. Curtis.

"Good." Mr. Curtis slapped James on the shoulder.

Suddenly, with a squawk, Mr. Baggins took off, up into the chandelier. A screech filled the air.

Mandy heard a groan from the crew.

"Okay, okay," Mr. Curtis shouted. "Leave him there for the time being."

Someone stepped forward with a black-and-white clapper board.

"Take your places!" Mr. Curtis ordered.

The man with the dagger in his chest lay backwards on the hall table. Someone ran over with a bottle. He splashed gooey red liquid on the floor.

"Not too much," Mr. Curtis called. "It's not a horror movie."

He beckoned to James. "Can you get your dog to lie by the fireplace, young man?"

"I'll try," James said.

Mandy held her breath. She suddenly remembered all the trouble Blackie had caused at this year's Welford County Fair, snatching Mrs. Ponsonby's hat and running wild in the show ring. "Oh, Blackie," she whispered. "Please be good!"

James led Blackie toward the big stone fireplace. He unclipped his leash. "Stay!" he commanded.

James fished around in the pocket of his jeans. He held up a dog biscuit. "Stay!" he commanded again.

Blackie lay down, head on paws. His eyes roamed the room. Mandy's heart was in her mouth.

Blackie stared up at Mr. Baggins. Mr. Baggins stared down at Blackie. James backed away from the dog, hand raised. Blackie lay still. *It's going to be all right*, Mandy thought. *It's really going to be all right!*

Ben took Mandy aside. "This is the scene just after the murder," he whispered. "Blackie . . . er, Black Rose and Mr. Baggins are the only witnesses."

"Oh," Mandy whispered. Miss Kent looked angry enough to stab someone for real.

"Then the murderess removes the dagger and hides it in the cupboard. But Black Rose sniffs it out."

"Oh, dear!" Mandy's eyes were wide. "I'm not sure . . ."

"What?" Ben asked.

"Nothing," Mandy said. She thought perhaps it was the wrong time to tell Ben that the only thing Blackie was good at sniffing out was his dinner!

"We got to this part before you arrived," Ben went on. "But Mr. Baggins took a sudden fancy to that beauty spot on Antonia Kent's cheek."

Mandy giggled. She wouldn't have missed this for anything!

"Silence!" Mr. Curtis yelled.

Antonia Kent took her position by the corpse. The clapper board clapped.

They were ready.

Antonia Kent pretended to look around warily. Then, still glancing over her shoulder, she began to remove the dagger from the man's chest.

A sudden commotion from the first-floor landing made her freeze in her tracks. The three cats came hurtling down the staircase. In front, a little gray mouse fled in terror. They sped across the hall and through the door.

Mr. Baggins squawked in alarm. *"She loves tea!"* he screeched. *"Where's Charley?"*

Antonia Kent screamed. "A mouse . . . a mouse!" Up went her long skirts. She jumped onto the table in one great leap.

It was all too much for Blackie. First the parrot; then the cats; now a screaming, jumping woman. He barked, leaped to his feet, tore off after the cats. His claws scratched the wooden floor as he slipped and scrambled his way to the kitchen.

"Cut!" Mr. Curtis yelled.

Mandy snorted with laughter. Mr. Curtis put his head into his hands. The man with the dagger in his chest stood up and lit a cigarette. In one corner, a young woman dressed as a Victorian parlor maid took a can of Coke from behind a potted plant and raised it to her lips.

Mandy wiped her eyes. James disappeared toward the kitchen after Blackie. Ben Burton was doubled over, laughing his head off. Antonia Kent swept up the stairs in a flurry of long skirts and hurt pride. The scene was ruined.

Mandy ran after James.

In the kitchen, George Sims was holding Blackie's collar. The Labrador was sitting at his feet, looking sorry for himself. James was telling him off.

"Blackie!" He shook his finger at the dog. Mr. Sims let go of his collar and Blackie lay down beside him.

George Sims scratched his head. "I thought it was Charley coming through that door," he said.

"I'm afraid not." Mandy gave Blackie a hug. He might not be a good actor, but he was great at cheering people up. She looked up at Mr. Sims. "Still no sign of Charley?"

Mr. Sims shook his head. "If she doesn't turn up soon I'll probably lose my job," he said, looking sorry for himself.

"We put a message out on the local radio," Mandy said. "And put posters up in the village."

"Well, thanks for your help," Mr. Sims said gruffly. "I know I was crazy to let her out. I'm just not used to animals."

"When are they sending your replacement?" Mandy began to feel sorry for George Sims. He really wasn't so bad. And she could see by the look on his face that he would never have frightened Charley on purpose.

Mr. Sims shrugged. "Tomorrow, I hope. There's something wrong with one of the horses now. I thought parrots were enough trouble." He shook his head. "I just can't cope with it. If I didn't have a wife and four kids, I'd quit the job."

Mandy suddenly had an idea. "Mr. Sims," she said, "if you like, James and I will help out with the animals. Just until the new person comes, that is."

George Sims seemed to cheer up a bit. A grin spread across his face. "Now, that's not a bad idea. The horses need mucking out, but —" His face fell. "— I couldn't pay you anything."

Mandy waved her hand. "No, we wouldn't want to be paid, would we, James?"

"Er . . . no," James said, although Mandy didn't think he looked very certain.

George Sims beamed. "All right, you're on." He looked over his shoulder. "I think I could run and get you a couple of ice creams."

Mandy grinned. "Thanks, Mr. Sims."

Just then Hammond Curtis came into the kitchen. Mr. Baggins sat on his shoulder. Mandy just managed to suppress a giggle. Mr. Curtis only needed a wooden leg and an eye patch and he'd look like Long John Silver!

"I think everyone's calmed down now," he said. "Thanks for bringing your dog, James. I'm sorry, I don't think he'll be suitable after all."

James's face fell. "I am *trying* to train him, honestly."

Mandy felt sorry for James — and for Blackie. He'd lost his big chance to be a star.

"Of course, what we really need," Mr. Curtis said, glaring at George Sims, "is Charley! If she's not found, I don't know *what* we're going to do!"

Mr. Sims hung his head.

Mr. Curtis put Mr. Baggins back on his perch. "You'd better round up the cats, George. Goodness knows where they've all gone to."

"And we'll go and find my dad, and ask him if we can stay and help with the animals," Mandy said.

Dr. Adam was just washing his hands under the yard tap.

"Dad," Mandy said excitedly. "We're going to stay and help George. Is that okay?"

"Yes, of course it is. I'll pick you up later if you like. How did Blackie's debut go?"

James blushed. "He failed his audition."

"Oh, dear." Dr. Adam's eyes twinkled. "I must say I'm not surprised. That dog's too intelligent to let anyone boss him around."

James brightened. "That's right," he said proudly. "Thank you, Dr. Hope."

A couple of hours later everything was spick-and-span. Mandy and James had mucked out and put clean bedding in the stables. They had fed the horses, and the cats, which they'd found in the cellar standing guard over a mouse hole in the baseboard. James had swept the yard while Mandy sat by the fire in the kitchen grooming the cats. She giggled, thinking about Blackie and Mr. Baggins and poor Antonia Kent. How could anyone be scared of a tiny little mouse?

When Dr. Adam arrived to collect them, Mandy and James were eating ice cream in the kitchen. Mr. Baggins was asleep, his head tucked under his wing.

"I don't know what I'd have done without them," George Sims said as Dr. Adam came through the door. "They can work for Animal Stars any time!"

"Can we come back tomorrow, Dad?" Mandy asked.

"Yes, fine. I have to go to Walton Market in the afternoon. I'll drop you off on the way," Dr. Adam said.

"Thanks, Dad." Mandy's eyes shone. "You're the best."

"Where's the tea?" Mr. Baggins mumbled sleepily.

Dr. Adam dropped James and Blackie off at their gate on the way back to Animal Ark.

"See you tomorrow, James," Mandy called, waving good-bye.

When they arrived home, Dr. Adam went off to make out his report. Mandy greeted Jess in the kitchen. The terrier was in her basket. She looked up and wagged her tail as Mandy came in but didn't climb out. Mandy frowned. Jess really was out of sorts lately. She hoped her dad had been right when he said she was okay.

"A long walk might be what you need, Jess," Mandy said, stroking her wiry coat. "You're not getting enough exercise, that's the trouble. I'll take you in the morning if you're good."

She gave the dog a hug, then went through into the office. Simon was sterilizing the surgical instruments.

"Oh, Mandy," he said as she came in. "There was a telephone call for you."

"Who from?" Mandy asked curiously.

"I don't know. Ask Jean." Simon opened the sterilizer to a cloud of steam.

Mandy went through to Reception. Jean was sitting at her typewriter, a frown on her face. She was trying to figure out Dr. Adam's spidery handwriting on a sheet of paper beside her machine.

"Jean, Simon says there was a call for me," Mandy said eagerly.

"Oh, yes." Jean flicked through her message pad. . . . "Here it is. Betty from the animal sanctuary. She asked you to call her."

Mandy's heart leaped. It might be news about Charley!

"Use my phone if you want," Jean went on. "The sanctuary's number is on the bulletin board above your head."

Mandy was so excited she could hardly dial the number.

"Animal sanctuary, Betty speaking."

"Betty," Mandy said breathlessly. "There's a message for me to call you."

Betty recognized her voice. "Hi, Mandy," she said cheerfully. "I thought you'd like to know the SPCA has brought in a stray poodle. She might be right for your friend, Mrs. Platt."

"That's great, Betty," Mandy said, brushing aside her disappointment at there being no news of Charley. "Could we come up and see her?"

"Yes, sure," Betty replied. "Whenever you like."

"I'll ask if Mom or Dad can bring me. We'll come as soon as we can."

"Okay, Mandy. I'll be here," said Betty.

Mandy put the phone down. She looked at her watch. If her mom wasn't busy she just might take her up to the sanctuary.

Mandy hurried through into the kitchen, Dr. Emily was folding her white vet's coat.

"Mom!" Mandy burst out. "Is there time for us to go up to the animal sanctuary before the evening shift?"

Dr. Emily glanced up at the clock. "Yes, I think so. Why?"

"Betty just called. She has a poodle for Mrs. Platt. Can we go and see her?"

Dr. Emily put her vet's coat on the shelf. "That's great news. I'll get my keys."

She came back a minute later. "Come on, sweetheart. Let's go and take a look at this poodle."

Eight

Mandy fidgeted all the way to the animal sanctuary. Her eyes darted from side to side as they drove along, still looking for signs of Charley. To find Charley and a poodle for Mrs. Platt all in one day would be like a dream come true.

At the animal sanctuary, Betty ushered them into the house. The poodle, thin and weak, lay in a basket in front of Betty's fire.

"Oh . . ." Mandy knelt down beside the basket. She gently touched the poodle's matted gray coat. Her heart turned over with pity.

"She had been left tied to a tree over at Monkton Spinney," Mandy heard Betty saying to her mother.

"Luckily someone spotted her and took her to the SPCA. She probably wouldn't have survived another night."

"How could anyone do such a thing!" Mandy said, her voice barely a whisper.

She heard her mother sigh. "Don't ask me, Mandy. I don't know either."

Mandy looked up at Betty and her mother. They were standing watching her stroke the poodle. Dr. Emily's face was full of sadness.

"Do you think she'll be okay, Mom?" Mandy asked anxiously. She had seen abandoned animals before but never one who looked quite so thin and ill.

Her mother crouched down beside her. She quickly ran her hands over the little dog, then looked into her eyes and ears.

"It's hard to say," said Dr. Emily. "She's suffering from exposure." She lifted the dog's muzzle to look at her teeth. "A few good meals and a day or so of being warm and we'll take another look at her, okay?"

"Oh, *thanks*, Mom." Mandy gave her mother a hug. "She has to be okay, she just has to be!"

Mandy stroked the poodle gently. It raised its head weakly and licked her hand.

"There you are!" Mandy stood up. "I know she's a fighter!"

"She's had some warm milk and cereal," said Betty. "And what she really needs, too, is lots of love."

"Mrs. Platt will give her that, won't she, Mom?" Mandy said, trying to imagine Mrs. Platt's delighted face when they turned up with a new dog for her.

"She certainly will," Dr. Emily said. "But, Mandy, I think we'd better make sure the dog is going to get really well before we tell Mrs. Platt."

"Whatever you say, Mom. I'll come up and see her again. I'll bring my pocket money next time. It will help pay for her food."

"That is very kind, Mandy." Betty gave her a hug.

They left the poodle lying in her warm basket and went outside.

"I'm sorry, Mandy," her mother said. "We must get back. It's time for the clinic."

They waved good-bye to Betty and set off toward Welford. Along the lane, Dr. Emily slowed down while two girl riders trotted past.

"Hello, Dr. Hope," one of the girls called. It was Susan Collins, a new girl in the area. She had had a difficult time settling in at first, but she now looked completely at home.

Dr. Emily rolled down her window. "Hello, Susan. How's Prince these days?"

"Fine, thank you," Susan replied.

Mandy waved as the girls trotted on.

For the rest of the journey home, Mandy was very thoughtful.

"You're quiet, Mandy," her mother remarked.

"I was just thinking about Charley and that little poodle," she said gloomily. "Sometimes I think I'll never make a good vet. I get too upset."

Dr. Emily patted her daughter's knee. "Yes, you will, Mandy. I know you will. You'd make a very *bad* vet if you didn't care about your patients."

Mandy sniffed, feeling better. "Yes, I suppose you're right." She thought for a minute. She smiled at her mother. Mom always had the knack of saying the right thing. "You know, Mom," Mandy said, "I think I'll call the poodle Antonia."

Dr. Emily smiled. "That's a very grand name. Why Antonia?"

"After that actress at Bleakfell Hall. She reminds me of a poodle with her hair tied up on the top of her head like that."

"That's a little rude, Mandy," Dr. Emily said.

"No it's not," Mandy replied indignantly. "Poodles are beautiful. I think it's a compliment!"

*   *   *

The following morning, Mandy was putting out food for her rabbits when James arrived with Blackie. They were off on that walk Mandy had promised Jess.

The terrier barked with joy at seeing Blackie. The two dogs greeted each other with sniffs and wagging tails, then ran off, chasing madly around and around the lawn.

"Watch the plants!" Mandy called. "Control your dog, James!" she said with a grin.

"Fat chance," James muttered. He whistled to Blackie but the Labrador ignored him as usual.

"Where should we go for our walk?" Mandy asked.

James shrugged. "Up to you."

They went into the kitchen to fetch Jess's leash. Dr. Adam was reading his veterinary magazine at the table.

"Where are you two off to?" he asked as they came through the door.

"We're taking Jess on a long walk to try to get rid of that fat tummy." Mandy bent to hug the Jack Russell.

Dr. Adam shut his magazine and rose from the table. "Well, I must go. I have several calls to make. Careful where you go, you two. Take good care of Jess."

Mandy frowned as her father went out. That was a funny thing to say. He *knew* she always took great care of the little Jack Russell. Mandy shrugged. Oh, well, her dad did say funny things sometimes. She took Jess's leash from its hook.

"Come on, you two." Blackie and Jess were wagging their tails at each other and panting after their race around the garden. "Let's go."

They walked along the lane to the general store.

"I'm just going to get some candy." James produced a ten-pence coin from his pocket.

They tied the dogs up outside.

"Hello, you two," Mr. McFarlane said from behind the counter. "Any news yet about that dog from Bleakfell Hall, Mandy?"

Mandy shook her head sadly. "Not yet, but we're keeping our fingers crossed."

Outside, James gave Mandy five candies and they set off across the village green. Jess and Blackie strained at their leashes.

"Let's go past the War Memorial," Mandy said, pulling Jess back. "Down by the tavern and along the river. We can let them off their leashes along there."

"Great," James said.

They stopped briefly on the bridge to throw sticks into the river, then they climbed over the fence and wandered down to the river's edge. Mandy loved the sound of the water as it sang and bubbled over the stones. The level was high, swollen from last week's rain. Mandy unclipped Jess's leash.

"Off you go, and stay where we can see you!" she said sternly.

Jess bounded off, Blackie at her heels. They sniffed along the bank, darting to and fro as they caught the scent of a rabbit.

Suddenly Mandy saw Jess scramble down to the river's edge. Blackie followed, his tail waving like a flag.

Then, all at once, Mandy saw Jess stand stock-still. Her head was cocked to one side.

"What's Jess hear?" James asked.

Mandy frowned. "I don't know. Let's go and see."

They scrambled down the bank. Mandy saw the alert little terrier standing like a statue at the water's edge.

Suddenly Jess shot forward like a rocket.

"Hey!" Mandy yelled. She felt frightened that Jess might run off, and one missing dog was quite enough! "Jess! Jess!" she shouted. "Come back!"

But the terrier ignored her. She splashed across the stepping-stones and scrambled madly up the high bank on the other side of the river.

"Come on, James," Mandy said urgently. "We'd better go after her."

James whistled to Blackie. The Labrador bounded toward him. For once it seemed Blackie was going to be obedient. Then he saw Jess's white tail disappearing over the top of the bank. He gave a couple of loud barks and set off after her.

"Blackie!" James cried. He turned, but Mandy was already clambering down the bank, across the stepping-stones, and up the hill on the other side.

"Wait for me!" he called, running after her.

"Come on," she called. Her heart was pounding as she ran. "Jess! Jess!"

By now both dogs had disappeared. Gone!

Through the clump of trees there was no sign of either of them. A rock-strewn hill lay ahead.

Side by side, Mandy and James scrambled up the hill after the dogs. At the top they stood on a huge outcrop of rock. Below, the houses in the village looked small, like a doll's town.

Mandy listened. All she could hear was the far-away sound of a train. Surely Jess wouldn't be chasing that? She whirled around, looking in all directions. There was no sign of either dog. Where on earth had they gone?

Then, from behind a distant boulder, Mandy suddenly heard Jess's short, sharp bark.

She jumped down. "Come on, James, this way!"

They ran toward the sound of Jess's frantic barks. They dashed across the turf, scrambling over rocks.

"They're over there." James pointed. "Look, Blackie's tail is sticking out from behind that rock!"

"Oh, thank goodness." Mandy heaved a sigh of relief. Now that they could hear Jess and see Blackie's waving tail, she was beginning to feel angry with the naughty dogs. Jess would get a good talking-to when they finally caught up with her.

Behind the rock, Jess still barked — a high, excited kind of bark that Mandy had never heard before.

They ran around the other side, then stopped dead in their tracks.

"Oh!" Mandy stood, hand over her mouth in disbelief.

For there, lying on her side beside a big gray boulder, was Charley! Her hind leg was caught in a snare.

Mandy's heart missed a beat. She could hardly believe what she was seeing.

Charley's sad eyes looked up at her as if to say "Am I glad to see you!"

Mandy fell to her knees. Her throat felt choked

with joy and relief. "Charley . . . Charley . . ." She blinked back tears.

The dog's back leg was bleeding where the tight wire held it fast. Mandy touched her gently. Charley wagged her tail and licked Mandy's hand. She tried to get up but fell back as the sharp wire dug deeper into her leg. Mandy gasped as she saw the blood ooze.

"Oh, poor Charley!" She looked up at James, her heart filled with anger and pity.

"What are we going to do?" James gulped, kneeling quickly beside Mandy. Jess and Blackie were lying down, panting from their run.

Mandy wrenched off her jacket and laid it over the dog to keep her warm.

Mandy knew they had to get help. They would never manage to carry Charley back themselves. "I'm going to find Mom or Dad," she said quickly, her heart thumping in her chest. "Stay with her, James. Keep Jess and Blackie with you." She thrust the dog leashes at him.

Mandy sped away. The wind blew back her short hair. She flew down the hill as fast as her legs would carry her. She splashed over the stepping-stones, heedless of wet feet and the chilly wind blowing through her sweatshirt. Mandy's breath came out in gasps. Past the village hall, the

shops . . . the sleepy morning main street. Her heart seemed to be drumming, *hurry . . . hurry.*

She reached Animal Ark, thrust open the gate, and dashed down the front path. She burst into the reception area. The door hit the wall with a clang.

"Where's . . . Dad . . . Mom . . . Simon . . . anyone?" she panted to a startled Jean Knox.

Jean dropped her spectacles in surprise. "Mandy, what on earth's happened? You look —"

"Please . . . where's . . ." She was completely out of breath.

"Your dad just got back. He's in his exam room, but —"

Mandy didn't wait to hear anymore. She rushed through to the back room.

Dr. Adam was filling his bag with veterinary supplies.

"Dad! Dad! You have to come. Quick!" Mandy gasped. "We've found Charley!"

Dr. Adam's eyes widened in surprise. "Charley? Where is she?" As he was speaking, he closed his bag quickly and grabbed his car keys from the shelf.

Mandy tugged his arm. "Quickly . . . oh, please. She's up on the hill. I'll show you as we go."

They both ran through reception and out of the front door.

"If there are any calls I'll be back soon," Dr. Adam shouted to Jean Knox as they raced down the path.

They both leaped into the car.

"We went over the fence by the stone bridge," Mandy explained. "Jess ran off. She must have heard Charley whining." Mandy felt so upset she began to sob. "Oh, Dad, her leg's caught in a snare. It's horrible. Poor Charley."

Dr. Adam was bent over the wheel. The car roared up the main street and out toward the bridge. Mandy twisted her hands together anxiously. "Dad, hurry . . . please hurry!"

Nine

Dr. Adam screeched to a halt on the bridge. They both leaped out, clambered quickly over the fence, and ran along the riverbank.

"This way," Mandy panted as she plunged down the bank and splashed across the stepping-stones. She began the steep climb up the other side.

"Hang on!" her father called. Mandy was way ahead.

Mandy stopped and turned impatiently. "Come *on*, Dad, for goodness' sake!" She held out her hand. Her father took it and together they ran through the trees, out the other side, and on up the steep bank toward the place where Charley lay injured.

"How much farther?" Dr. Adam panted.

"Just there!" Mandy pointed to the pile of boulders past the steep outcrop of rock. "Charley's over there!"

At the sound of her voice, Jess and Blackie came bounding up. Jess barked madly, jumping up at Mandy as she ran.

Mandy and her father arrived at last, breathless and flushed with running all the way from the road.

James leaped to his feet, looking very relieved. "I thought you were never coming!"

"We came as quickly as we could," Mandy panted.

Dr. Adam knelt beside the injured Labrador. Charley wagged her tail feebly and whined. Mandy knelt beside them, clasping her hands together anxiously.

"Now then, old girl," Dr. Adam said gently. "Let's have a look at you." He eyed the snare with disgust. "Who on earth . . . ?"

James shrugged. "Don't ask me," he said. "Some idiot, I guess."

Dr. Adam took pliers from his bag. A couple of quick snips . . . the wire was gone.

"She's been trying to bite it off," Dr. Adam said almost to himself as he examined the wound.

"How long do you think she's been here, Dad?" Mandy felt better now that her father was here. If anyone could make Charley okay, he could.

Dr. Adam shook his head. "Not that long, thank goodness. She's thin. Been out on the hills, I should think. It's my guess she was heading back to the village. If she'd been here all the time, I'm afraid she'd be dead by now."

He quickly covered the wound with a rough bandage. "That'll keep it clean while we carry her back to the car," he said. "I'll dress it properly when we get her to the Ark."

Dr. Adam fastened his bag and handed it to Mandy. "Here, you carry this." He put his arms under the injured dog and lifted her up. She lay quietly in his arms. Her head lolled to one side. Big brown eyes looked at Mandy. Her tail wagged feebly. "You lead, James," said Dr. Adam.

They set off down the hill in single file, James in front, Mandy behind, her heart pounding anxiously.

A couple of times Dr. Adam slipped on the damp turf. Mandy gasped and dashed forward to steady him, afraid he would stumble and fall with Charley in his arms. After that she stuck beside her father like glue, guiding him over the uneven ground.

In front, Blackie and Jess trotted beside James as good as gold. Mandy was sure that somehow they realized the seriousness of the situation.

Crossing the river was worse. The stones were slippery at the best of times without having to carry a heavy dog in your arms. Dr. Adam couldn't see where he was stepping, and Mandy had to hold his arm to guide him across. He walked forward hesitantly, putting one foot in front of the other slowly to feel for the stepping-stones. Once he slipped, his foot going with a splash into the rushing water. Mandy gasped, her heart in her mouth.

Mandy heard her father mutter something under his breath as he fought to regain his balance. Steady at last, he stumbled on across. Mandy was never so glad to feel her feet on dry ground once more.

They scrambled up the bank and walked quickly along to the low fence. Mandy helped her father over.

At last they reached the car. Mandy opened the tailgate and Dr. Adam placed Charley gently inside.

Mandy climbed in with her. "I'll stay in the back," she said. Now that Charley had been found, Mandy didn't want to leave her side for a minute.

James and the other two dogs clambered into the

front of the vehicle. Dr. Adam drove slowly and carefully home.

"I'll phone Bleakfell Hall when we get back, if you want," James offered. "Tell them we've found her."

"Thanks, James," Mandy said gratefully. "They'll be so pleased." She held Charley's head in her lap. The dog looked up at her, then licked her hand.

When they arrived at Animal Ark, Dr. Adam took Charley directly into the treatment room. Mandy held the dog's head while her father bathed and dressed Charley's wounded leg and gave her an injection of antibiotics.

"Will she be all right, Dad?" Mandy asked anxiously.

"She'll be fine. The wound's not very deep, thank goodness."

James went off to phone the hall with the good news. "Ben's very pleased," he said, coming back into the room. "He's going to tell the others."

Dr. Adam carried Charley into the kitchen. He put her down on the floor. Jess came over to lick the Labrador's face. Charley hobbled toward the fire and into Jess's basket.

"Oh!" Mandy laughed. "Sorry, Jess . . . it looks as if you've lost your bed."

But Jess wouldn't have it. She climbed in and curled up beside Charley.

"Make her a bowl of warm milk and biscuits," Dr. Adam suggested. "She can have some meat later on."

Mandy warmed a saucepan of milk on the stove and poured it over a bowl of dog meal. She took it across to Charley. The Labrador lapped it up hungrily, licking the bowl clean in just a few seconds.

"That's better," Mandy said, stroking Charley's head. "Now try to get some rest. Come on," she said to James. "Let's leave them both to have a good sleep. They deserve it."

Later that afternoon, after James had gone home, Charley had visitors. Mandy went to answer the knock at the door. Hammond Curtis stood there with Ben Burton and Antonia Kent. Behind them stood George Sims.

Mandy invited them through into the kitchen. George Sims crouched down beside the dog basket. Mandy was pleased when Charley wagged her tail at him. He patted her head awkwardly.

"I should tell you off," he said gruffly. "But I suppose it was my fault you ran away." Charley sniffed the sleeve of his jacket. He patted her head again then stood up. "Thanks, young lady," he said. "I'm very grateful."

Mandy blushed. "It's all right, Mr. Sims," she said. "Jess did it, really." Mr. Sims patted Jess's head.

"The new trainer's arriving later today," Ben said. "George is going to pick her up at the station before he leaves."

Dr. Adam came in from the garden. He shook hands with Mr. Curtis and Ben. Antonia Kent offered her cheek to him for a kiss. Mandy almost giggled as her dad looked a bit flustered.

"How long will it be before Charley can work again?" Mr. Curtis asked.

"Next week, I should think," Dr. Adam replied. "She'll limp for a while, but not badly."

"Can we leave her here for you to look after, Mandy?" Mr. Curtis asked. "The new trainer's coming today but I'd be happier if Charley stayed with you." He winked at Mandy.

"Well . . ." Dr. Adam's eyes twinkled as he looked at his daughter. "I suppose it will be all right."

Everyone laughed as Mandy threw her arms around her father's neck. Her heart brimmed with joy as she kissed him soundly on the cheek. She felt honored to be trusted with a movie star dog!

"We'll get on with the scenes she doesn't appear in," Mr. Curtis said, looking relieved. "But as soon as she's better, it's back to work."

Antonia Kent opened her handbag. She took out

a black-and-white photograph of herself dressed in the white silk dress she wore in the murder mystery. She took a pen and quickly signed it.

"Here you are, darling." She thrust the picture in front of Mandy. "Have this for your bedroom wall."

"Oh!" Mandy said. "It's great. Thank you, Miss Kent. My friends at school will be really jealous."

Mr. Curtis clapped his hands. "Okay, everyone. Back to work."

"Slave driver," Antonia Kent said, giving Mandy a wink behind Mr. Curtis's back.

Charley and Jess barked good-bye.

A little over a week later, Charley was ready to go back to work.

That afternoon Mandy rushed out of school as fast as she could. She was in a terrible hurry. There were chores to do, English homework and math, and she had to make Charley look beautiful for her return to Bleakfell Hall.

"Hey, what's the rush?" James called as Mandy jumped on her bike and pedaled furiously away from the school gates.

"It's Charley's last day at Animal Ark," Mandy called over her shoulder. Her backpack bumped on her back. "I have to get her ready. We're taking her back this evening."

"Well, you could at least wait for me!" James yelled as Mandy got farther and farther away.

Mandy waited for him to catch up.

"She looks great," Mandy said. "Her leg's healed beautifully." She suddenly felt sad. "Jess is going to miss her like anything."

"She'll be going back home in a few weeks, too," James reminded her.

"I know," Mandy said sadly. Animal Ark would seem really empty without Jess and Charley.

They biked the two miles to Welford in no time at all. James stopped by Mandy's gate.

"Good luck tonight," he said.

Mandy smiled. "Thanks. I'll feel really upset taking her back," she confessed.

"You can always borrow Blackie," James said generously.

Mandy managed a cheerful smile. She squared her shoulders. It was no good moping around. There'd be lots of other animals who needed her help. "Thanks, James," she said warmly.

"See you tomorrow!" James waved and rode off down the lane.

Mandy left her bike by the shed and went into the

kitchen. Charley got up from her place by the fire and came to greet her. Mandy threw her bag down and gave the dog a hug. She looked into the deep brown eyes.

"You look great, Charley. But it's back to work for you, I'm afraid."

Charley barked.

Mandy looked around. "Where's Jess?" Suddenly, she heard a strange noise from the broom closet. A kind of snuffling, then a tearing noise. Something fell with a clatter and all at once Jess appeared with a yellow rag in her mouth. She let it drop to the floor, put her front paw on it, then started trying to tear it up.

Mandy burst out laughing. "Oh, Jess, you are funny." She picked Jess up and pried the rag away from her. She hugged her close. "You're a real monkey." Mandy suddenly noticed just how tubby the terrier was. She had been so busy looking after Charley during the week that she really hadn't paid much attention to Jess.

Mandy put Jess on the table and felt her tummy. Underneath she was a bit swollen. Mandy frowned. She knew it was silly, but it really looked as if Jess . . .

Just then her mom came into the kitchen.

"Mandy," she said with a smile on her face.

"Betty's outside in the car. She has a surprise for you."

Mandy's heart leaped. A surprise . . . that could only mean one thing: the poodle. She quickly put Jess down on the floor and ran outside.

Betty stood beside her old station wagon. And beside Betty, on a brand-new blue leash with a blue leather collar, stood Antonia, the poodle. She wagged her tail when she saw Mandy run out. Mandy bent to scoop the little dog up in her arms. Her eyes were bright and healthy, her coat soft and fluffy. She looked plump and well, the picture of health.

Mandy's throat was so full of happiness that she couldn't speak.

"I thought you'd like to take her to Mrs. Platt yourself," Betty explained.

"Oh, I would." Mandy looked at her with shining eyes. Then she looked at her mother. "Could I call her now, Mom? I have time to go over before dinner. I can groom Charley later."

"If you like, sweetheart."

Mandy ran back inside. "Jean, can you give me Mrs. Platt's number?"

Jean thumbed through the card index and came up with Mrs. Platt's telephone number.

"Thanks." Mandy quickly dialed. After two rings she heard Mrs. Platt's voice at the other end.

"Mrs. Platt," she said breathlessly. "It's Mandy Hope."

"Hello, Mandy." Mrs. Platt sounded pleased to hear from her.

Mandy quickly explained about Antonia. She heard Mrs. Platt draw in her breath.

"Oh, Mandy." Mrs. Platt's voice trembled a little. "How lovely. Yes . . . please bring her over right away."

Mandy ran back outside. "It's okay!" she cried. "I can take her now. I won't be long, Mom." She took the leash from Betty's hand. "Thanks, Betty."

Mandy felt really proud to be walking along with Antonia. She had helped to save the little dog's life and was taking her to a wonderful new home. It was a great feeling.

Antonia trotted meekly beside Mandy, as good as gold, all the way to Mrs. Platt's house. When they arrived, Mandy spied Mrs. Platt watching eagerly from the window.

The door opened. Mrs. Platt stood with a wide smile on her face.

"Come in, come in." She wrung her hands in delight. Mandy felt her heart turn over as she handed Mrs. Platt her new pet. Mrs. Platt cradled the poodle's soft coat against her face. Then she held the dog away from her to get a better look.

"She's wonderful, Mandy! Thank you so much." She hugged the dog to her again, then laughed as Antonia licked her face.

Mandy's throat ached. It was really great to see Mrs. Platt so happy. "Her name's Antonia," she told her.

Antonia wagged her tail and licked Mrs. Platt's nose.

"What a grand name! She's beautiful, Mandy." Mrs. Platt put Antonia down on the floor and gave Mandy a quick hug. "I certainly won't be lonely anymore," she said, smiling. Then her smile broadened. She pointed. "Well, bless me. Look at that!"

Antonia had jumped up onto Mrs. Platt's fireside chair. "Antonia!" Mandy chided.

"Well, who can blame her after all she's been through," Mrs. Platt said. "Though, I don't think I'll fit very well into her basket!"

Mandy was still smiling as she said good-bye. Mrs. Platt scooped Antonia off the chair and went with her to the door.

Mrs. Platt kissed Mandy's cheek. "Thank you again, Mandy. I'll never forget your kindness." She and Antonia watched as Mandy went out of the gate. A little way down the road Mandy turned to wave. She didn't think she would ever forget the sight of Mrs. Platt standing with Antonia tucked

comfortably under her arm as if they had been friends forever.

After dinner, Dr. Emily drove Mandy and Charley up to Bleakfell Hall. Jess went along for the ride.

The new animal trainer greeted them at the back door. She was a young woman with short red hair. She wore a pair of denim overalls over a checked shirt. A button on the collar said "Stop Animal Experiments."

"Hi, I'm Sue." She bent down. "Hello, Charley, I'm so glad to meet you at last." Charley wagged her tail happily. Sue fondled Charley's neck and gave Jess a pat.

Mandy looked at her mom. She gave a sigh of relief. Charley would be okay now. She and Sue were already friends.

"Dr. Hope," Sue said, "one of the horses cut herself today. Would you take a look?"

"Yes, of course," Dr. Emily said.

"Would you take Charley indoors for me, Mandy?" Sue asked.

"I'd love to."

Mandy took Charley and Jess into the kitchen. She'd been dying to see Mr. Baggins again. And the cats, of course — and everyone else.

Mr. Baggins sat on his perch. The cats were asleep by the fire. Charley and Jess went straight into the pantry. When Mandy looked, they were lying side by side on Charley's blanket. *I'm definitely not the only one who's going to miss Charley*, Mandy thought.

"*Right, everyone*," said Mr. Baggins. A noise like hands clapping together came from his throat.

Mandy couldn't help giggling. Mr. Baggins sounded just like Hammond Curtis. She wondered what *he* thought about Mr. Baggins's new saying.

"*In your places and two sugars*," the parrot squawked.

Mandy ruffled the bright feathers. "Been behaving yourself, Mr. B?"

"No, he hasn't!" Ben Burton came through the door. Charley came out of the pantry to greet him. "Charley! Great to see you, girl." Charley licked his hand.

"I'm really going to miss Charley," Mandy said.

Ben put his arm around her shoulders. "She looks great, Mandy. You've all done a really good job. Hey, why not come up to see the filming tomorrow. Bring James if you like."

"I'll ask Mom," Mandy said, feeling more cheerful. "But I'm sure it'll be okay."

Mandy and her mom were driving back to Animal Ark when Mandy remembered she was going to ask about Jess.

"Mom . . ." She gazed at her mother thoughtfully. "Is Jess . . . ?"

She noticed a twinkle in her mother's eye as she glanced at her.

"Is Jess what, Mandy?"

Mandy shifted in her seat. "Is Jess by any chance . . . ?"

Dr. Emily laughed out loud. "Come on, Mandy. Spit it out."

"Is Jess . . . ?"

"Yes, Mandy," Dr. Emily said, still laughing. "Jess is going to have puppies!"

Ten

"I thought so!" Mandy shouted gleefully. "Mom, why didn't you tell me?"

"We thought we'd keep it as a surprise. We might have known you'd notice she was getting more than just pudgy."

Mandy clasped her hands together. "Mom, isn't it great? What's Auntie Mary going to say?"

Dr. Emily made a wry face. "I don't know. I expect Tad is the father."

Mandy laughed. "I thought Jess was missing him. I didn't know they were *such* good friends!" She turned around to look at the little terrier curled up on the back seat. "Oh, Jess, you clever thing!" She felt she could burst with excitement. "When, Mom . . . when is she having them?"

"Now, calm down, Mandy," Dr. Emily said, patting her daughter's knee. "We're not quite sure . . . pretty soon, though.

"We must get things ready," Mandy said. "She'll need somewhere to have them. She likes the broom closet, I found her tearing up —"

Mandy's mother laughed again. "Mandy, hold your horses. She's not quite ready. Don't go emptying out the closet just yet."

"But she'll need somewhere," Mandy insisted.

"We'll find her somewhere, don't worry," her mother soothed.

Back at Animal Ark, Mandy skipped into the office with Jess. Dr. Adam was just clearing up after the last patient.

"Dad, Mom's told me about Jess!"

Her father smiled broadly. "We thought you'd probably guess."

"I did. I just had so much to think about I kept forgetting to ask. Oh, Dad, I'm so excited." She picked Jess up gently and patted her stomach. Then she hugged the terrier close. Charley didn't need her now, but soon there would be lots of other dogs to look after. Tiny, gorgeous Jack Russell puppies. She just couldn't wait!

*   *   *

Next morning, Dr. Adam dropped them off at Bleakfell Hall for the day, complete with picnic lunch.

Mandy couldn't wait to tell Ben the good news about Jess.

"Congratulations, Jess!" Ben said when he heard. "Sue said Charley's been moping around a little. I think she's been missing her."

They found Sue grooming Charley in the kitchen. Charley looked great, with a beautiful shining coat and moist nose. Mandy felt proud to have been the one to help rescue her.

Mr. Baggins greeted them with his usual squawk.

"Better leave Jess in here," said Sue, lifting Charley down from the grooming table. "Charley will need all her concentration this morning."

"Stay here, Jess," Mandy began. But Jess was already curled up by the fire, fast asleep.

Mandy took a couple of pieces of orange from a plate on the table.

"Come on, Mr. Baggins," she called. "Time for work." Mr. Baggins flew onto her shoulder.

They filed along the passageway and into the big hall.

"You'd better be good today, Mr. Baggins," Mandy whispered.

"Yeah, yeah," said Mr. Baggins.

In the big hall, Mandy placed the parrot gently on her perch. Everyone was ready.

"Right over here with Charley, please." Mr. Curtis stepped forward.

"You take her over." Sue handed the leash to Mandy.

"Right . . . take your places," said a voice.

Everyone started to move into their positions.

"Did I say move?" Mr. Curtis shouted. His face looked red with annoyance. "Everyone stay where you are."

"Right . . . take your places." His voice came again.

The actors and crew looked at one another. Mandy burst out laughing. "It's Mr. Baggins," she spluttered. Beside her, James put his hand over his mouth to control his laughter. All the crew was laughing, too — even the man with the dagger sticking out of his chest.

"Right . . . take your cup of tea," Mr. Baggins squawked suddenly.

Even Mr. Curtis was laughing by now. He wiped his eyes and waved his hand in the air. "That's enough, thank you, Mr. Baggins. *I'll* give the orders, if you don't mind!" He pushed his cap to the back of his head. "Never work with children or animals!" he said, grinning.

Then filming began in earnest. Before they knew it, it was almost lunchtime. After thirty-six takes, they had finally gotten the stabbing scene right.

"How would you like to be stabbed thirty-six times?" James whispered.

Mandy nudged him. "Shh!"

Mr. Baggins had been unusually quiet. He sat on his perch, a piece of orange skin in his claw. Once he tucked his head under his wing and went to sleep. No one seemed to notice. Except Antonia Kent. She kept a wary eye on Mr. Baggins, whatever he did.

"Could you take Charley back to the kitchen please, Mandy?" Mr. Curtis sat on the top of a stepladder, looking down. "Come back and watch the rest of the day's shoot if you want."

"I'd love to," breathed Mandy. "Thanks."

She quickly took Charley back to the kitchen. "Stay," she commanded, pushing her inside the door and closing it firmly. She didn't want to miss anything. Sue had already gone off to groom the horses.

It was another hour before Mr. Curtis shouted, "Okay, everyone, take a break. We're outside this afternoon, don't forget."

Everyone breathed a sigh of relief.

"Come on," James said. "I'm starving. Let's have our picnic!"

In the kitchen, the dogs were nowhere to be seen. The pantry door was slightly ajar.

"I bet the dogs are in there." Mandy pushed open the pantry door. She peeped in. Charley was sitting in one corner. She pricked up her ears and looked at Mandy. She whined softly. It was as if she was trying to tell Mandy something, something very important.

Then there was another sound. A whine and a series of tiny squeaks. Mandy opened the door a little more and went inside. She stopped suddenly. Her mouth fell open.

For there beside Jess, on Charley's blanket, were four squirming bundles. Tiny puppies, their eyes closed tight. Two black-and-white, two brown-and-white. So small they would fit into Mandy's palm. Jess was trying to lick them all at once. She glanced up at Mandy. "Look," she seemed to be saying. "Aren't I clever?"

Mandy's eyes felt as if they were popping out of her head. "James . . . here — quick!"

Jess, with four tiny puppies. It was just too good to be true!

James made a face. "Wow! Aren't they . . . um, funny."

"They're not *funny*," Mandy said, feeling indignant. "They're gorgeous."

"They'll look a bit better when they're dry," James muttered.

"Shh," Mandy said. "Jess will be insulted if she hears you."

"They're lovely, Jess," James said quickly. "Wonderful."

Soon all the film crew knew about the puppies in the pantry.

"We'd better leave her now," Mandy said when they had all taken a peek. "When Dad comes back we'll ask him what we should do."

Just as she spoke, she heard her father's car pull up in the yard.

She ran outside. "Dad! Dad, guess what?"

Dr. Adam got out of the car. "What now?"

Mandy pulled his arm to drag him inside. "Jess's had her puppies. In the pantry!"

"The pantry! Well, trust Jess. She always did like her food."

Dr. Adam came in to examine the pups. "They're all fine," he said. "We don't want to upset Jess, so we'll leave them here for tonight, if that's okay?" he said to Sue. "We'll collect them first thing tomorrow."

Suddenly Jess wagged her tail furiously. There, peeping from behind Dr. Adam's legs, was Charley. Jess whined and Charley pushed through into the pantry.

"I think Charley better stay out," Dr. Adam began.

Mandy touched his arm. "No, Dad," she whispered. "Look!"

Charley was licking one of Jess's puppies. Mandy stood watching, her hands on her hips.

"She's going to be their auntie," she said.

Everyone laughed. Dr. Adam gave his daughter a

hug. "Imagine having a movie star for an auntie," he said, a broad grin spreading across his face.

"We'll come back first thing," Dr. Adam reassured Mandy as they drove back to Animal Ark. "Jess is in good hands for tonight."

"In good paws, you mean," James piped up from the backseat.

The next day the film crew was packing up when they arrived to collect Jess. The rest of the movie would be made at the studio.

"I will really miss you all," Mandy said to Ben, giving him a hug.

"If you change your mind about being a vet, Mandy," Hammond Curtis said as he came down the stairs, a suitcase in his hand, "just give me a call. I'll find you a job as an animal trainer."

"Thanks, Mr. Curtis," Mandy said, shaking his hand. "But I don't think I will."

Sue walked in with Mr. Baggins in a cage. Charley followed at her heels. Mandy poked her finger through the bars of Mr. Baggins's cage. "Now, you behave yourself, Mr. Baggins."

"Two cups of sugar," Mr. Baggins said, looking annoyed at being shut in.

Mandy bent to hug Charley, sad at having to say good-bye. "Bye, Charley, I'll watch for you on TV."

Jess was safely tucked in the back of the car with her pups. Mandy squared her shoulders as she watched Charley clamber into the Animal Stars van. Jess and her little family needed her now. Her job with Charley was over.

"Come on, Dad," she said. "Let's get Jess and her babies home."

Mandy turned to take one final look at Bleakfell Hall as they drove through the wrought iron gates and headed for home.

Ahead, the winding road led down to the village. Mandy felt full of anticipation. Four puppies to care for until Aunt Mary came home from Australia! And Jess, of course. What fun they were going to have.

She rolled down the window and took a deep breath of sharp, clear air. She could see the village now, nestling peacefully among great stretches of meadowland. The familiar church spire rose comfortingly from the bundle of houses and shops. She would feel really special walking Jess and her four puppies across the village green for all to see. And when it was time for them to go back home, Mandy knew there would be plenty of other animals needing her care. She grinned to herself. *Life*, she thought happily, *is absolutely great!*

ANIMAL ARK®

Dog at
the Door

Ben M. Baglio

Illustrations by Jenny Gregory

Special thanks to Pat Posner.

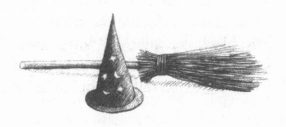

One

It was Halloween; Mandy Hope had been to a costume party in the town hall and now, as she hurried down the lane toward Animal Ark, she was remembering all the ghosts and skeletons and other creepy things she'd seen! She'd passed the row of houses behind the Fox and Goose where reassuring lights glowed from behind closed curtains. But the moon had just gone behind a cloud.

Mandy shivered and wished she'd let her best friend, James Hunter, walk home with her. She blinked to get used to the darkness, then peered ahead. Something moved stealthily out of the ditch at one side of the road. She gasped and faltered to a standstill as it came creeping toward her.

Then she smiled and crouched down, holding a hand out in front of her. "Jet! What are you up to? You nearly frightened the life out of me!"

The little black cat meowed and came eagerly toward her. As Mandy picked her up, she heard light footsteps and found herself caught in the beam of a flashlight.

"Mandy! You look really frightening in that outfit!" said Elise Knight, laughing. Elise lived in one of the houses Mandy had just passed.

"I'm the wicked witch of Welford!" Mandy whispered in a low, deep voice. "I should have borrowed Jet," she added with a chuckle. "She'd have made a fantastic witch's cat!"

"She just came for a walk with me and Maisy," explained Elise. "She comes with us every evening now. Although sometimes she doesn't stick so close by."

"Well, she really scared me!" said Mandy. She put the little black cat down so she could pet Maisy, Elise's dalmatian. "She suddenly appeared from the ditch. All I could see was a weird black shape creeping toward me!"

"It was brave of her coming up to you in that outfit!"

said Elise. "You'd think seeing that broom would have made her run."

"It's Grandpa's," said Mandy. "I think it helped me win a prize for my costume. But the others looked great, too! I left them at the end of the road. They went to trick-or-treat around town."

"I'd better get home so I can have a few treats ready in case they knock on my door," said Elise. "I don't want anyone playing any tricks on me!"

"And I've got to hurry, too, so I can have dinner ready for Mom when she comes home," said Mandy. "She's been at a veterinary convention in York all day."

Mandy walked her fingers across Maisy's nose. Maisy was deaf and had been trained to recognize hand signals. This one was Mandy's special way of saying "good-bye" to the dalmatian.

Only the dim night-lights were on in Animal Ark's clinic, a modern extension built on to the back of the old stone house where the Hope family lived. Mandy walked along the side of the building to go in the front entrance.

As she went around the corner, she thought she heard a rustling noise in the rhododendron bush. She couldn't see anything and she didn't hear the noise again. But she still went inside as quickly as she could.

The sound of music filled the small hallway. It was coming from upstairs. Mandy was glad. That meant her dad hadn't been called out. He'd be lying on the bed resting his sore ankle and maybe reading *Veterinary News* while he listened to the radio. He'd been up all the previous night with Duke, Dan Venable's shire horse, who'd had a nasty bout of colic. In his distress, poor Duke had kicked Dr. Adam in the anklebone.

Mandy went upstairs and stopped in front of the door to tell her dad she was home, but Dr. Adam was fast asleep with his sore ankle propped up on a pillow and his magazine lying open on the bed beside him. Mandy smiled and went to get out of her costume.

Before long, she had dinner ready. The soup she'd taken from the fridge was heating in the pot on the stove and there were cheese sandwiches all ready to grill.

"Now all we need is Mom!" Mandy murmured to herself. "It's eight o'clock; she said anytime between eight and eight-thirty." Then she frowned. Had she heard a knock at the front door or not? It wouldn't be her mom — she'd have used her key.

There it was again. Not a knock exactly, more of a muffled thump.

"It must be trick-or-treaters!" said Mandy as the thumping became more persistent. "All right, I'm coming," she called. She picked up a handful of candy bars to give them and went to the door.

But when she opened the door, Mandy felt her smile fade and her eyes widen in disbelief. A distraught and panting golden retriever was pulling at its leash, trying to reach the door. The end of the leash had been looped through one of the fancy wrought-iron whirls of one of the big flowerpots and the dog couldn't get it loose.

When the dog saw Mandy, it whined and strained harder at the leash, dragging the flowerpot along with a series of thumps. *So that's what I heard*, thought Mandy, stepping quickly forward.

"It's all right, everything's going to be all right." Her voice was quiet and soothing as she bent down in front of the dog.

She let it sniff her hand before stroking its soft golden head. The dog was still whimpering, but it had stopped straining quite so hard at the leash and was gazing at Mandy with imploring eyes.

"Don't worry. I'm going to unfasten you. I can't do it from here. The leash is pulling too tight. Just hang on a minute. I'll have to move around behind you."

Mandy straightened up slowly; any sudden movement would make the dog even more scared. She placed her hands carefully around the dog's body so she could unclip the leash from its collar.

Mandy bit her lip as she realized the dog was pregnant. She often helped her parents in the clinic and sometimes went on home visits with one of them. She'd seen and handled quite a few dogs who were having puppies, so she knew the signs. And from the feel of things, this poor golden retriever was very pregnant; her sides were round like a barrel and her stomach felt low and droopy. Mandy was a little worried about trying to move her on her own.

But the dog suddenly stepped backward, releasing the tension on the leash. "Good girl! I can take off the leash now! That's right, just keep still for a second," said Mandy.

After two or three attempts, Mandy managed to move the tiny knob on the clasp of the collar and release the metal ring. "There." She breathed at last. "I did it."

The dog sat down and Mandy ran her free hand over the dog's plump side. "Come on," she persuaded. "We're going inside." The dog struggled to her feet. "That's a good girl," praised Mandy. "Come on." The dog whined heartbreakingly and pulled in the opposite direction from the door.

Mandy's heart lurched; the poor dog sounded so distressed, but she knew the sooner she got her in and tried to calm her, the better it would be.

"No! *This* way," she said in a firmer tone, giving the

collar a sharp tug. Mandy heaved a sigh of relief as the dog suddenly decided to stop struggling and allowed herself to be taken inside.

Mandy kicked the front door shut behind them and led the dog down the hall and into the kitchen. She shut the kitchen door, too. She had a feeling the dog would want to try to get away again.

Mandy walked the dog over toward the stove. "You sit here." Mandy tapped the floor in front of the warm stove. "I want to see if there's a name tag on your collar. It would be much better if I knew what to call you, wouldn't it, girl?"

To Mandy's surprise, the dog sat down. There was no name tag, but Mandy did notice a triangle of black on the dog's creamy-gold chest. "That's an unusual mark," Mandy told the dog. "It might help in finding out who you belong to. But you do need a name; I'll call you Goldie. Now, I'm going to get you some water, then I'll go and wake Dad."

As soon as Mandy let go of her collar, Goldie started to wander around the kitchen, sniffing in corners and under the table and around the chairs. Then she started whimpering and whining as she scratched at the stone floor.

Mandy couldn't bear it! She knelt down in front of the dog and took hold of her front paws. "Don't do that,

Goldie," she begged. "Everything will be all right, I'm sure it will." The dog whined and licked Mandy's hand. But then she pulled her paws free and began to scratch again.

"I'm going for Dad *now*," said Mandy. She didn't want to leave the dog alone, but she knew she had to get help.

Mandy started to get up; the dog stopped scratching at the floor, whined louder and harder, and banged her head against Mandy's stomach.

"Oh, Goldie! I only want to leave you for a minute," said Mandy, trying to hold the dog's head still. "I've got to go and get some help. Dad might be able to give you something to calm you down a bit."

The dog let her head lie in Mandy's hands. But the look in her eyes was such a lost, bewildered, hurting look, Mandy couldn't bring herself to try to get up again. "We'll just have to sit here like this till Mom comes home or Dad wakes up," she said, and she thought she saw the dog's tail wag ever so slightly.

Then Mandy heard the sharp, shrill sound of the telephone. It only rang twice and Mandy let out a long breath. Her dad might be able to sleep with the radio playing, but the telephone ringing always woke him instantly.

Sure enough, a couple of minutes later, the kitchen

door opened and Dr. Adam came in. "So it wasn't a prank call!" he said, shaking his head. "Somebody just called to ask if we'd found a dog at the door," he added. And he walked slowly to where Mandy was kneeling with the golden retriever's head in her lap.

Two

As Dr. Adam came closer, the dog began to tremble and tried to wriggle herself even closer to Mandy. "She's really upset, Dad. I was going to come and get you but she got herself into such a state, I was scared to leave her."

Dr. Adam nodded. "Keep talking, Mandy. If she realizes me being here isn't worrying you, she might accept it, too."

Mandy stroked the dog's head and face with gentle fingers. "It's all right, Goldie," she said quietly. "We're going to help you." Mandy was still kneeling back on her heels and she wished she could move into a more comfortable position.

But the dog whined and kept wriggling; by now her chest and most of the front of her body was over Mandy's legs. "Keep still, girl," Mandy pleaded. "You might injure your puppies, wriggling like this. There, that's better, that's right, nice and still. You've stopped trembling! Are you going to make friends with Dad now?"

"Puppies?" whispered Dr. Adam, crouching down beside them.

"I think she's very pregnant, Dad." Mandy gulped. "She was tied up to one of the heavy flowerpots and she was dragging it along behind her, trying to reach the door."

Dr. Adam looked grim but his voice was gentle and reassuring as he spoke to the dog. "Hello, girl. There's a good dog, come on, let me have a look at you."

The dog looked at the hand he was holding out, then raised her head to look up at Mandy.

"It's okay, Goldie. Let Dad check you over." Mandy took Dr. Adam's hand in hers and drew it closer to the dog's face. "There, see, that's it . . . you're letting him pet you now . . . there's a good girl."

"I don't suppose there was an address on the name

tag?" Dr. Adam asked as he ran his hands over the dog's back and sides.

"There isn't a name tag." Mandy shook her head. "I just had to call her something. I don't know why, it didn't seem right saying 'dog' or 'girl' all the time. Not when she was feeling so alone. And, who —"

Mandy forced herself to stop talking. She wanted to ask "Who could have done a thing like this?" But she knew the anger would have shown in her voice and that would have worried the poor animal even more. Instead, she watched with anxious eyes while Dr. Adam continued to run his hands over the dog.

"Her abdomen is very saggy," he said, glancing up at Mandy. "You're right, she is *very* pregnant. In fact," he stroked his beard thoughtfully, "I think the pups are due any day now. I'll need to give her a more thorough examination. But for now . . . has she had anything to drink?"

"I got the milk out of the fridge, but that's as far as I got," Mandy told him. She sighed with relief as the dog moved off her legs.

"Don't move too far away from her," said Dr. Adam. "She's calmed down a lot and her breathing's not so panicky. I'll warm some milk and bring it over."

Dr. Adam placed the bowl of milk in front of her a few minutes later. At first, the dog just stared at it. Then Mandy saw her lick her lips and she held her breath as Goldie got to her feet. But she just sniffed at the bowl and then turned her head to gaze at Mandy with reproachful eyes.

"What's the matter, girl? Don't you like milk? Maybe she wants water, Dad. I think she wants *something.*"

But the golden retriever didn't even bother to sniff at the bowl of water when it was offered.

"Come on, Goldie," Mandy said, slowly petting the dog. "At least drink a little."

Finally, the golden retriever bent her head down to the bowl.

"Well, she's not overly enthusiastic, but at least she's drinking it," said Mandy.

As they watched the dog slowly lapping, Mandy asked her dad about the phone call.

"I'm almost sure it was from a phone booth," said Dr. Adam. "I could hear traffic in the background. It was a woman, and she sounded upset, but she only asked if we'd found a dog at the door before hanging up."

"Do you think Goldie's *her* dog? Do you think she abandoned her? Or could she have *stolen* Goldie and panicked when she realized she had a pregnant dog on her hands?"

Dr. Adam didn't have time to answer. Goldie suddenly lifted her head from the bowl and stared intently toward the door.

"It's Mom!" said Mandy, moving swiftly. "I'd better warn her to come in quietly." She intercepted her mom at the door and explained the situation.

"I can't leave you two alone for a second, can I?" Emily Hope was shrugging off her outdoor coat as she spoke. She wasn't looking at her daughter or her husband; her green eyes were on the dog.

Mandy caught her father's gaze. The golden retriever hadn't moved, but she was looking at Dr. Emily and her long, feathery tail was moving ever so slightly.

"Are you coming to say hello?" Dr. Emily stayed where she was, crouched down, and held her hand out. "I want to see if she'll come to me," she said quietly. "Do we know her name?"

"I call her Goldie," Mandy replied.

"I don't think your mom's going to have to call her anything," Dr. Adam whispered.

Mandy nodded and smiled. The dog was walking slowly but surely toward Dr. Emily.

"She's a beauty," said Dr. Emily. "Well cared for, too, from the look of her. But she's worried and disorientated, aren't you, girl! You're with strangers and there are no familiar smells, or toys, or rug for you. Poor Goldie."

"I don't think Goldie really *is* her name," said Mandy.

"It will do for now." Dr. Emily was still concentrating on the dog, who was moving closer and closer.

Mandy held her breath as she watched to see what would happen. When Goldie reached Dr. Emily, she sat down. Then, with her head slightly to one side, she lifted a paw.

Mandy felt a great big lump in her throat while she watched the two of them. The dog's brown eyes held such a sad look as she sat there with her paw trustingly in Dr. Emily's hand. They stayed like that for a few seconds, then Goldie withdrew her paw and stood up. She looked over toward Mandy and Dr. Adam before walking over to them.

"An encouraging sign," murmured Dr. Adam. "Don't move yet, Mandy. Let the dog play it her way."

This time the dog gave a little grunt as she sat down and held up a paw. She was looking at Dr. Adam, so he stepped forward first.

"Still wary of me, aren't you, girl!" he murmured, noting the slight trembling and the speed at which the retriever withdrew her paw. "I don't think she's used to men," he added, glancing at his wife as he moved away.

"Mmm, she definitely seems to relate better to females." A small smile touched Dr. Emily's lips as Goldie shuffled, still sitting, a couple of inches closer to Mandy.

Mandy knelt down in front of Goldie before taking her paw. She was pleased to see that the dog's eyes were starting to lose their hurt expression. "She must be feeling safe with us now," said Mandy, using her free hand to play gently with the soft fur on Goldie's chest.

"She needs a closer examination than the one I gave her," said Dr. Adam. "And we need to check to see if she's been microchipped."

Mandy knew that a lot of owners had a numbered microchip injected painlessly into their pet's neck. Most vets, police stations, and branches of the SPCA had a special scanner they could use to reveal the number. "I hadn't got around to thinking of that!" said Mandy. "If Goldie *has* been microchipped someone will be able to trace her owner, won't they?"

Dr. Emily nodded. "Either way, we'll have to inform all the authorities as soon as we know. I think it would be best if you and I handled her, Mandy. Let's see if we can get her to come through to the clinic."

"You could finish making dinner, Dad," said Mandy. "The sandwiches are all ready to toast. Poor Mom must be starving!"

"I am," agreed Dr. Emily. "But as always it's —"

"Animals first!" laughed Mandy and Dr. Adam together.

"No microchip," reported Dr. Emily, after she'd run the scanner over Goldie's neck. "And no name on her collar, either. Put it back on, Mandy. Then you can hold her steady while I listen to her heart and lungs."

Mandy watched Dr. Emily's expression carefully and smiled when her mother gave a satisfied nod. "No problems there," she said. "Ears, eyes, mouth, and nose are fine, too. I think she's about eighteen months old. And this is probably her first pregnancy."

"Her nails feel naturally short" — Mandy leaned over to feel for herself and Dr. Emily continued — "so it seems as though she's used to walking on sidewalks or rough roads. Indoor dogs, or ones who only have a yard for exercising in, usually need their nails trimmed with clippers."

"Goldie's turned out to be a good name for her," chuckled Mandy. "She's being as good as gold. She doesn't seem to mind being up on the examination table at all."

"Not up till now." Dr. Emily smiled and reached for a pair of rubber gloves from the cart. "She might not be so happy at this next part, though. I want to take her temperature."

Mandy watched as her mother got a snub-nosed glass thermometer, then spoke soothingly to Goldie. The dog flinched a bit but she didn't struggle. "There, I'm proud of you," Mandy whispered.

"It won't take long, girl," murmured Dr. Emily.

"Is her temperature okay?" asked Mandy half a

minute or so later when her mother removed the thermometer.

"Slightly below normal, just a little over ninety-eight
point six."

"Is that something to worry about, Mom?"

"Not in the way you think. A normal temperature is
around one hundred or one hundred two. But in a pregnant dog, a dropping temperature is one of the signs
that the pups are within a day or two of being born."

"Dad thought they were due any day," said Mandy as
she helped Dr. Emily lift the heavy dog from the table to
the floor. "What are we going to do, Mom? What if nobody's reported her missing? Where will she go to have
her pups?"

Dr. Emily took a leash from the hook on the door and
clipped it onto the dog's collar before replying. "One
thing at a time, Mandy. We'll take some food in with us.
You can make her a meal while Dad and I sort a few
things out. Come on, girl," she added, patting the top of
her leg to encourage the dog to follow her.

She passed Mandy a can of special care dog food and
a packet of dry food from the display in the reception
area and the three of them walked through the connecting door back into the kitchen. But Goldie whined
anxiously and pulled toward the back door.

"Shall I take her into the yard, Mom?" Mandy asked. "I'll keep her leash on but she can't get out anyway. The gate's shut; I came in that way."

"Yes. Keep a good hold on the leash, though I don't think she'll try to run off. She might just have to go to the bathroom. Leave the door open and call out if you need any help."

Sniffing here and there, the golden retriever walked around the yard for a while before crouching down. "Good girl," praised Mandy. "Should we go back in now and get you something to eat?"

Goldie seemed only too anxious to go back inside. And when Mandy unclipped the leash, she went straight for the spot in front of the stove.

Dr. Emily was munching a raw carrot. "Just something to snack on," she said. "Your dad's gone to make a few phone calls. The kettle's boiled and I've put some yeast extract in that jug. You can make some gravy to soak the dry food in."

"How much of everything?" Mandy asked.

"Just soak a very small handful of the dry food. Then mix it with a quarter of the canned meat."

"Are we not giving her much in case the food doesn't agree with her, Mom?"

Dr. Emily smiled. "That would be a reason, normally. But even if we knew what Goldie's usual diet was, we'd still only give her a small portion to prevent her from feeling bloated. At this stage of pregnancy it's best to feed a dog little and often, rather than giving her one or two main-sized meals. And it wouldn't surprise me if Goldie didn't want anything to eat at all."

"Because she's in a strange place, Mom?"

"That could be a reason, of course. But refusing food is another sign that the pups are only a day or two away from being born." Dr. Emily smiled. "We'll see what happens when you give her some."

"Who's Dad calling?" asked Mandy as she opened the can.

"The police, the dog warden, the SPCA, Betty Hilder, and the Golden Retriever Rescue." Dr. Emily smiled. "Though, unless it was a dog thief with an attack of guilty conscience who called, which is extremely unlikely, I very much doubt there'll be any report of a missing golden retriever that matches the description of this dog."

"What comes next, then?" asked Mandy. She kept on mixing the dog food but turned her head to look down at Goldie. The dog was lying on one side, her body slightly curled and her legs stretched out. She'd crossed one front paw over the other, her head was resting on the floor, and she was watching Mandy.

Mandy stopped what she was doing and kneeled

down beside the dog. Goldie licked Mandy's hand and gave a little whine.

I just hope that nobody's coming to take her away to the dog pound, thought Mandy as she played gently with Goldie's ears.

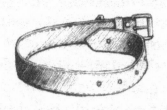

Three

"It's all arranged," said Dr. Adam. He was limping slightly as he walked back into the kitchen.

"What is?" Mandy asked anxiously.

"Betty Hilder says she could have Goldie and her litter at the animal sanctuary. She thinks she'd probably be able to find homes for the pups when they're old enough. And the Golden Retriever Rescue would be willing to take Goldie. That's unless someone claims her, of course, which I doubt."

"We won't be taking Goldie to the animal sanctuary tonight, will we, Dad?"

Dr. Adam smiled at his daughter. "No. Unless she's

claimed, Goldie's staying here to have her pups," he said.

"That's great!" said Mandy, dashing over to give him a hug. "Does Mom know? She went to take a quick shower. What's the matter?" she added as her dad gave a small gasp.

"You knocked me off balance a bit, sweetheart, and my ankle isn't feeling so good."

"Oh, Dad! I'd forgotten all about Duke kicking you. Tell you what . . ."

Mandy took the first-aid box down, then handed Dr. Adam a tub of anesthetic cream. "Sit down and rub some of this on your ankle while I finish with dinner." She turned to glance over at the golden retriever. "I don't think Goldie wants hers."

"Don't worry about it, Mandy. Expectant moms often go off their food a couple of days before the pups are due."

Mandy nodded. "That's what Mom said. But I'm worried that she feels too strange and unhappy to eat."

"Well, we'll see how things develop. In the meantime, let's try to make sure she drinks a reasonable amount of fluid."

Dr. Adam gave a little groan as he started to rub the cream in, and immediately Goldie waddled over to him.

She sniffed at his ankle, then, whining a little as though in sympathy, she licked his hand.

"Well, I don't know whether you feel sorry for me or if you just like the smell of the cream," Dr. Adam said softly. "But you're a good, brave girl, aren't you!"

"She's thanking you for letting her stay to have her pups," said Mandy. She smiled as Goldie allowed Dr. Adam to rub the top of her golden head before turning to waddle away. "Dad, do you think her owner *did* abandon her? How could anyone bear to? She's such a loving, gentle animal!"

"She's also having puppies," Dr. Adam replied grimly. "Maybe her owner hadn't bargained for that!"

"But they'd have noticed before now!" said Mandy. "I think she was stolen and the thieves panicked when they realized she was pregnant."

"In that case, she'll be reported missing." Dr. Adam shook his head. "Only time will tell, Mandy."

Mandy nodded. "Look, she's settling down in front of the stove again. I'll get my big beanbag for her later. We can put an old blanket and a sheet over it. And what about —"

"Mandy! Dinner?" prompted Dr. Adam, smiling. "I'm sure that soup is more than ready by now, and I toasted the sandwiches while you and Mom were examining

Goldie. They're on a baking tray in the oven. If we don't eat them soon, they'll be soggy."

"It'll be a bit of a struggle getting them out," Mandy chuckled. "There isn't that much room between Goldie and the oven door."

In the end, Mandy had to kneel down and stretch over the big dog to get the tray of toasted sandwiches out. "It's all right, just you keep still," whispered Mandy.

Goldie blinked sleepily, then yawned; other than that, she didn't move a muscle.

"That soup smells good!" Dr. Emily hurried in, looking pink and warm. Mandy hid a grin. Her mom's cheeks were clashing terribly with her red hair, which was tied up on top of her head. "You look pleased, Mandy," Dr. Emily said. "I guess that means your dad got the okay for Goldie to stay a while?"

Mandy nodded and carried the soup bowls to the table.

"What I want to know," said Mandy, once they were all eating, "is why you're letting Goldie stay at Animal Ark for the next few days. You're usually so strict about not taking in strays. Not that I'm complaining, of course," she added with a happy smile.

"Special circumstances," Dr. Adam replied. "If it's the dog's first litter, and we think it is, she might need help when the pups start to arrive. Especially after what she's been through this evening. Letting her go to another strange place with another bunch of strangers, well . . ." Dr. Adam shook his head.

"Your dad and I agreed that it would have caused her too much distress," said Dr. Emily. "And moving Goldie around could send her into labor before she's completely ready."

"I think it's unlikely she'll start for a day or two," said Dr. Adam. "But first thing tomorrow, we'll have to organize things. We should fix up a good place for her to have the pups and try to get her familiar with that place before anything happens."

"What do you mean, fix up a good place?" Mandy asked.

Dr. Emily smiled. "It will be easier to keep an eye on her if she's in the house," she said. "Besides, she might settle in better if she feels like part of the family while she's here. Though I think it would be sensible to confine her to the kitchen. It's close to the yard and it's the best room to arrange a birth area in."

"I'll call James first thing in the morning," Mandy said eagerly. "He'll be really glad to come and help. That's if you don't think seeing another new face will upset Goldie."

"She'll probably be happy to meet James," said Dr. Emily. "Golden retrievers are popular family dogs because they like having people around them. And she'll be able to smell Blackie on him, which should help."

Blackie was James Hunter's black Labrador. James had had him since he was a tiny pup, so he was used to handling dogs. He loved animals almost as much as Mandy did; the two of them had often worked together helping ill or injured animals.

When they'd cleared the dinner dishes away, Mandy got the big beanbag from the corner of her bedroom, as well as a soft old blanket and a sheet. "This is your bed, girl," she told the dog. Goldie lifted her head to glance at it, then closed her eyes and went back to sleep.

"Just leave it there. She might decide to use it later," said Dr. Emily. "And listen, Mandy, I don't want you to keep coming down in the night to check on her. I'm sure she won't go into labor just yet, but I'll look in on her a couple of times anyway. All right?"

Mandy knew from her mother's firm tone that she really meant what she said.

"All right," she agreed. "But how about if I get up early? I'll take Goldie into the yard if she wants to go and I'll give her some milk afterward. I can get all my chores done early as well, then I'll call James. That would be okay, wouldn't it, Mom?"

"Fine," Dr. Emily replied, and Mandy went happily to bed.

*   *   *

The next morning, James arrived at Animal Ark ten minutes after Mandy had called him. She'd told him not to knock on the back door but to come right in. "That way, Goldie will think you're one of us," she'd said.

So James, slightly out of breath and his eyes bright behind his glasses, walked in and went straight over to sit at the kitchen table. "Dad's changing the front wheel on my bike," he said. "I ran all the way here." James lived at the other end of the town.

At the sound of his voice, the golden retriever lifted her head from her paws. She looked at him steadily for a moment, then lowered her head again.

James smiled. "Not exactly a big hello, but at least she isn't bothered that I'm here. She's very pretty, Mandy. She's got such a gentle-looking face."

"She's got a nice, gentle nature, too," said Mandy. "She really likes it there in front of the stove, James. I took her out in the yard early this morning, then persuaded her to drink some milk when we came back in. She didn't want any food, but Dad said not to worry about that. After she'd had her milk she went straight back there to lie down. She's completely ignored the beanbag bed I made for her."

"She's probably used to lying in front of a stove wherever she's come from." James looked from Goldie to Mandy, a look of disbelief on his face. "Do you think she *has* been abandoned, Mandy?"

Mandy shrugged helplessly. "Dad's called all the places he contacted last night and there's still no report of a golden retriever missing from home," she said. "But if she was stolen, it might have been miles out of our area."

James scowled and shook his head. "It doesn't take long for information to reach other counties," he pointed out. "They use computers to do that."

"Well, all we can do is to make her feel as good as possible," said Mandy. "And to fix up a special place for when she has the puppies."

"I've been thinking about that!" Dr. Adam came in just in time to hear Mandy's last words. He smiled at James, then pointed to a large cabinet a couple of yards away from the stove.

"We could pull that out. I'm sure we can find somewhere else to put it temporarily. And I bet one of those special boxes for when a dog or cat has a litter would fit perfectly in the space. The single cupboard will separate it from the stove, so that area will be nice and warm without being too hot."

"Have we got a spare one in the clinic?" Mandy asked.

"No. We need to keep ours in case of any emergencies. But luckily," Dr. Adam grinned, "the man who works for the company that makes them lives in Walton."

Walton was only two miles away from Welford; Mandy and James went to Walton Moor School there. They weren't in the same class; James was a year younger than Mandy.

"I've already called him," Dr. Adam continued. "He's agreed to bring his sample model over. All we need to do is assemble it."

"Dad! You're brilliant!" said Mandy. "Come on, James, help me drag the cabinet out!"

"Uh, Mandy." James shoved his glasses farther onto his nose. "Doesn't your mom keep dishes in that cabinet?"

"Yes, but . . . Oh, I see what you're getting at!" Mandy laughed. "You're right, James. We'll have to empty it first!"

"That's up to you two," said Dr. Adam, ruffling Mandy's hair. "I've done my part for now. I've got to make a couple of home visits. One of them's to Yindee. *Another* upset stomach!"

Mandy chuckled. Yindee was a Siamese cat with a habit of eating wool. No matter how hard her owner tried to hide wool sweaters from the Siamese, Yindee somehow managed to find every new hiding place.

She'd claw at the garment until the wool started to un-ravel, then bite off and eat all the loose bits.

"Make sure you keep your jacket on while you're there, Dad!" Mandy glanced meaningfully at the warm wool sweater Dr. Adam was wearing.

"Will do," he replied cheerfully. "Hello, girl," he added softly. Goldie had raised her head again and was look-ing at him. "Do you want me to pet you? Have you de-cided I'm not too bad after all?"

"She wasn't sure of Dad at first," Mandy told James as they watched Dr. Adam petting the dog.

"I bet she came around soon though," said James. "Both your parents are great with animals!"

As Mandy nodded, she noticed that Dr. Adam's hands were moving slowly over Goldie's barrel-like sides.

"Everything *is* okay, isn't it, Dad?" she whispered anxiously.

"As far as I can tell, everything seems fine, sweet-heart. Just make sure you take her outside as soon as she shows any sign of wanting to go."

"Okay," said Mandy. "We'll empty the cabinet and see if she wants to go out before we start moving it." She smiled as Goldie pawed at James's sneakers.

A look of delight appeared on her friend's face and he bent down to pet the dog. Mandy guessed he'd been longing to do that, but James was good with animals, too; he'd known to wait until Goldie *wanted* him to pet her.

By the time Desmond Barratt, the sales representative, arrived at the back door with the special box, Mandy and James had finished preparing the small area it was to go in.

"I won't come in, Mandy," Desmond said quietly. "It might upset the poor girl, seeing another stranger. The box is easy enough to assemble; everything slides into place. There's an instruction sheet with it so you shouldn't have any trouble."

Before long, the parts of the box were spread out all over the kitchen floor. Mandy and James were on their knees, reading over the instruction sheet, when Goldie got up and walked toward them.

"You know, Mandy," James said thoughtfully, "that leather collar looks awfully heavy for her to wear all the time."

"You're right, it does!" Mandy got up. "I'll go over to the clinic and get a lightweight one for her."

Jean Knox, Animal Ark's receptionist, glanced up when Mandy hurried through the connecting door. She knew all about Goldie, of course. If anyone happened to call about the golden retriever during office hours,

she'd be the one to answer the phone. "Everything okay?" she asked. "No problems? Your mom's with a patient but I could get Simon for you." Simon was the nurse.

"No, no problems, Jean," Mandy assured her. "But Goldie's wearing a heavy collar. She could use a lightweight one. Will it be okay if I take one from the sales display?"

"I'll buy it for her, Mandy. I'd like to do something to help."

"Thanks, Jean," Mandy smiled. "I'll tell Goldie that it's a present from you. I'll have a blue one, please."

Mandy hurried back to the kitchen with the new collar and showed it to Goldie. "This will be comfier for you," she said. "You owe James and Jean a lick!"

Mandy removed the leather collar and put it on the floor beside her. Then she put the new one around the dog's neck. Goldie whined and walked slowly toward the back door.

"You take her, Mandy," said James. "I think I've figured out where everything goes, and it'll be easier putting it together with Goldie out of the way. She was getting interested in all the different pieces while you were gone. She kept sniffing them."

"That's good!" said Mandy as she opened the back

door. "Let's hope that means she'll be happy to use it when it's ready."

Goldie made her way to the end of the yard and went to the same place she'd used before. "Good girl," Mandy told her. "You're starting to make a nice little routine for yourself, aren't you! How about staying out a while longer? Give James time to put your special box together?"

But James suddenly appeared at the back door. "Mandy! Mandy!" he called urgently. "Come here — quick!"

Four

"What's up, James?" Mandy demanded, racing to the back door and turning to wait for Goldie, who was meandering slowly up the path.

"I was picking her leather collar up off the floor and I suddenly thought of looking at the underside," James said quickly.

"Mom and I looked there after we checked to see if she'd been microchipped." Mandy sighed. "I thought someone had called to —"

"Mandy!" James interrupted tersely. "There *is* a name on it!" He dangled the collar in front of Mandy's eyes. "I'd never have seen it if I hadn't been looking really closely. I think somebody scratched it on with the point of a needle or something!"

"Where? Let me see!" Mandy almost snatched the collar from him in her impatience.

"There!" James pointed triumphantly to some very faint, scratched lettering.

Mandy squinted in concentration; she had to hold the collar at several different angles before she could make the letters out. "Looks like K . . . I . . . M . . . S . . . L . . . E . . . I . . . O," she said doubtfully. "That doesn't sound like a name!"

"I don't think the last two are letters. I think they're numbers!" James told her. "There's a space after the E; maybe somebody was going to scratch the address on as well. And it isn't an S there, it's a B!

"Whoops!" he added as the golden retriever nudged his legs with her nose. "Sorry, girl, are we in your way?" James moved aside to allow her to walk through the door.

"B," said Mandy. "That would make it" — Mandy figured it out — "Kimble." she said. "Wow, James! You're a genius!" Mandy just managed to stop herself from hugging him; James got embarrassed so easily.

"There's a Jessica Kimble in the first grade at school, isn't there?" Mandy went on excitedly. "Her dad breeds birds and I'm sure they don't have a dog. But it's an unusual name. She might have a relative who does. We could call and ask. She lives in Walton."

"That's what I thought!" James nodded. "And if she doesn't, we can look for Kimbles in the phone book."

"Keep an eye on Goldie," said Mandy. "I'll go and tell Mom about your discovery and I'll get the phone books. I'll bring all of them, in case we need them. We've got one for every county in North Yorkshire!"

"Well, I'm glad it's a fairly uncommon name," James murmured to Goldie. "Hey, no, come away from there, girl. I've still got the front part and one of the side parts to put in place!"

The dog had gone to the partially assembled box and looked as if she was about to try to get into it. James knelt down and rubbed his face against the soft fur on the retriever's chest. She whined, and when James lifted his face, she licked his cheek.

"Oh, Goldie!" James had to take his glasses off and give them a good rub.

Mandy seemed to be taking her time, so with the golden retriever watching his every move, James finished assembling the box. "We should let Dr. Adam or Dr. Emily check it before you get in," he said. "I'll lift it onto the table for now."

Goldie watched him with mournful eyes, and James swallowed hard. The dog looked so sad!

"Sorry to have taken so long, James." Mandy returned, carrying four telephone books. "Mom called Jessica's dad; he's one of our clients. They don't have any Kimble relatives in this part of the county, so it's down to searching for ourselves. Mom said to start checking in the local directory," she told James. "But she doesn't want us to call anyone. She says it will be best if she does that. Office hours are finished, so she'll be here soon."

"Well, the local one only covers places within fifteen miles or so from here. If we don't find the right Kimble in that, I hope she'll call all the Kimbles in the rest of the county!" James said fiercely as he crouched down next to the dog.

Mandy gazed at him in astonishment. James was usually so calm and even tempered.

"Sorry," he muttered. "I know your mom will do that if she has to. It's just that . . ." James buried his face against Goldie's chest again. "She's such a good dog," he said in a muffled voice. "I think she likes the box. She tried to get in it!"

"It looks great, James," Mandy told him, then she flipped through the pages of the local directory until she came to the K's. "There's five entries under Kimble."

she said. "Two in Walton — but one's Jessica — two in Glisterdale, and one in Upper Barnall. So that's four to try. Oh, I hope Mom doesn't take long!"

"Impatience should be your middle name!" Dr. Emily spoke from behind her daughter and Mandy turned to grin at her.

"I didn't hear you come in," she said.

"I'm not surprised. You were too busy talking. Did you say there are four Kimbles to try?"

Mandy nodded as her mom pulled out a chair and sat down. "*If* we happen to find Goldie's owner," she said, "I'll have to report to the SPCA and let them take things over from there." She smiled and added gently, "I know you're hoping we'll be able to return Goldie because she was stolen. But if someone claims her, we'll need to be very sure that is what happened."

"You mean if she hasn't really been stolen, the owner might take her back and abandon her somewhere else?" asked James.

"I'm afraid so, James. That's why we'd have to let people who are used to handling this sort of thing deal with it." Dr. Emily got up and went over to the phone.

When Mandy read out the first number, James got up from the floor where he'd been sitting with his arm around Goldie and joined her at the kitchen table. Their eyes were glued to Dr. Emily as she spoke to someone on the phone. Even though they could only hear one side of the conversation, it was obvious that this Kimble didn't know anything about a golden retriever, missing or otherwise.

The second call was no good, either. Mandy read the third number out. This time, Dr. Emily seemed to be having trouble making herself understood.

"I'd like to speak to Mr. or Mrs. Kimble, please," she repeated. Then she gave the number she'd dialed. "Yes that number is listed next to the name Kimble. Initial . . ." She glanced at Mandy who told her. "Initial P," Dr. Emily said into the phone. "Oh, I see. Yes, well, I'm very sorry to have troubled you."

She replaced the receiver and grimaced at Mandy and James. "There's no Kimble there and there never has been," she reported. "And he doesn't know anyone called Kimble, either. I think he was telling the truth," she added wryly.

"It must be a misprint," said Mandy. "Let's try the last one."

"The last *local* one!" James corrected.

Goldie had wandered over to the table and plunked herself down in between him and Mandy. James was petting her but he kept his eyes on Dr. Emily. From the look on her face this phone call was more promising.

"You say your son's got a golden retriever?" said Dr.

Emily. "And she disappeared three weeks ago? Yes, yes, please, I would!" She reached for the pad and pen next to the phone.

Mandy clutched at James's arm. This could be it! If Goldie had been stolen three weeks ago, and the thief hadn't realized the dog was having pups until yesterday . . .

Dr. Emily turned quickly from the phone. "She's looking up her son's phone number. She can't remember it. I think she's very elderly," she added with a whisper.

Then she said, "Yes, I'm here, Mrs. Kimble!" Dr. Emily started to write.

But Mandy saw her mom's hand falter; saw her shake her head. She glanced quickly at James just as Dr. Emily said, "Mrs. Kimble? Does your son live in *Australia*?"

Emily Hope had recognized the area code immediately; the Hopes had done a six-month exchange with a veterinary practice in New South Wales and they still kept in touch with the Munroes at the Mitchell Gap clinic.

"Australia! How could anyone think that a dog lost in Australia could end up here!" Mandy groaned despairingly. She was so disappointed. James let out a huge sigh and reached for one of the other phone books.

"Cheer up, you two," said Dr. Emily. "Poor Mrs. Kimble was only trying to help! I told you she sounded elderly," she said, glancing reprovingly at her daughter.

"Sorry, Mom," said Mandy. "I suppose at any other time I'd have found it funny," she admitted. "But I was so sure we were going to find the right Kimble this time."

She turned to Goldie. "Hey, what's the matter, girl? You shouldn't jump up like that, not in your condition!"

Goldie was trying to get her front legs onto Mandy's lap. She was looking intently at Mandy and she was panting slightly; her long pink tongue lolling out at one side of her mouth.

"Maybe she's trying to get into the box," said James, glancing up. "She did try to get in it before, Dr. Emily, but I wanted you to check it first to make sure I've done everything right."

Dr. Emily smiled. "Okay, I'll do that now. But it looks fine, James."

James blushed, then turned to Mandy and said, "There's only one Kimble in this phone book! I haven't —"

"James!" gasped Mandy. "Say that again, will you! Just the first part."

James gave her a puzzled look, but he did as she'd asked. "There's only one Kimble in this phone book," he said.

Goldie jumped up again. "I *was* right!" cried Mandy. "I

knew I hadn't thought of it! Mom! James! You know what? Oh, we've been so silly, and all because of Jessica!"

Dr. Emily and James stared hard at Mandy. What on earth was she talking about?

"We just assumed that Kimble was her owner's last name because of Jessica Kimble," Mandy said. "But it isn't, is it, girl? It's *your* name. You're named Kimble, aren't you!"

The golden retriever gave one quick, sharp bark. Kimble it was!

Five

"I'm afraid you're right, Mandy." Dr. Emily sighed as she stroked the excited-looking dog. "All right, calm down. That's right, you go and have a drink of water."

"What do you mean, Mom, you're *afraid* I'm right?" Mandy asked. "I think it's fantastic that we know her real name."

"I know what you mean, Dr. Emily," said James. "It's good for Kimble but not so good for us. We're right back to square one. There's no way we can trace her owner now."

Mandy looked crestfallen. She'd been so happy when

182

the golden retriever had reacted to hearing her real name, she hadn't thought about the rest of it. But maybe they weren't back to square one.

"I'm not so sure, James," she said after a while. "We can tell the SPCA and the police that she's named Kimble. If she's been reported missing her owner would have given the dog's name, too!"

"That's a good point, Mandy. I'll call them now." Dr. Emily ruffled Mandy's hair.

"And it *is* good that we can call Kimble by her real name," said James. "That could help her settle down better."

Mandy nodded. "As soon as Mom's finished on the phone we'll get the box fixed up for her."

The box was just over a square yard. It had a floor but no top. The section at the front was lower and hinged so it could be pulled down. Dr. Emily sent Mandy and James through to the clinic to get a pile of newspapers for lining the floor of the box.

"Because her pups are almost due, we won't give her a blanket or a sheet to lie on," said Dr. Emily. "A little while before she goes into labor, she'll probably want to make a nest and will start looking for something to tear up. So if the newspapers are there, ready for her, she won't get anxious wondering what to use."

"You look busy," came a voice from the doorway.

Mandy looked up with a smile. "Hi, Dad!" she said. "Is Yindee okay?"

"She managed to open the closet door this time," Dr. Adam told them. "She'd chewed a hole about this size" — he made a circle with his thumb and index finger — "in one of Mrs. Anderson's best Yorkshire wool blankets. I can never be sure if it's eating the wool that upsets the cat's stomach or feeling guilty for what she's done. Mrs. Anderson swears Yindee knows when she's been naughty!" Mandy and James laughed.

"It's possible it's some sort of vitamin or mineral deficiency that makes her feel the need to eat wool," Dr. Adam continued. "More than likely it's just a habit, but it's good to check. I've made an appointment for tomorrow. We'll run a couple of tests. What's new with Goldie? Anything?"

Mandy ran over to give him a hug and to tell him the news about the dog's name.

"So it's Kimble, huh?" said Dr. Adam looking across at the golden retriever. "No doubt about that," he added, laughing, as Kimble thumped her tail on the floor.

"Come and look at the box!" Mandy dragged her father to the table. "James did all the assembling," she said. "We're going to put it in its place now that we've lined it."

"The newspaper will be warm for the pups to lie on, won't it?" asked James as he and Dr. Adam lifted the box off the table. "*And* easy to change when it gets soiled."

Dr. Adam nodded. "Yes! Warmth is very important," he said. "If we weren't putting the box in such a cozy place, we would have had to cover the open top with a square of wood and a thick blanket, or use a heat lamp. We'll still have to keep checking on the temperature, but I'm almost sure it will be okay without any of that."

"What should the temperature be, Dr. Adam?" asked James; he was always eager to learn.

"Seventy degrees is the ideal, James. It very rarely falls below that in here at this time of year with the stove going."

The Hopes didn't use the stove very much during the summer months, as it made the kitchen much too hot. Instead, they used the microwave. Mandy, though, was always pleased when the time came to relight the big, friendly stove. She especially loved the coziness of their kitchen in winter.

As soon as Dr. Adam and James moved back from the box, Kimble walked over eagerly. Without hesitation, she stepped over the low front part to settle herself on the bed of newspapers.

"Do you think she might have had a bed like this at home?" James asked.

"Yes, I think that could be the case." Dr. Adam stroked his beard thoughtfully.

Mandy looked at him. "There really is something strange about the whole thing, Dad!" she said. "Kimble's obviously been very well looked after. She seems to be used to lots of love and attention, and it looks as though she's been used to this kind of box."

"Which means her owner must have been preparing for the birth," James added. "I can't believe such a caring owner would abandon her."

"But if she was stolen you'd think we'd have heard from her owner by now." Mandy nodded. "There was that phone call to make sure we'd found her," she said. "That was strange. If it was her owner, it's a shame she didn't tell you what Kimble likes to eat, Dad! I know you said not to worry about her not eating, but maybe she just doesn't like what we're giving her."

"I stopped at Grandma's on my way home," Dr. Adam told her. "She was making stew so I've brought a few chunks of meat home to chop up. Kimble may well be used to some raw meat in her diet. We'll give it to her in a while, but first we'll leave her alone until she's settled in her box. Meanwhile, *I'd* eat almost anything that was offered!"

"Oh, no!" gasped James. "I hadn't realized it was so late. I'll have to go, Mandy. Dad and I are going swimming this afternoon, then we're going to visit my aunt. Will you leave a message with Mom if there's any news about Kimble?"

"Of course I will," Mandy promised. "But you're not staying at your aunt's, are you, James?" she added anxiously. James sometimes spent a couple of days with his cousins during school vacations.

"Not this time," said James.

"So you'll be able to come tomorrow morning?"

James grinned. "Nothing could keep me away!" he said.

That's okay then, thought Mandy as she closed the door behind him. *There's something important James and I need to talk about.*

Kimble stayed happily in her box for an hour or so. Then she got out and walked over to Mandy. She lay her head on Mandy's knee and wagged her tail.

"Are you trying to tell me something?" Mandy asked as she played gently with Kimble's soft golden ears. "Are you hungry? Should we try some of the meat that Dad got for you?"

Mandy mixed the raw meat with a small portion of canned food. She decided not to bother adding anything else. If Kimble ate this meal she'd try adding dry food to the same mix next time.

Kimble ate about half of what Mandy gave her before going to the door and whining to go out.

Dr. Emily was in the garden planting some tulip bulbs. She smiled when Mandy told her that Kimble had eaten a little bit, then suggested that Kimble might like a slow, short walk down the back path. "Put her leash on though, Mandy, and if she shows any reluctance to walk, bring her right back."

"I'll turn back well before we reach the houses anyway," said Mandy. "She might get overexcited if we meet any of the other animals. We don't want her getting into a fight with Tom!"

Walter Pickard lived in one of the houses behind the Fox and Goose and he had three cats. The two females, Scraps and Missie, were friendly, gentle creatures, but Tom was big and fierce and thought nothing of taking on any cat or dog he saw.

"Yes, it wouldn't be good for Tom to set eyes on her," Dr. Emily agreed.

Both Mandy and Kimble enjoyed their short walk. October had been a mild month; the trees were still dressed in their glorious autumnal leaves of yellow, orange, russet, copper, and crimson. The little green flowers were still blossoming on ivy hedges and Mandy saw a blackberry bush still full of juicy berries. Perhaps she'd come and pick some for Grandma after she'd taken Kimble back.

Kimble didn't seem in any hurry to turn back. She was ambling happily along, pausing every now and then to sniff and scratch in the hedges' undergrowth, her tail moving slowly from side to side.

Watching her, Mandy grew thoughtful again. Who could possibly have left her at the door of Animal Ark, and why? "I'll find out, Kimble," she promised aloud. "I don't know how yet, but James and I will think of some way to do it."

Six

Mandy and Kimble were in the backyard when James arrived the next day. He saw them from over the gate. Mandy had let Kimble off the leash and she was walking slowly along the edge of the flower bed, sniffing and scratching at every plant and, now and then, whining anxiously.

"Hello, Kimble," called James. But Kimble didn't even glance toward him. She was too intent on what she was doing.

"You don't look very happy about things, Mandy! Kimble's still okay, isn't she? Your parents haven't changed their minds about her staying here, have they?"

Mandy gave him a weak grin. "No, they wouldn't do that. But you're right about me not feeling too happy. Kimble won't settle indoors at all. She'll come in with me, but two minutes later she'll be scratching at the door to come out here. She's done everything she needs to, so it isn't that."

"Maybe she thinks the box is just for sleeping in. Could she be looking for somewhere to have the pups?" James suggested.

"I wouldn't have thought so," Mandy sighed. "Mom checked her earlier and said she didn't think anything was about to happen just yet. But she does keep whining, so I suppose she might be going into labor."

"Maybe she's pining for her real home and owner, Mandy. She's bound to do that, even with all the love and attention she's getting here. Trouble is, if nobody's called, it looks as though she *has* been abandoned."

"I guess," Mandy nodded. "I want to talk to you about that, but I can't concentrate while Kimble's behaving like this. She hasn't made any attempt to get out of the yard. You'd think she would if her mind was on her real home. She just keeps doing that!" Mandy sighed, and they both gazed to where Kimble was sniffing and scratching.

"Has your mom or dad seen the way she's acting?" James asked.

"No, Mom's been called out and Dad's busy with patients," said Mandy. "And I didn't want to leave her while I went into the clinic."

"I'll go in and see if I can talk to Simon," suggested James. "He might come up with something."

"That's a good idea, James!" Mandy took her eyes off Kimble to smile at him. James turned slightly red and hurried off in the direction of the clinic.

When Kimble reached the far end of the flower bed, she lifted her head and looked around the rest of the yard. After that she turned and made her way over to Mandy. "Do you want to go back indoors?" Mandy asked softly.

Kimble whined, then pawed at Mandy's leggings.

"Oh, Kimble, I really don't know *what* you want," murmured Mandy. The dog moved away and wandered over to the wire run where Mandy's three rabbits played in warm weather. The nights were very cold now so Mandy had moved the hutch into the garage.

Kimble whined, lay down, and tried to get her front paws underneath one of the pieces of wood that supported the wire mesh. There was a small mound of hay in one corner of the run. Kimble seemed to be very interested in it.

Mandy picked the hay up — it was only a handful — and put it between the dog's front paws. Kimble sniffed it, pawed it apart, then looked up at Mandy. She looked bewildered, but all Mandy could do was pet her.

When James came quietly toward them, he was holding a ball, a rubber bone, and a rubber ring.

"Simon thinks she could be searching for something to retrieve!" he said.

"Of course!" Mandy sighed. "Why didn't I think of that! It's in a retriever's nature to pick things up and take them to their owner as presents! I remember reading about it in one of the books we got from the library when we were trying to train Blackie."

James's Labrador was adorable, but he wasn't very obedient. James and Mandy often tried to get him to behave better and had read all sorts of books on dog training.

"Let's put each toy in a different place," said James.

"Okay. I'll hide the ring inside that clump of hay. She seemed extra interested in that," said Mandy.

James didn't hide the bone and the ball; he put them at the edge of the flower bed, a few yards apart. He walked back to Kimble, bent down, and put his arms around her neck. "Go fetch me a present, girl," he whispered into her ear.

One at a time, Kimble fetched the rubber bone, the

ball, and the ring and laid them at Mandy's and James's feet. "Maybe that *was* it!" said James as he petted Kimble's head. "Her tail's really wagging, Mandy."

But the next second, Kimble had returned to the clump of hay. She pawed and sniffed at it, then whined and looked mournfully at Mandy and James.

"I just remembered something else!" cried Mandy. "Wait here, James. And you, too, Kimble."

Mandy came back with an armful of hay. She hurried to the rabbits' run, kicked it carefully with her foot to tilt it on one side, and put the hay down. "Come on, James. We'll wait by the back door," she said.

Once they were there she called, "Okay, Kimble. Find them for me."

"Find what?" James demanded.

"Wait and see," Mandy said, smiling. "I'm sure I've figured it out. Yes . . . yes . . . Look!"

Eyes bright, and her tail wagging really hard, Kimble ambled up the yard toward them. She was holding something in her mouth, but James couldn't see what.

"Hold your hand out, James," whispered Mandy.

James shot Mandy a look, but he did as she'd asked.

"Give it to James. Good girl," Mandy encouraged, and gently and carefully, Kimble deposited an egg in James's hand. She gave a small "wuff," then waddled away back to the hay.

Mandy laughed at the expression on her friend's face. "There was something in one of the books about a golden retriever who used to find and collect duck eggs every day for her owner. Remember?"

"Mandy! That was brilliant!" said James. "Look, here she comes with another egg. How many have you hidden?"

"Six!" Mandy chuckled. "They'll probably still smell newly laid to her," she continued, taking the second egg from Kimble and praising her. "At least, five of them might. Libby Masters brought them this morning."

Libby's family kept free-range hens; the Hopes were among their regular customers.

"I don't suppose Kimble minds if they're newly laid, free-range, or store-bought eggs," said James. "She just seems happy enough to be fetching them."

But that was where James appeared to be wrong. Kimble only brought five eggs and when Mandy went to look, the sixth egg was on the grass and not in the hay where she'd put it. "Kimble found it but she wasn't interested in it!" she called to James.

"Well, she's happy again now," said James, pointing to Kimble. The dog had gone inside and was having a long drink from her water bowl.

"She still isn't very interested in food," said Mandy. "And she's not eager to drink milk, either."

"That dog who collected eggs," said James. "Didn't she like to eat scrambled eggs? I wonder. . . ." He looked thoughtfully at Kimble.

"Good idea, James. I'll go through to the clinic to check with Dad or Simon if it's okay to give her some."

Mandy was almost deafened when she went through the waiting room. Mrs. Anderson had brought Yindee in and the Siamese didn't like being confined in her carrying box.

"Mandy! Am I glad to see you!" Jean Knox had to raise her voice to be heard over the angry yowls. "Simon's helping your father with a dog who isn't too happy about having his wound dressed and that noise is driving us all crazy. Mrs. Anderson says Yindee will settle down all right if we put her in one of our big cages!"

"Okay! I'll take her through to the residential unit." Mandy grinned and grabbed a white coat.

"I'm so sorry about this, Mandy!" said Mrs. Anderson, handing Mandy the carrying box. "Yindee doesn't like being confined in a small space." She looked really embarrassed as Yindee continued to yowl and a couple of dogs started to yap loudly.

"Don't worry. I'll soon have her in a nice big cage," said Mandy.

After washing her hands at the little sink in the unit,

Mandy carefully opened the carrying box and lifted
Yindee out. "You really are beautiful, even though
you're so noisy," Mandy said. Yindee, her bright blue
eyes almost crossed and her brown ears pointing
straight up, gave one more yowl and swished her long,
dark brown tail from side to side.

When Mandy put Yindee in the cage along with a cat-
nip toy from the carrier, the Siamese gave a tiny meow
of approval and began playing with it.

Mandy went back to the waiting area. The door to the
exam room opened just then, and a sad-looking basset
hound, straining at his leash, almost dragged his owner
out. Mandy quickly excused herself from Mrs. Anderson and popped into the exam room to ask her dad
about giving Kimble some scrambled eggs.

Dr. Adam said it would be all right and added that he
wouldn't mind having some for lunch. So Mandy hurried back to James and the two of them went to work,
beating eggs and slicing bread for toast.

"We won't make ours until Mom and Dad come in,"
said Mandy. "But we could make a small portion now,
just for Kimble."

James nodded. "If she eats it, she could have some
more when we have ours," he said.

To Mandy's and James's delight, Kimble cleaned her

plate. Then she climbed into her box, plopped herself down, and fell asleep.

"Whew!" sighed Mandy. "This morning was hard work! All that thinking and figuring things out!" She glanced at James and grinned. "But if you agree with what else I've been thinking, we've got a lot more thinking to do!"

"Tell me already!" said James. "You're not making sense."

"Okay. Here goes. You agree that Kimble must have come from a loving home and that her owner obviously cared a lot for her?"

"Definitely!" James nodded hard. "You can tell that by the way she acts. She enjoys being petted and spoken to. I'm sure if a dog wasn't used to that it would take a while for it to respond. I still can't believe that her owner has abandoned her!"

"I think it *was* her owner who abandoned her," said Mandy. "And I don't think it has anything to do with her having pups. But we'll know that when they're born."

"How?" asked James.

"If they're pedigree golden retrievers we'll know for sure," Mandy stated. "Because that would mean the pups' father is a golden retriever, too. He'd have been chosen specially by Kimble's owner."

"Who'd be looking forward to the puppies arriving," said James.

"Exactly!" Mandy nodded. "So *I* think there must be a special reason for Kimble being abandoned, and the only way we'll find out what it is, is by . . ."

"Finding the owner!" James finished for her. "But how, Mandy? How can we do that? The only thing we think we know about her is that she keeps hens or ducks and lets Kimble collect their eggs! And that's not enough to help us!"

"I said we'd have a lot more thinking to —" Mandy broke off abruptly, her eyes growing large as she stared toward Kimble's box.

James spun around. "Oh, no!" he whispered.

Kimble was scratching at the newspaper in her box, tearing it up, and pawing it into a small mound. As James and Mandy watched, she started panting heavily.

"Kimble?" said Mandy in a low voice. Kimble paused in her scratching and glanced up.

"She's got a sort of lost look in her eyes," said James.

Kimble went back to ripping the paper. Her paws were moving faster this time, and suddenly she gave a couple of anxious whines.

"I'm going to get Mom or Dad," said Mandy.

Seven

Mandy dashed out of the kitchen and flew through the door and into the clinic like a whirlwind. "Jean! Is Mom back? Where's Dad?"

"They're in the residential unit," said Jean. The door was swinging shut almost before she'd finished answering.

"Mom! Dad! I think Kimble's getting ready to have her pups! She's panting really hard and ripping up the newspaper. She looks frantic!"

"She's not the only one," Dr. Emily said kindly. "Calm down, honey. There's usually a long time between the dog making a bed for the pups and actually having them."

Dr. Emily's matter-of-fact words calmed Mandy down. She managed a wobbly smile. "I know that, Mom," she said. "I was more or less okay till she whined."

"We'll go and have a look at her," said Dr. Emily, walking to the sink to wash her hands. "I'll leave your dad to settle Morgan down."

"Morgan?" asked Mandy.

Dr. Adam pointed to a cage. "A monster of a mouse with an ingrown claw," he said. "Yindee must have caught his scent. She started hissing and poor Morgan turned into a mass of quivering jelly. He'll be all right. He's hiding in his sleeping quarters."

"I'll come and talk to him later," said Mandy. "Give him some TLC." Mandy's parents often said that her TLC — tender loving care — was as good as medicine.

Dr. Adam nodded and smiled. "That's right, Mandy. Don't keep all your famous TLC for Kimble."

"I think it will be an hour or two at least before anything happens," Dr. Emily told Mandy and James after she'd had a quick look at Kimble. "She's feeling worried and anxious right now. Becoming a mom is a new experience for her."

"What can we do to help her, Dr. Emily?" asked James.

"Just let her go on ripping the newspaper and don't worry about her panting." Dr. Emily smiled. "It's nature's way, James."

"It's the look in her eyes that gets to us, Mom," said Mandy.

"Well, don't let it. What she needs at this stage is gentle sympathy. If you two want to stay with her," Dr. Emily smiled again to soften her words, "she mustn't be encouraged to feel sorry for herself. Understood?"

Mandy and James nodded. "That's okay then," Dr. Emily continued. "And, James, if you want to stay and see the pups being born you'd better check with your parents. It could be a long job."

"Do you mean it, Dr. Emily? Can I really stay?" James's face was flushed with pleasure.

"As long as you and Mandy being here doesn't upset Kimble, yes, you can," she replied. "We'll have lunch now, I think, then I'll probably have time to see to Morgan before Kimble's ready to give birth."

"James and I will make lunch," said Mandy. "It's all ready to cook. Dad said he wanted scrambled eggs."

"Fine. Call us when it's ready. I'll go and see if I can juggle this afternoon's workload around a bit and try to make sure either your dad or I can be on hand. Oh, and if Kimble wants a drink, that's all right, Mandy, but I think water or *cold* milk would be better. Sometimes warm milk can make a dog feel sleepy, and that could deaden her labor pains. Then she might not recognize when it's time for her to bear down to push the puppies out," she explained.

"If Kimble couldn't push would you have to deliver the pups by operating on her, Mom?" asked Mandy.

"Possibly," replied Dr. Emily. "Or sometimes special injections can help. But don't worry about something that probably won't happen. Most dogs manage perfectly well on their own."

"Come on, Mandy. Let's finish making lunch," said James as Dr. Emily left the room. "It will take our minds off Kimble for a while," he added.

Mandy smiled. It was really good that James was here with her.

"Okay," said Mandy when they'd eaten lunch and cleaned up. "We might as well make use of the waiting time, James. Let's make a list of ideas for finding Kimble's owner."

Dr. Emily had checked Kimble again and told them to call her if there was any change, adding that she'd come back in half an hour anyway.

James glanced at the golden retriever. "I know we're not supposed to feel sorry for her," he said. "But it's hard not to, Mandy. She looks so . . . so . . . far away from us."

"I know," Mandy agreed quietly. "I guess a dog having her first litter always looks like that. It's probably worse for Kimble because she's in a strange place. That's why we've got to work on this list!"

"Right!" said James, picking up a pen. "Your parents have contacted all the official authorities, so we've got to think of people who come into contact with dogs in other ways. Like the groomer in Walton!" he said, writing it down. "Jane and Andrew, the owners, don't only groom dogs, they sell pet food. We get Blackie's food from them. They deliver it. They probably cover quite a wide area."

"James, you're brilliant!" said Mandy. "They'll know lots of dogs!"

"So they just *might* know Kimble!" said James. "We could go and see them tomorrow."

Mandy nodded. "And there's the traveling library. Everyone talks to Mrs. Chambers about their dogs and takes them on the van to see her. And she brings her dog to Animal Ark, so we'll have her home number on record."

"Mailmen!" said James. "They know everybody's

dogs. We'll ask our mailman to put a sign up in the post office and see if he'll get other offices to put one up, too! Something like 'Do you know the owner of this dog?' with a description of Kimble underneath."

"And a photograph," said Mandy. "We can get film for Dad's camera when we go into Walton tomorrow."

"Now we're beginning to get somewhere!" said James.

"I think Kimble is, too!" Mandy said softly. "She's squatting, James. She looks as if she's straining a bit. I'll go and get Mom."

Mandy forced herself to walk unhurriedly out of the kitchen and managed to keep calm when she went into the exam room to get Dr. Emily; Jean had warned her that her mother was attending to Morgan. Mandy didn't want to startle either of them.

"All right, Mandy. I've just finished checking on Morgan. He'll feel a lot better now that his claw isn't digging into his pad. You take some of the small towels, packets of rubber gloves, and garbage bags for soiled bedding. And white coats for you and James," she added. "Scrub your hands thoroughly. I'll put Morgan back in his cage and be right with you."

James looked really glad to see Mandy. "Nothing's happening," he said as he put on his white coat. "I was just worried it might."

"I was only gone a couple of minutes," Mandy smiled.

"Yes, well, it seemed like ages," said James, shoving his glasses farther onto the bridge of his nose. "Kimble's looking at us, Mandy. Do you think she wants to be petted, or should we leave her alone?"

"We'll ask Mom when she comes," said Mandy. "She'll be here soon."

"She isn't straining for real yet, but I think she soon will be," said Dr. Emily when she checked Kimble. "I think maybe she would like you close by. Some dogs like being left alone to get on with things, others like someone within reach. Just kneel or sit by the box and see what she does."

Kimble stretched her head out and sniffed first at Mandy's shoulder, then at James's. Then she moved back, circled the box two or three times, and lay down.

"She might feel comfier lying down for the birth," Dr. Emily said quietly.

"She's stuck one paw over the edge of the box," whispered James. "Do you think she wants me to hold it, Dr. Emily?"

"Could be." Dr. Emily nodded. "You can take it in turns, a few minutes at a time. And I think we should get prepared now.

"Warm water, rags, the small towels, and rubber gloves, Mandy, and a cardboard box and heating pad in case we need to separate the pups from Kimble for any reason. Anything else we might need is on my exam tray on the table."

Kimble made a small whimper of protest when, after ten minutes or so, James let go of her paw so Mandy could hold it. "All right, Kimble," Mandy whispered. "I'm here for you now."

A short while later, Kimble's paw jerked, then tensed in Mandy's hand. Mandy turned her head to look up at her mom.

"Well, pup number one is about to arrive, I think," Dr. Emily murmured, her eyes on the dog. "Here it comes," she said.

Then she shook her head. "Kimble doesn't understand what she should be doing. I'll have to show her."

"What is she supposed to be doing?" asked Mandy.

Dr. Emily glanced very briefly at Mandy and James, her eyes soft as she noticed their earnest but worried expressions. "She should be licking the puppy," she said. "Feeling Kimble's tongue would rouse the pup and encourage it to take its first breath. So the important thing," she continued, working as she spoke, "is to tear the membrane over the puppy's nose — pass me a paper towel from my tray, James — then to open its mouth and clear the mucus away with the paper towel and clear its nose as well."

Mandy and James hardly breathed as Dr. Emily held the tiny puppy upside down. "It allows any fluid to drain," she explained; then she smiled as the puppy coughed.

"I'll lay him next to Kimble now and see if she'll take over. There, Kimble, what do you think? Your firstborn is a tiny boy pup. Let go of her paw now, Mandy," said Dr. Emily without changing the steady and comforting tone of voice.

"What should she do now, Mom?" Mandy used the same soft tone. "Bite off the cord?"

"Yes, then lick the puppy. But I don't think she's going to do it. I'll have to rub the pup hard with a towel. Don't worry if he screams, I want him to. Once Kimble hears him protesting she might take some interest."

The little pup squealed alarmingly; Kimble got to her feet and James and Mandy looked at each other in delight. It was working!

But it wasn't! Kimble lay down again with her back to them.

"All right, not to worry," said Dr. Emily. "I'll take care of it."

"We'll put him in the cardboard box with the heating pad and a layer of towels," she said.

"What about feeding, Mom?" Mandy asked anxiously. "Isn't it important for him to have some milk as soon as possible?"

"It is, but we mustn't force the puppy on her. Not just yet," said Dr. Emily. "When the second pup arrives, Kimble might react differently. She might deal with everything herself. Then we can put both pups to suckle at the same time."

The second puppy was born twenty minutes later. Kimble put her nose close but again she didn't attempt to tear the sac.

"Do you want to do it, Mandy?"

Mandy took a deep breath and nodded. She could

hardly believe her mother was trusting her to do such an important job.

"Okay. Make sure Kimble can see what you're doing . . . use your thumbnail to break the membrane over the pup's nose . . . that's it. Open its mouth and" — Dr. Emily passed her daughter a paper towel — "clear the mucus away. And from the nostrils, that's right."

"Now do I hold the pup's head down?" asked Mandy, and her mother nodded. The tiny creature didn't cough, though. It appeared to be lifeless.

"I'll take over." Dr. Emily took the pup and gently but firmly tapped its rear end. Nothing happened and Mandy heard James swallowing hard.

"This looks cruel," Dr. Emily warned them. "But it sometimes works . . ." And, holding the pup by its back legs, she swung it from side to side.

Mandy bit hard on her lip and James knelt upright, his body rigid, his glasses slipping down his nose. But just then the pup made a noise like a strangled sneeze. They both felt like cheering!

Dr. Emily smiled her relief and Kimble got to her feet and nosed at Dr. Emily's hand. "She wants it!" Mandy gasped in delight as the golden retriever licked the pup from head to tail. "This time she really does want it. Is it a girl or a boy, Mom?"

"A girl," said Dr. Emily.

Suddenly, the puppy squealed and squealed; James and Mandy looked into the box, then, in alarm, at Dr. Emily. She laughed at the expression on their faces. "It's all right, Kimble's not eating the pup. She's bitten the cord off. That often makes a pup yell."

James took his glasses off and rubbed them on his white coat. "Whew!" He grinned. "This is a real nail-biting experience."

"The pup needs rubbing with a towel," said Dr. Emily. "Do you think you're up to it, James?"

James's glasses were back in place in a flash. He took the towel from Dr. Emily, knelt over the box, and whispered, "Don't worry, Kimble. I'm just going to finish drying your pup. I'll put her back in a minute, I promise."

Kimble watched James with huge anxious eyes and Dr. Emily smiled in satisfaction. "Hold on a second before you put her back, James." She reached into the cardboard box for the firstborn pup. "Her maternal instinct seems quite strong now. We'll put both puppies to suckle together. Ready, James? Here we go."

Kimble nosed halfheartedly at the boy pup, then turned all her attention to the second one. "She's not too keen on the poor guy, but at least she's letting him feed," said Dr. Emily. "Pour some milk, Mandy. We'll leave them for a few minutes, then see if Kimble will have a drink herself. Then we'll change the newspapers."

Kimble lapped eagerly at the cold milk. "It's the first time she's really seemed to enjoy it," James commented.

"Are we leaving the puppies in with her while the rest are being born, Mom?"

"Maybe. We'll wait and see. If Kimble gets too restless or there are any problems, we'll move them. She's settling herself down, so I think it will be a while before any more arrive. And unless she shows signs of needing us, we'll leave her alone."

Dr. Emily passed through to the clinic to check that everything was running smoothly. It was time for afternoon office hours; Animal Ark was busy, but her husband and Simon were coping.

James and Mandy made themselves milk shakes and sandwiches and sat at the table to discuss their plans for the following day. They decided they'd go to the post office and ask about putting a sign up. It would be easier than trying to catch their own mailman. After that they'd bike into Walton, buy film for the camera, then stop in at the groomer.

"We can ask the owners if they know anyone with a golden retriever who might be the father," Mandy suggested. "I think the pups could be pedigrees."

"It's hard to tell when they're such tiny things and their eyes are closed and their ears are so close to their heads," said James.

"You're right." Mandy nodded but she was more convinced than ever that Kimble's owner had planned for the pups.

She got up to take their used dishes to the sink, glancing into the box as she went past. "James," she whispered urgently. "Kimble's had another pup. She knows what to do now."

"It's very still," James said dubiously. "Do you think it needs shaking like the other one did?"

Mandy heard the door open and turned in relief. "Mom! There's a third puppy and it isn't moving."

Dr. Emily hurried to the box and lifted the pup. She stared at it for a long second, then lifted her eyes to Mandy and James. Mandy's face clouded over. She knew immediately what her mother was going to say.

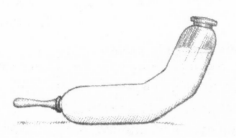

Eight

"This little one didn't make it, I'm afraid," Dr. Emily said. She spoke briskly but her green eyes were soft and sympathetic.

"It's a shame it had to happen just as Kimble had learned how to do everything all by herself," said Mandy in a choked voice.

Her mother nodded and turned her attention to Kimble. "She's all right," she said a few minutes later.

"And she's getting out of her box, Mom! Is that because she doesn't want to know the other pups now?"

"She might feel the need to exercise," said Dr. Emily. "Some dogs like a little walk around in between pups arriving. She's going to the door, Mandy. Put her collar and leash on and take her into the yard. Only stay out a minute, though. It's cold outside. I'll stop by the clinic while you're gone."

Mandy nodded and blinked. She guessed her mom was going to take the dead puppy out of the way. "Coming, James?" she asked.

To her surprise, James gave her arm a quick squeeze as she opened the door. "There's still the first two, Mandy," he said. "And however many more she has. They'll be all right, just you wait and see."

"You're right, James. I'll think positively!" said Mandy. And as they let Kimble walk slowly around the yard, she thought what a good friend James was.

When they went back inside, Kimble wandered over to her water bowl; Mandy and James waited anxiously to see if she'd go to her box when she'd had a drink.

"It's okay, she's going," said Mandy. They watched Kimble climb in and settle herself down close to the two pups. She licked the girl pup and ignored the boy.

"She doesn't seem to like him at all," Mandy said sadly. "Poor little . . ." She glanced at James. "They ought to have names," she added.

"How about Jake?" said James, his eyes on the boy pup.

"That was quick!" said Mandy.

James nodded. "I was thinking about it when we took Kimble outside," he said. "Do you like it?"

"Yes, it sounds just right," said Mandy. "What do you think of Pippa for his sister?"

"That sounds just right, too," James replied with a grin.

'There's a strong possibility we'll have to help rear Jake," said Dr. Emily after she'd returned and put him to suckle. "Good girl, Kimble, let him feed. That's right. Good dog."

An hour went by before Kimble showed signs of having another puppy. She started getting restless, standing up, then circling around. "Let's move Pippa and Jake into the other box, Mandy," said her mom. "I know you'd both love to cuddle them, but it's best to handle them as little as possible."

Mandy and James nodded, then quickly but carefully each picked up a pup and laid the tiny bundles side by side in the heated box.

Kimble didn't have any trouble delivering the next pup but she didn't attempt to tear the sac; she didn't even look at it.

"This one's a boy," said Dr. Emily, working quickly. "He's small and weak. I think we'll have a fight on our hands to save him."

"Felix?" Mandy asked James. "Shall we call him Felix?"

"Okay," said James. Then he burst out, "Kimble looks so sad and confused, I hope there aren't too many more pups."

Dr. Emily was examining Kimble. She glanced up at James. "Don't worry too much about her, James," she said. "Dogs do sometimes react like this when it's their first litter. She'll probably feel happier about things in a day or two. And I can't feel any more pups. I think Felix was the last one."

A little while later, Kimble let Dr. Emily help Felix to feed from her but showed no interest in him at all.

Mandy sighed. "Would Kimble be acting differently toward her babies if she were with her owner, Mom?"

Dr. Emily nodded. "Possibly. I'm going to check her over again and change the bedding, then we'll leave her in peace and quiet. She might come around to accepting them wholeheartedly in an hour or so. Meanwhile, Mandy, I think your dad would appreciate a hand in cleaning up after office hours."

"I'd better be going," said James. "Blackie hasn't seen me today. He'll be sulking."

"So will my rabbits," said Mandy. "I'll go and see to them first, Mom, before I go and do my chores in the clinic."

Playing with her rabbits, feeding them, and settling them down for the night soothed Mandy a little bit. And scrubbing and disinfecting the exam tables and counter-tops, mopping the floors, and tidying the waiting area helped, too.

After a while, Dr. Adam joined Mandy in the residential unit. "Better now?" he asked, ruffling her hair.

Mandy nodded. "A little bit. I know I shouldn't get so upset when things go wrong. Kimble's got two healthy puppies and the little one *might* make it. I just wish she would show more interest in them. I'm sure she would if she was in her own home. But James and I are going to try to do something about that!" she added determinedly.

"That's my girl," laughed Dr. Adam. "I'm sure if anyone can do anything, you and James can. Now, Mom wants us to take feeding bottles and some feeding formula with us." Mandy knew that the formula was especially for hand-rearing. It was as close as possible to the mother's milk, containing everything a puppy needed.

"The tiniest pup is too weak to suckle from Kimble, so he's going to need extra feeding and a lot of attention," Dr. Adam continued. "You can be on duty till midnight, then Mom or I will take over. Okay?"

"Okay!" Mandy agreed.

*   *   *

It was hard work trying to coax the tiny puppy to feed from the banana-shaped feeding bottle. Dr. Adam had enlarged the holes so Felix wouldn't have to suck too hard. But he only took a little bit before falling asleep.

"If that's all he'll take at a time, we'll have to feed him hourly," said Dr. Adam. He stroked his beard and looked at Mandy, his eyes serious.

"I know, Dad," Mandy sighed sadly. "We'll be lucky if he survives. I'm not giving up on him yet, though!"

Mandy tried flicking Felix's back paws gently to wake

him but it didn't work; so she rubbed all around his abdomen with a warm wet piece of cotton to help him digest the milk formula.

"Shall I put him in with Kimble and the other two, Dad?" she asked.

"Yes. Although she isn't taking any notice of him, she does let him lie close," said Dr. Emily. "Snuggling up to her and his brother and sister will give him comfort and help to keep him warm."

Kimble raised her head to gaze at Mandy when she placed Felix in between the other two. Mandy felt her heart lurch. Kimble looked more forlorn than she ever had before. "Is she just tired out, Dad?" she whispered, stroking the dog's big golden head.

"There's more to it than that," Dr. Adam replied. "I think she's missing her home and her owner more than ever. She's okay physically at the moment, but the birth dehydrated her and I'd feel a lot happier if she'd drink more. You could try giving her some lukewarm milk, Mandy. I'm going to help your mom with some paperwork now. Call us if you need us."

By midnight, Mandy could hardly keep her eyes open. She'd managed to persuade Kimble to drink a little and she'd fed Felix another three times. He hadn't drunk much, but at least he'd had some. Kimble had suckled the other two pups. She'd licked and cleaned Pippa each time but ignored the boy pup. So Mandy had rubbed Jake with warm wet cotton and he seemed to be okay.

Dr. Emily had said good night some time earlier. "Dad's doing first shift. I'll come down at three o'clock," she'd told Mandy after hearing the progress report and checking Kimble and the pups.

When Dr. Adam arrived to take over from Mandy, she had just made some cocoa. "I'll take mine up with me," she said, walking over to have one last look at Kimble and the puppies.

Suddenly, Kimble jumped to her feet. She got out of the box and stood looking at Mandy. Then she whined!

"What's wrong, sweetheart?" asked Mandy, bending low to pet the dog.

Kimble raised her head and sniffed; then she tried to reach Mandy's mug. "Do you want some cocoa?" said Mandy. "Is that it? Sorry, girl, but that's not good for you."

"Let's try some milk, instead," Dr. Adam said. He poured some in Kimble's bowl. Mandy smiled at her dad as Kimble halfheartedly lapped at the milk. Feeling a little happier about Kimble, Mandy took her cocoa and went up to bed.

"But your parents do think Jake and Pippa will be okay?" James said. He and Mandy were on their way to the post office and Mandy had given him a full report on Kimble and her family.

Felix was still alive but it was a real effort to get him to feed and Mandy knew there wasn't much hope for him.

Mandy nodded. "Even though Kimble won't have much to do with Jake, she lets him feed. One of us has to clean him and rub him to help him digest the milk, though. She's not overly loving toward Pippa, either, but she *is* looking after her. We've just *got* to find her owner, James. I'm sure she'd be a great mom if she wasn't pining so much!"

The man Mandy and James were told to speak to at the post office seemed unfriendly; Mandy's heart sank when he asked them brusquely what they wanted. She gave him her best smile and explained the situation as briefly as possible.

"Anyone who'd do a thing like that isn't worth being found!" he snapped. "Surely, if the poor dog had been stolen, the owner could have traced her by now." He gazed thoughtfully at Mandy, then, to her astonishment, said, "I'd give her the sort of home she deserves. My old dog was sixteen when she died. I'd had her since she was a pup. You don't get over losing a good friend and companion that quickly. But it was almost a year ago now."

"Yes, but . . ." Mandy bit her lip and glanced at James for help. He took over briskly and efficiently.

"Kimble's pining badly," he said. "For her sake, and the puppies' sake, it's worth trying to find the owner. We're sure Kimble came from a very caring and loving home, and we need to find out what happened to make the owner abandon her."

"All right. You win. You can bring some signs. I'll put a couple up here and I'll circulate some to other post offices. That is" — he held a hand up to stem Mandy's flow of thanks — "as long as you guarantee that if the owner comes forward, he or she will be questioned thoroughly before being allowed to have the dog back."

"If and when we find the owner, the SPCA will take over," Mandy told him.

"Fine. That's fine. I'd like you to make it clear on the sign that's what will happen. Perhaps you'd better ask anyone who has any information to get in touch with their local SPCA."

James nodded. "We'll do that," he said.

"Good. And make it known that I'd be willing to give the girl a loving home if nobody claims her. Now go ahead and get those signs done. I'll expect you back first thing tomorrow. And just make sure you get good photos of the dog. We don't want any cases of mistaken identity."

"I thought we were going to have a big problem with him at first," said Mandy as they biked off. "But he's nice under that gruff manner."

James smiled. Anyone who cared about dogs was okay as far as he was concerned. "You do realize we'll have to go and buy the film, come straight home and take the photos, then go back into Walton to get them developed?" he asked.

Mandy glanced questioningly at him.

"Otherwise," James pointed out, "we won't have the photos in time to take the signs to the post office tomorrow morning. If we don't take them then, he's likely to change his mind."

"It's no problem, really," said Mandy. "Apart from making the trip twice," she added with a grin. The road to Walton was a hilly one. "Then," she continued, "we can stop at the groomer while we're waiting for the film to be developed."

When they got back to Animal Ark, Mandy made up some milk formula to feed Felix, while James took photos of Kimble. Dr. Adam's camera was easy to use; it automatically adjusted itself, so James didn't have to worry about getting the pictures in focus.

"He's all skin and bones, Dad!" sighed Mandy as she cradled Felix in the palm of her hand. "He won't lick my finger when I run it around his mouth, and I've put a tiny drop of milk on his nose, but he isn't wrinkling it or anything! He's just lying here helpless, and I can't help him!"

"The little fellow's getting weaker," said Dr. Adam as he watched Mandy gently squeezing the corners of the pup's mouth, trying to help him suck at the bottle. "I'll go and get a syringe. We might be able to dribble a drop of milk into his mouth with that."

Dr. Adam returned, emptied the milk from the bottle into the small plastic container he'd brought as well, then filled the syringe a little.

"Okay, put your hand under his chin to support it. I'll see what I can do."

Mandy watched hopefully as her dad held the end of the syringe that looked like a miniature plastic straw against one corner of Felix's mouth. "Is it easier for him to swallow if the milk goes in through the side of his mouth?" Mandy asked.

Dr. Adam nodded. "This tiny tube is at a slight angle, pointing toward the back of Felix's throat," he said. "So as long as I don't press the plunger too hard and release too much at once, there's less chance of the milk just trickling straight out again."

"He swallowed, Dad. I felt his throat move," said Mandy.

But when Dr. Adam carefully released another drop of milk it trickled back out almost right away.

"Poor little Felix," whispered Mandy as she dabbed gently at his mouth with some cotton. She gave a deep, sad sigh and looked across at James. "Take a photo of him, James," she said huskily. "When we find Kimble's owner we'll at least be able to show her a picture of the youngest pup."

Dr. Adam nodded and squeezed her shoulder. "I think the other two will make it through all right," he said. "We can't win every time, you know. No matter how hard we try."

"I know, Dad. It still hurts, though! Still, there are all the other animals to think of." Mandy gave him a wobbly smile. "What's new in the clinic. Any admissions?"

"Yes. One of Johnny Foster's guinea pigs. It had a nasty splinter in its cheek. Simon got the splinter out, but we're keeping Brandy in overnight to make sure there's no infection. Morgan the monster mouse is going home later, and your mom is taking blood samples from Yindee right now."

"Did Libby bring any more eggs?" asked Mandy after she'd put Felix into his heated box. "Kimble's going toward the back door. If she wants to go out it might cheer her up if we hid a couple in the hay for her to retrieve."

"Yes, they're in the pantry," said Dr. Adam. "We'll make some scrambled eggs for Kimble to eat. She needs some nourishment. She's not had much to drink."

So Mandy got two eggs and hid them in the hay. Kimble collected them when Mandy asked her to. But she didn't wag her tail either time when she dropped them into Mandy's hand.

James watched with a sad look on his face. Then he said abruptly, "I can't bear to see her like this. We've *got* to find her owner. Let's get this film back to the photo shop, Mandy. The sooner we do that and get to the groomer, the better!"

Nine

At the groomer neither Jane nor Andrew, the two owners, recognized the description of Kimble. "We don't have many golden retrievers in for grooming," said Jane, who was busy clipping a black poodle. "We deliver pet food to one house where there's one. He's won lots of prizes and he's fathered quite a few litters. But he's getting older now; I don't think he could be the father."

"We'll ask his owner if she's ever seen a dog like Kimble at any of the shows," said Andrew. "I know she still goes to them, even though she doesn't enter her dog anymore. If you let us have a photo, we'll show it to her and anyone else we can think of."

Mandy smiled and asked Andrew if it would be okay to pet the dog he was combing out.

"He's terrific, isn't he?" said James. "I always think chows look so dignified."

"He's named Leo," Andrew told them. "It suits him, doesn't it? He does look like a lion."

"Does he live around here?" asked Mandy. "I've never seen him before. He doesn't come to Animal Ark."

"He lives in Sheffield but his owner works in Walton and brings him in once a month," said Andrew. "He likes you, Mandy," he added as Leo licked Mandy's hand. "Would you like to finish combing him out?"

"We need to come back here anyway with some photos," said James when Mandy hesitated. "You stay here and groom Leo while I go to the photo shop."

"So," Mandy said to her parents a couple of hours later, "Jane and Andrew have a photo to show around and James has gone home to make the signs for the post offices."

It was almost time for evening office hours. Dr. Adam and Dr. Emily were having a quick cup of coffee before it started, and Mandy was preparing a meal for Felix as she talked.

"I'll call Mrs. Chambers later," she continued, "and ask her if anyone who uses the library van has a dog like Kimble, and if none of that works, well, I can't think of anything else at the moment!"

"The two of you have certainly come up with some good ideas." Dr. Emily walked over to look at Kimble, who was lying quietly with her puppies. "Let's hope one of them produces a result. Kimble is really down in the dumps."

Dr. Adam nodded. "See if you can persuade her to drink some milk after you've fed the pup, Mandy. If she doesn't start taking more fluids soon we'll have to put her on an intravenous line to prevent dehydration."

"If that happens, would we have to bottle-feed Jake and Pippa, Dad?" Mandy asked.

"We may have to anyway," Dr. Adam replied. "I've got a feeling the poor girl is on the verge of rejecting them completely."

When her parents had gone through to the clinic, Mandy sighed and looked sadly down at Kimble. Then she shook her head. *I can't let her see I'm worried,* she thought. *It might make her worse.*

Mandy tried to keep calm and cheerful but it was hard work; the tiniest pup hadn't taken much milk and Kimble moved out of the box when the other two started suckling from her.

"I bet you're thirsty, Kimble," Mandy said encouragingly. "Let's have some milk, okay?"

Kimble was lapping halfheartedly at her milk when there was knocking on the back door. Mandy hurried to open it and Elise Knight dashed in with Jet in her arms and Maisy walking behind.

"I came the back way because it's quicker," she gasped. "Jet's swallowed one of my pearl earrings, Mandy! It was my fault. She knocked it off the dresser and started playing with it. When she picked it up I tried to get it out of her mouth. But she swallowed it. I'm so scared it will get stuck somewhere inside her."

"How big's the earring?" asked Mandy, taking the black cat from Elise.

"I brought the other one." Elise gave it to Mandy.

"Okay, I'll take her through to the clinic," said Mandy. "Don't worry, Elise, it's not a very big pearl."

When Mandy returned to the kitchen, she smiled reassuringly at Elise. "Mom says not to worry, she'll give Jet some castor oil. She says leave her with us for tonight, though, and —" Mandy broke off with a gasp as she noticed what Maisy was doing.

The dalmatian was sitting close to the box, staring down intently, her head tilted to one side. "She's looking at the puppies!"

"Puppies?" Elise asked. "Whose?"

"Kimble's." Mandy pointed to the golden retriever. Kimble was lying down by her bowl, her big head resting on her front paws as she gazed mournfully into space.

"I was so worried about Jet I didn't even see her," said Elise. "What's wrong with her, Mandy? She looks so sad!" Then she added urgently, "Maisy's got her head right in the puppies' box! Kimble won't like that! She might go for her."

"I don't think she will," said Mandy. "She's too sad to bother. But I'll keep an eye on her while you get Maisy."

"Okay!" Elise took a couple of steps forward, then paused. "Maisy's licking the puppies," she said, glancing across at Mandy.

Mandy nodded. "Just take it nice and slow," she replied quietly. She knew Elise was trying to figure out the best way of moving the deaf dog without making her jump.

But before Elise had time to move again, one of the pups squeaked.

Kimble was on her feet and at the box in a flash, the instinct to protect her litter suddenly strongly aroused in her. She barged into Maisy, pushing her away, and climbed into the box.

Elise took hold of Maisy's collar and Mandy froze and held her breath.

Then she said, "Kimble's licking them. *All* of them!" Half laughing and half crying, she watched Kimble's

pink tongue working its way over the pups' squirming
bodies. Even tiny Felix was squirming a little. One
of them was whimpering with pleasure but Mandy
couldn't tell which it was. She didn't dare go too near.

Maisy's tail was wagging and it brushed against
Mandy's leg. "Oh, Maisy!" Mandy knelt down and held
the dalmatian's head in her hands. "You're a good, good
girl. You've made Kimble realize that she does love her
puppies after all!"

Elise shook her head in bewilderment. Mandy grinned, then told her the whole story. "So if you hadn't had to bring in Jet, Maisy wouldn't have seen the pups and Kimble wouldn't be loving them like she is now!"

Mandy glanced again toward the box. Kimble was letting Jake and Pippa feed while she licked Felix. "We're not sure that one is going to make it," she said sadly, "but at least he'll have had some love from his mother!"

"Oh, Mandy!" Elise gave her a quick, firm hug and wiped away a tear.

Dr. Adam came in a few minutes later to tell Elise that Jet had been given a dose of castor oil, and all being well, Elise would be able to take her home first thing in the morning.

"Should I go and see her or not?" Elise asked him. "I don't want to upset her."

"I would leave her," advised Dr. Adam. "She's in a cage next to Yindee. They're 'talking' away to each other. A fine pair they are," he said. "A wool-eater and a pearl-eater. Yindee's test results are all okay," he added to Mandy. "So I guess the wool-eating is just a habit!"

"Let's hope she doesn't give Jet any ideas then," chuckled Mandy.

"You look as happy as a clam, Mandy," he said, noticing Mandy's smile.

Mandy nodded and told him what had happened. Maisy woofed with delight when Dr. Adam took her head in his hands to praise her. "We'll send for you if Kimble loses interest in her pups again," he told her, his mouth close to one ear so she could feel the vibration of his voice even though she couldn't hear it.

"Maybe she won't have time to lose interest again," said Elise. "Maybe Mandy and James's efforts to find her owner will pay off quickly."

"Oh, I hope so," sighed Mandy. "Once I've called the librarian and James and I have taken the signs to the post office, we won't be able to do anything but wait!" Mandy was never very good at just waiting for things to happen; she liked to be doing something to help them happen.

Elise and Maisy left and Mandy glanced up at her father. "I was about to feed Felix before all that happened," she said. "Should I try now, Dad, or leave him while Kimble's loving him?"

"Being licked by Kimble could just stimulate him enough to give him the incentive to take some milk," he replied thoughtfully. "But I doubt he's up to suckling yet." He crouched down and spoke softly to Kimble as he stroked Felix with one finger. Kimble didn't stop licking the pup but she wagged her tail and didn't try to nudge Dr. Adam's finger away.

"I don't think Kimble would mind if you tried feeding him from the syringe while she's licking him," he said.

So Mandy half filled the syringe and knelt down by the box. "Is this okay, girl?" she asked Kimble. "Can I try to feed your pup? There, I'll put one hand under his front paws so I can hold his head up a bit with my thumb. That's right, you lick his stomach. Now I'm going to put this in his mouth. It's got milk in it, see?"

Kimble gave a small whine, then licked Mandy's hand before returning her attention to licking Felix's stomach.

"It's working, Dad!" Mandy whispered after a while. "I felt his little throat move when he swallowed. That's it, Felix. Swallow again, and again. His tongue's moving now! He's getting the idea, Dad. He's taking quite a bit. And now he's wrinkling his nose. Whoops!"

Mandy chuckled as Felix sneezed. Kimble pushed Mandy's hand away with her paw, then sniffed anxiously around the pup's mouth and nose. "He's all right, Kimble. I haven't hurt him," Mandy assured her.

Kimble sniffed and licked for a while. Then she scooped Felix along with one paw and tucked him firmly against her stomach next to Pippa and Jake.

"She's telling me that it's time for Felix to sleep," said Mandy. "I'll give him some more in an hour or so. Kimble looks a bit happier now, doesn't she? But she's still got that sort of questioning look in her eyes. As if she's wondering what she's doing here."

Dr. Adam nodded. "I'm almost sure the pups are pedigreed goldens," he said. "So that makes it likely that Kimble was abandoned for a reason other than her being pregnant."

"We've got to try to find out what that reason was!" said Mandy. "Oh, I still haven't called Mrs. Chambers." She glanced at the clock. "I'll do that now. She should be home from her library rounds."

"Remember, Mandy," said Dr. Adam, "*if* Kimble's owner is traced, it will be the start of another long haul."

"At least we'd have something else to start *on*!" said Mandy. "Okay, I know," she added, catching her dad's warning glance. "It'll be up to the SPCA. But you never know, they might need a bit of help."

Ten

Mandy dashed downstairs, brushing her hair as she went. She'd overslept and she and James had arranged to meet early to take the signs to the post office. They were going to walk there and take Blackie with them.

I'll have to feed Felix first, though, she thought, hurtling into the kitchen.

"Morning, Mom. Morning, Dad," she said, walking toward the box.

"Hang on a minute, Mandy," Dr. Emily said quietly.

Mandy stopped dead. Her heart sank as she saw the

look on her mom's face. "What's up?" she whispered. "Something's happened, hasn't it?"

Dr. Emily nodded. "Yes, it's bad news, honey," she said. "I'm afraid Felix died about an hour ago."

"Oh, Mom!" Mandy walked slowly to the table and sat down. "I know we didn't expect him to make it at first," she said. "But then when Kimble started mothering him properly and he started taking some milk —" Mandy felt like her heart was breaking. Anguished, she turned to look at her mom.

"He took a lot from the syringe every time I fed him last night. He even —" Mandy gulped and dashed her hand across her eyes before she continued. "He licked my fingers, Mom. He seemed to be getting stronger. I thought he had a chance. What happened? Why did he die? Would it have made any difference if Kimble had taken to him right away?"

"I don't think it would have mattered, Mandy," said Dr. Adam. "He was just too weak. If he had lived, I doubt he'd have been able to lead the active sort of life a retriever should. Sometimes, hard though it seems, nature does know best."

Mandy nodded. She knew her dad wasn't saying that just to try to make her feel better. Her parents were always honest with her. "It still hurts when it happens though," she said. She looked at her mother. "He wasn't — did he feel anything, Mom? Was he in pain?"

Dr. Emily's green eyes were misty when she replied, "He died peacefully, Mandy." She reached across the table to give Mandy's hand a quick squeeze. "He was snuggled up to Kimble. I think she sensed what was about to happen. She was licking him very slowly and gently. One second he was breathing and the next second he wasn't."

"What did Kimble do when it happened?" Mandy asked, her eyes wide. "Do you think she was upset, Mom?"

"That's the next thing," Dr. Emily said. "Kimble is rather distressed. No," she added quickly, "don't go to her, Mandy. She's feeling a bit overprotective of the other two pups at the moment."

"She growls if we go near," said Dr. Adam. "So we're best just leaving her completely alone."

"Is that something to worry about?" asked Mandy. "Or is it good that she's feeling protective?"

"It could be something to worry about." Dr. Adam nodded. "She wasn't really eating or drinking enough before. Now she might refuse to leave her puppies at all. And if she doesn't like us going near her box, she might not eat or drink from a bowl we put in it. A protective mother dog sometimes loses trust even in people she knows well."

"And she'll see us as strangers more than ever now," Mandy said sadly.

"But thanks to Maisy, at least Kimble cares about the pups now," said Dr. Adam. "It could be that instinct will tell her to take nourishment so she can keep feeding them. We'll just have to wait and see."

Mandy sighed. "It's like taking one step forward, then two steps back," she said.

Her parents smiled and Dr. Adam stood up. "Time for me to take some forward steps," he said. "It's my farm rounds today."

"Yes, and if I'm going to be on time to meet James, I'd better have my breakfast, then get started on my chores," said Mandy, reaching for the cereal box.

James and Blackie were already waiting at the Fox and Goose crossroads. Blackie greeted Mandy with enthusiasm. She cuddled and petted him while she broke the sad news to James about Felix.

"Well, if your parents think it was for the best, then I'm sure it was," said James. "We've just got to do our very best for Kimble now."

Mandy gave him a quick smile, then gently pushed

Blackie down. "I suppose so, James. But it still makes me feel a little sad." She admired the signs James had made and they hurried off to the post office.

"I just hope the manager hasn't changed his mind about helping us," said James as they rang the bell on the door of the small single-story building.

But he hadn't. He even said he'd take a couple of signs to other post offices himself on his way home.

"That's that," said James as they walked back up the path and through the gates. "There's nothing more we can do for now."

"Then let's go to Lilac Cottage," suggested Mandy. "There's an awful lot to tell Grandma and Grandpa about!"

To Mandy's surprise, the sound of country music greeted them as they arrived at the back door of her grandparents' house.

"We're starting square dancing at night at the town hall," explained Grandma after she'd greeted James and Mandy and petted Blackie. "They hold square dances in Walton already and a few members of the badminton club have been going. It seemed silly to have to go there when we can hold our own sessions here."

"That was your grandma's decision, of course," Grandpa smiled. "She's organizing it all."

"Which is why I bought the *Teach Yourself Square Dancing* video," said Grandma, waving toward the television. "I thought I'd better get a little practice in before the first session. But that's enough of my news. Sit down and tell us what's been happening at Animal Ark!"

Twenty minutes later, Grandma's phone rang. "It'll be for you, Dorothy," said Grandpa. "It almost always is."

But when she'd gone to answer the phone, Grandma called from the hall. "It's for you, Mandy. It's Jean Knox. Sounds urgent!"

Mandy leaped to her feet and dashed out, followed closely by James and Grandpa.

"Jean! Jean! How did you know we'd be here? What's wrong? Is Kimble okay? Has something happened to the pups?" Mandy asked the second she had the receiver in her hand.

Grandma, Grandpa, and James waited anxiously to hear what Jean had called about.

"Someone called Animal Ark," Mandy reported quickly, once she'd gotten off the phone. "She said the dog is called Kimble and she likes a warm drink of something called 'Malto' at eight o'clock every night."

"Was that it?" said James. "Nothing else?"

"That was it," replied Mandy. "Jean said she didn't

have time to mention the puppies. She's sure the call came from a phone booth, just like the first one did. That might be to stop us from trying to trace the call."

"It doesn't help, does it?" James sighed as they went back into the kitchen.

"Well, it proves that it was Kimble's owner who left her at the door," said Grandpa. "Nobody else would know to call Animal Ark."

"And we know what to give Kimble to drink," said Mandy. "At least, I think we do. I've never heard of Malto."

"It's a malted powder," said Grandma. "You pour hot milk onto it, like making cocoa, but it's better for dogs. I used to give it to your dad when he was little, Mandy. He loved it. But I haven't seen it for years. I didn't know they still made it."

"We could see if Mrs. McFarlane has any," suggested James.

They said a quick good-bye to her grandparents, James put Blackie on his leash, and they hurried off. "I'll come with you, then take Blackie home," said James.

Mrs. McFarlane ran the Welford general store. Her store sold all kinds of things — a real general store.

The door squeaked loudly when Mandy dashed into McFarlane's. James was tying Blackie up outside; the door squeaked again as he dashed in after Mandy.

"My, you two seem to be in a hurry," said Mrs. McFarlane.

"Hello, Mrs. McFarlane," panted Mandy. "We *are* in a bit of a rush."

"Well, what can I get you then?" The woman smiled.

"Do you sell something called Malto?" asked Mandy.

"It's a malted powder used to make a drink," James put in.

"I don't stock Malto," Mrs. McFarlane told them. "But this makes a malted-tasting drink." She took a can off the shelf and passed it across the counter.

"We could try it, Mandy," said James. "It might taste the same as Malto."

Mandy nodded and gave Mrs. McFarlane some money. "Let's hope it does taste the same," she said.

"Hang on a minute," Mrs. McFarlane called just as Mandy and James were about to leave. "I've just thought of someplace where you might get Malto. I can't remember the name of the store, but it's an old-fashioned specialty drugstore in York. It's down a cobblestone side street just past Mason's, the big furniture store in the main shopping area."

"That's great! Thank you, Mrs. McFarlane," said Mandy.

James nodded in agreement. "If Kimble won't drink

this," he said, "we could catch a train to York tomorrow!"

A few minutes later, Mandy dashed into the clinic. "I've got a malted drink for Kimble," she told Simon breathlessly. "Do you think it'll be okay to give her some?"

"It's worth a try," said Simon. "Your mom looked in on her before she went out on a call. She said Kimble had drunk some water but hadn't touched the milk and sugar. And she still doesn't like anyone getting near her and the pups, Mandy, so I wouldn't talk to her at all. Don't let Blackie anywhere near her, either!"

"It's okay. He's not here," said Mandy. "James is taking him home. So I'll just make the drink, put it as near to the box as I can, and leave Kimble alone."

Before long, Mandy was pouring warm milk onto a tan-colored powder. It smelled very malty and she glanced at the box to see if there was any reaction from Kimble.

Kimble had her head over the side of the box and Mandy was sure the golden retriever's nose was twitching. Moving as casually as she could, Mandy put the bowl on the floor, then went outside.

When James arrived, Mandy was peering in the kitchen window. "I'm watching to see if she'll drink it," she whispered. "She's just getting out of the box, James."

Noses pressed to the window, the two of them watched hopefully as Kimble stretched, then moved toward the bowl. Halfway there, she stopped and turned to look back at the box. Then she moved forward again.

She put her head down to the bowl and sniffed. Her tongue came out and she lapped. But only for a moment. Kimble pushed the bowl away with her nose and walked quickly back to her pups.

Mandy and James sighed so hard that their breath made misty patches on the window.

"So tomorrow morning we go to York!" said Mandy as they turned away. "Because even if anyone calls the SPCA with information about Kimble's owner, Kimble will be with us for a while longer."

"I can't see what good it will do if they do find the owner," said James. "If she'd wanted Kimble back she'd have said so when she called."

But Mandy shook her head. "I *can't* believe she doesn't want Kimble," she said stubbornly. "I'm positive there's a mystery here, James. And somehow we're going to solve it."

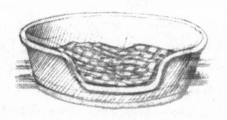

Eleven

"*Apothecary!* Isn't that an old name for a druggist, James?" Mandy pointed to the lettering on the window of a tiny shop on the other side of the narrow cobblestone street.

"Yes! That's got to be it," said James. He let out a huge sigh of relief. They'd spent over an hour searching the side streets of York for the store. Mrs. McFarlane's instructions on how to find it hadn't been too good.

They crossed the road and pushed open the door, smiling when an old-fashioned bell rang loudly above their heads. The man behind the counter looked like a kindly, ancient wizard with a long gray beard and blue, twinkling eyes. He was very strange looking!

"Hello," said Mandy when she'd found her tongue. "Do you sell Malto?"

"That's an unusual request," said the man. "Normally I'd have to order it specially for you. But you're in luck. I got some in for my one and only regular customer. She's a mail-order customer and I send her half a dozen cans at a time. But she called to say she wouldn't be needing her order just yet. That was Tuesday. So it will be safe to let you have some."

"Could we just have three cans, please?" asked Mandy, her voice high with excitement.

"The box is in the back. I'll go and open it up. Have a look around while you're here. I welcome browsers. People tend to think of me when they want something special or unusual. I stock a lot of old remedies, perfumes, herbs, soap, bath cubes, shaving cream, powdered drinks, licorice roots, herbal candy, cherry gums . . ." He waved in the direction of the tightly packed shelves and went off through a beaded curtain.

Mandy's eyes were shining as she turned to James. "The order was canceled on Tuesday!" she whispered. "*One* day after Kimble was left at the door."

James nodded.

"So are you thinking what I'm thinking?" Mandy asked.

"Yup! His mail-order customer could very well be Kimble's owner. We'll have to turn the conversation to dogs, Mandy, then see what his reaction is. If he's a dog lover he might be willing to tell us something."

When the man appeared with the cans of Malto, Mandy couldn't think of a subtle approach. "Actually, we're buying this for a dog," she told him as she handed him some money. "On Monday night, someone left her at our door with her leash fastened to a heavy flower-pot."

"We thought she might have been stolen, then abandoned," said James. "But nobody's reported her missing. She's a great dog and she's making herself sick pining."

"Then someone called, told us the dog's name, and said she liked Malto. We were wondering" — Mandy gulped before continuing in a rush — "we were wondering if your customer might be the owner!"

The man was silent for a moment. "Hmm. You could be right," he said at last. "She came here once, about a year and a half ago if I remember correctly. I think she did mention that she wanted the Malto for her new puppy. I've been sending it to her ever since."

"That proves it. It is her. It's *got* to be!" Mandy cried, turning to James. "Mom said Kimble is about eighteen months old, didn't she?"

James looked at the man and nodded hard.

"So could you . . . please, could you give us her name and address so we can check?" Mandy asked breathlessly.

The man shook his head. "I'm sorry. I can't possibly give out information like that. It would be a breach of confidence."

"Just the area where she lives would do, sir," said James.

"No. No. I'm sorry. It's out of the question."

"But Kimble might *die* if she keeps pining!" said Mandy. "Could you call her and ask —"

Mandy's plea was interrupted by the ringing of the shop bell. "You'll have to excuse me while I attend to this customer," the shop owner said as an anxious-looking woman hurried in.

"What are we going to do, James?" whispered Mandy. "How can we persuade him to help?"

James gave a deep sigh and shook his head.

As the store owner reached for something from one of the jars behind him, the lady turned to Mandy and James. "I'm sorry if I barged in. My young daughter doesn't travel very well and I need something for motion sickness. We've got a long journey ahead of us."

Before Mandy had time to say anything, the door flew open and a boy about James's age said urgently, "Mom! Mom! Come quick! Barry's got a bone stuck in his throat."

"Where is he, Jason? Where have you left him? Where's Julie?" the woman asked, hurrying toward the door in a panic.

"I'm here, Mom. What can we do about Barry?" It was a little girl's voice — high-pitched and frightened.

"We'd better go and see if we can help!" The druggist came from behind the counter and, followed closely by James and Mandy, went to the door.

On the sidewalk at the little girl's feet was a small Yorkshire terrier. Strange bubbling noises came from his mouth and he was rubbing his face along the ground.

"Poor Barry!" said the little girl. "He's trying to move the bone."

"A dog!" said the shop owner, shaking his head. "I don't think I —"

"A vet! We need a vet!" The lady was crouching down beside the dog. "I won't be able to remove the bone myself!"

Mandy moved swiftly to the distraught woman and crouched down beside her. "Don't worry. I think I can help," she said quietly. She scooped the terrier up into her arms. "Come on, Barry. Let's get you inside."

As Mandy walked to the counter, James cleared a space for the dog. Mandy put the terrier down and James moved to hold his body steady.

"It's all right, boy," Mandy murmured, "I'm going to open your mouth and look at your throat. There's a good dog. It's okay."

"Can you see it? Can you see it? Is Barry going to choke?" the woman asked anxiously.

"It's not a very big bone. Barry picked it up off the street," said Jason.

"Poor Barry!" wailed his little sister. "Can you get the bone out?"

"Shh!" said Mandy. "Please don't talk, you'll make Barry struggle." She looked over to the shop owner. "Could you let me have a pair of tweezers, please?"

"Are you sure you know what you're doing, young lady?"

"Her parents are vets," James told him. "She often helps out in the clinic."

The man pursed his lips, thought for a while, then disappeared through the bead curtain. When he came back he passed Mandy a pair of tweezers.

A couple of minutes later, with a triumphant smile, Mandy placed the small bone on the counter. James stood the terrier up, and the little dog shook his head, then looked at Mandy and yapped.

"Yes! It's gone," she laughed. She turned to the owner and said, "His gums might be a little bit sore but the bone wasn't digging in too much. It was just lodged across his mouth."

Jason moved forward to lift the dog. Then he and his sister cuddled and petted him.

"Thank you so much," their mother said to Mandy and James. "I don't know what we'd have done if you hadn't been here!"

"You're so smart!" said the little girl, looking up at Mandy. "I guess you must like dogs an awful lot."

"I like all animals," Mandy replied with a smile. "And Barry is great," she added, stroking the terrier's head.

"He was naughty, though, picking up that bone," said Julie. "We never let him have little bones like that! We'd better carry him back to the car in case he finds any more."

"Yes, and we'd better hurry," said her mother. "The parking meter will run out."

She paid for her purchase, and after thanking Mandy and James again, the family hurried away.

The store owner looked thoughtfully at Mandy and James. "That was extremely impressive," he said. "You've certainly got a way with dogs, young lady."

"I can't do any more to help poor Kimble, though," said Mandy. "Not unless we can trace her owner and find out why she had to abandon her dog," she added, gazing at him with a look of appeal.

"Hmm. Well. Before you leave, perhaps you wouldn't mind returning the items on my counter to their correct positions!" The man's voice was gruff but his eyes were twinkling. Then he spoke very quickly. "I believe

Kimbleton is a nice town. You should go there some-
time."

"Kimbleton?" said Mandy, an idea beginning to dawn.

"That's right," said the man, giving a secret smile.

"I thought Mandy was going to kiss him!" said James. "I
had to grab her and get her out of the store."

It was six o'clock. Mandy, her parents, and James
were sitting at the kitchen table, watching Kimble drink
her second bowl of Malto.

Mandy laughed as she looked at the dog, then toward
the door, then back at the dog again. "I thought I was
hearing things when the man mentioned a place called
Kimbleton. Then to find it's only twenty miles away
from us, and that Simon has an aunt who lives there.
Oh, I do wish he'd hurry up!" Mandy's eyes swiveled to
the door again, willing the nurse to return from calling
his aunt.

Dr. Adam smiled and touched his daughter's arm.
When she looked at him he put his finger to his lips,
then pointed. Kimble was walking slowly toward her.

Mandy hardly dared to breathe; a little earlier when
she and James had walked into the kitchen, Kimble had
growled at them from the box. But now, was Kimble
ready to be friends again?

"Oh, Kimble," Mandy murmured softly as the golden

retriever came and laid her big head on her knee. "It's all right, girl, everything's going to be all right. Will you let me pet you now?"

Mandy slid her hand slowly toward Kimble's nose. Kimble nuzzled into it and wagged her tail. Then she turned and went over to the box. She climbed in, settled down, and licked her two puppies all over.

"Aunt Hannah does know Kimble's owner!" said Simon, coming into the kitchen. "She's named Vera Morley, and she lives alone in an isolated house. Aunt Hannah hasn't seen her for a week or so, but she knew Kimble was having pups so she thought Vera was staying in to be on hand.

"My aunt just can't believe what's happened," Simon continued. "She said Vera thinks the world of Kimble. Apparently, she is a real animal lover, which is how she knew about Animal Ark. Aunt Hannah told her I work here."

"So what do we do now?" asked James.

"We should let the SPCA know and leave it to them," Dr. Adam replied. He glanced at his wife and raised his eyebrows.

"We should," Dr. Emily confirmed. "But maybe this Vera Morley would find it easier to explain things to one of us first."

"Mom!" Mandy leaped up and threw her arms around Dr. Emily's neck.

"It will have to be tomorrow. I'm on call this evening and your dad's got an important meeting."

"And if I don't go now, I'll be late," said Dr. Adam, standing up.

"I promised Aunt Hannah I'd drive over soon for a visit," said Simon. He glanced at Dr. Adam, who smiled. "So it may as well be now," concluded Simon. "Why don't you and James come with me?"

"Simon! You're the best!" cried Mandy. She raced over and gave him a hug.

"Is it okay if I call home, Dr. Emily?" James asked. But his eyes were on Mandy as he moved quickly toward the phone.

Mandy laughed again. "It's okay, James; I won't hug you," she promised.

"From what Simon's aunt said about Vera Morley, it sounds as if something drastic happened to make her leave Kimble here," Dr. Emily warned, her voice serious. "But even if the situation has changed since she left her, the outcome of it all won't be up to us, Mandy. You've got to remember that."

Dr. Emily looked apologetically at Simon. "It's not that I don't trust you, Simon. It's just that I know

Mandy." She turned back to Mandy and said, "So no promising her she can have Kimble back. Is that understood?"

"Yes, Mom," Mandy answered seriously. "I'll be sensible, I promise."

An hour later, Simon pulled his van up outside Vera Morley's house. There were no streetlights in the road, but an old-fashioned lantern hanging outside the porch cast a friendly glow over the large front yard. The house was low and long with two stories and there were lights behind the curtains at the tiny downstairs windows.

"Let me do the talking first, Mandy. Okay?" said Simon as they got out of the van. Mandy nodded and they opened the wooden gate and walked up the path.

Simon knocked on the door, and before long they heard a chain being put into place. The door opened slightly, and a small woman with an anxious look on her face and dark shadows under her brown eyes gazed up at them.

Simon explained quickly that he was Hannah Mitchell's nephew. Vera Morley gasped and her hand went to her mouth.

"The one who works at Animal Ark?" she asked, fumbling to release the door chain. Simon nodded and then introduced Mandy and James.

"You've come about Kimble," said Vera Morley, reaching out for Mandy's hand and almost pulling her in. "Is she all right? Please tell me she's all right. Has she had her puppies? Oh, you've no idea how worried I've been. I couldn't think of any other safe place to take her. I thought . . . I thought it would just be for a day or two . . . but . . . Oh, you must think I'm so irresponsible and uncaring."

"Perhaps we could all go and sit down somewhere where you can tell us about it," suggested Simon.

Vera nodded and led them into the front room.

"I will tell you about it," she said, once they were all sitting around the fire. "But, please, tell me about Kimble first." She pointed to a dog bed on the floor in an alcove next to the hearth. "You've no idea what it's felt like, just staring at Kimble's empty bed night after night, wondering if she was missing me, wondering if she'd had her pups. She's such a softie at times. I knew she'd need me. I promised her I'd be with her when she had her pups."

"We were with Kimble when she had her pups!" James burst out. "Mandy and her mom and me. Kimble was worried and bewildered. Mandy and I held her paw to comfort her, and when she had the puppies she didn't know what to do. We had to show her and help her and —" James broke off suddenly as he noticed the tears rolling down Vera's cheeks.

And when Vera looked across at Kimble's bed and murmured, "Oh, Kimble. I'm so sorry," Mandy's heart went out to her.

"Kimble had four puppies," she said. "There's Jake and Pippa — they're coming along nicely. The third one was stillborn and the fourth one was tiny and weak. We called him Felix. I'm afraid he didn't make it, either."

"But is Kimble all right?" Vera asked, and Mandy glanced across at Simon.

"We think she's going to be now," said Simon. "Dr. Adam and Dr. Emily were worried she'd become dehydrated; she hasn't been eating or drinking as much as she should. But Mandy and James got her some Malto this afternoon, like you suggested, and she had two bowls before we came here."

"Is she enjoying being a mother or is she still feeling too confused?" asked Vera.

"She didn't take to the pups very well at first," said Mandy. "But then . . ." Mandy went on to tell Vera about what happened when Maisy had licked the puppies. "And after that, Kimble became a really loving mom. She was really upset when little Felix died. She wouldn't let anyone go near her or the pups after that."

"Until this evening," said James. "After she'd had some Malto, she went over and put her head on Mandy's knee."

Vera wiped her eyes, then said, "I'll tell you why I left

Kimble. Maybe you'll understand even if you can't for-give me."

Then Vera explained everything.

She told them she rented her house. There was a clause written into the lease stating that no dogs were allowed. But the owner of the house had agreed to waive that clause for Vera.

"Mr. Samuels had known me for a long time," she said. "He knew I wouldn't let a dog wreck the place or go chasing sheep — the fields behind the house belong to a sheep farmer. He got to know Kimble well and he knew my sister, too. She died a year ago. She was blind and her guide dog, a golden retriever related to my Kim-ble, meant everything to her. She left me some money when she died, and I donated it to the Guide Dog Asso-ciation. Then I thought it would be nice to let them have a puppy or two to train."

"Did that make you think about letting Kimble have puppies?" Mandy asked. "We guessed the puppies had been planned for."

Vera Morley nodded, then took a quivering breath be-fore continuing. "Mr. Samuels gave me the go-ahead and even said he'd like to adopt one of the puppies. But then . . ."

The rest of the story came out in an anguished rush. A month ago, the landlord had fallen ill and been rushed to the hospital. His nephew had taken over managing the business; Mr. Samuels owned quite a few properties that he rented out. There'd never been anything put in writing about Vera being allowed to keep a dog. The nephew told her she'd have to get rid of Kimble or get out of the house.

"I told the nephew that his uncle had given me permission to have Kimble," said Vera. "But he told me he was in charge now and *he* wasn't giving permission. I ignored him at first. I thought Mr. Samuels would soon be back and it would all blow over. But then the nephew told me his uncle had to have an operation.

"And last Sunday morning he came again and said if Kimble wasn't out of here by the next day, he'd deal with it himself. He said the authorities would be on his side. He said they'd come and take Kimble away!"

"But why didn't you go and see Mr. Samuels?" asked James. "You could have gone on Sunday and he could have explained everything to his nephew!"

"I tried that, James," Vera said, her voice anguished. "Mr. Samuels was very sick. They wouldn't let me see him. I couldn't think of what to do. I knew the nephew would be around first thing the following morning. I was terrified he'd bring someone with him to take Kimble away!"

James took his glasses off and rubbed them furiously

on his sweater while he stared into the fire glowing cozily in the hearth.

Vera sighed and ran her fingers through her hair. "In the middle of the night I suddenly remembered everything Hannah had told me about Animal Ark. I got up early, put Kimble in the car, and drove toward Welford. Then, when it was dark, I came and left Kimble at the door," she whispered. "I thought she'd be safe there for a day or two while I found somewhere else to live. When I'd done that I was going to come to Animal Ark and explain everything."

Vera sighed. "I've spent the whole week going to real estate agents and calling numbers from newspapers," she said. "It was useless. I couldn't find anywhere that would allow dogs."

"But why didn't you go to Animal Ark and tell Mandy's parents what was happening?" asked James. "They might have been able to think of something!"

"Believe it or not, I was going to come this afternoon," said Vera. "I was just about to go out when the mailman came. He said something about a notice that had been put up in the local post office late yesterday afternoon. Said there was a photo of a dog just like Kimble on it, and if anyone knew the dog's owner they were to inform the SPCA. I don't think he dreamed for a minute that it *was* Kimble."

She glanced sadly at Simon. "I gave up all hope of everything then. Even if I could find somewhere else to live now, somewhere where I could have Kimble, the SPCA wouldn't let me have her back. Not after I'd abandoned her."

Vera stumbled out of her chair. "I don't know how you found out about me. But I'm grateful to you for coming and for everything you've done for Kimble and her pups. But I'd like you to go now. Give Kimble my love, tell her I miss her, and most of all, tell her I'm sorry I let her down. And please, please, try to find her a good home. And the puppies as well, of course."

Mandy and James looked at Simon for guidance.

Vera looked at Simon, too. "I really do mean it, Simon. There's no other way!"

Twelve

"Do you think we should have left her?" asked Mandy as they walked back down the path. "She was so upset!"

"I know," said Simon. "But I think if we'd stayed she'd have gotten even more upset."

"I think there might be something we can do, though," said Mandy.

James nodded. "I think so, too."

"I'm sure we've all had the same idea," said Simon as he unlocked the van door. "And that's to find out which hospital Mr. Samuels is in!"

"We need to try to get in to see him before we go back

to school on Monday," said James. "We won't have much spare time to do anything."

"We should have asked Vera," said Mandy.

Simon shook his head. "No, we shouldn't have, Mandy. I don't want her to know what we're thinking of doing," he went on. "Because it wouldn't be good to raise her hopes in any way."

"But how are we going to find out where Mr. Samuels is?" asked Mandy.

"I suppose we could call the local hospitals and ask if he's there," said James. "There won't be many, will there?"

"We need a bit more information before we start calling around," said Simon, turning on the ignition. "Knowing Mr. Samuels's first name would help. And my Aunt Hannah is sure to know it! So if you buckle up," he said, pointing to their seat belts, "we'll go and ask her."

"It's almost nine o'clock. Isn't it a little late to go visiting?" asked James.

"Aunt Hannah will be delighted to see us," said Simon.

Simon's Aunt Hannah *was* delighted to see them. She led them into the kitchen and said they were just in time for dinner. She bustled around making hot chocolate, asked Mandy to make herself useful by cutting some fruit, and set Simon and James to work making and buttering toast.

"Eat first, talk after," she commanded when she'd seated them all to her satisfaction. Mandy and James grinned and obeyed willingly when Aunt Hannah added, "Well, get started then. What are you waiting for?"

When they'd finished, Mandy said it was the most delicious supper she could ever remember eating.

James agreed. He'd managed to drink two huge mugs of hot chocolate.

"Good. I'm delighted you enjoyed it! Now, get on with it, Simon," Aunt Hannah said brusquely. "Tell me what happened to make Vera Morley give up the dog she loves."

"I know Kenneth Samuels's nephew," she snorted when Simon had told her everything. "He's a really nasty person. He wants Vera's house for himself. He always has, ever since Vera moved in five years ago."

"I suppose it's too much to hope that you know which hospital Mr. Samuels is in?" Simon asked.

"I saw him this afternoon with my own eyes," his aunt retorted. "I'm a volunteer at Highlands Hospital. Today was my day for visiting. Kenneth is still sick, but not so sick that I couldn't talk with him. There's nobody else to visit him. The nephew doesn't bother and he's Kenneth's only relative."

"Well . . ." Simon began. Then he shook his head. "No," he murmured. "Even you couldn't arrange that!"

"Sure I could. I'm already one step ahead of you."

She looked over at James and Mandy. "Okay, you two. Get some paperback books. And a few flowers, maybe, and some fruit. Be here at two-thirty tomorrow. You two are going to be temporary hospital volunteers. You'll visit folks who don't have anyone else to go to see them."

"Like Mr. Samuels?" asked Mandy.

"That's right!" said Aunt Hannah with a chuckle.

The next day, Mandy and James felt nervous as they followed a nurse down the hospital ward. They were carrying flowers from Grandpa Hope's garden, two jars of raspberry jelly from Grandma's cupboard, and some paperback books that James's father had let them have.

Simon had driven them to his aunt's house and she'd told them that she'd cleared their visit with the head nurse. Mr. Samuels would be expecting them.

But, thought Mandy as they made their way to Mr. Samuels's bed, *he has no idea why we're really here!*

"Think of Vera Morley and Kimble," James whispered. He'd guessed what was worrying Mandy. Mandy nodded and shot him a grateful glance.

"Your young visitors are here, Mr. Samuels," the

nurse said cheerfully. Then she turned to James and Mandy. "Ten minutes. No longer. Okay?"

"Okay," agreed Mandy, hoping that ten minutes would be long enough. There wouldn't be any time to waste!

Mr. Samuels thanked them for their gifts, then looked puzzled. "It isn't often that people your age can find the time to do this kind of thing," he said.

Mandy bit her lip as she met his gaze. "I'm sorry," she said at last. "We *are* here under false pretenses, Mr. Samuels."

"But it's because we're trying to help someone!" James blurted out. Then, blushing boldly, he reached into his pocket, pulled out a photograph, and handed it silently to Mr. Samuels.

"This is Kimble, isn't it? Vera Morley's dog? I'm very, very fond of both of them. I did wonder..." Mr. Samuels shook his head. "No reason why she should have come, of course."

"If you're wondering about Vera," Mandy said softly, "she did try to see you, but they wouldn't let her in. You weren't well enough for visitors on the day she came."

"That's a shame. I would have enjoyed a visit from her. She could have told me all about Kimble. Has she had the pups yet? And —"

Mr. Samuels broke off again and looked at James.

"You said you were trying to help someone, young man? I think you'd better tell me what this visit is really about."

"It's about your nephew," James said, getting to the point. "He told Vera Morley that she'd have to get rid of Kimble if she wanted to stay in her house."

"That's ridiculous!" said Mr. Samuels. "Surely she told him that I'd agreed to let her have Kimble there."

"She did!" said Mandy. "And he told her *he* was in charge and he wasn't giving her permission to keep Kimble. He said he'd get the authorities to take Kimble away."

"They haven't done that, have they?" said Mr. Samuels, his face turning red as he sat bolt upright in the bed.

"Not yet," said James. "But they might!" And he and Mandy went on to tell Mr. Samuels everything else that had happened.

"We saw Vera last night and she's given up all hope of having Kimble back," Mandy ended.

Mr. Samuels heaved himself to the edge of his bed and called loudly for a nurse.

"Mr. Samuels! What on earth's the matter?" the nurse asked. "I hope you two haven't been upsetting him," she added, glaring first at James, then at Mandy.

"*You'll* upset me, nurse, if you don't get me to a

phone! I've an important call to make. And you'll have to allow my friends here a few minutes extra with me. We've a very important matter to sort out."

"Are you . . . are you calling your nephew?" Mandy asked when the nurse bustled away to get a wheelchair.

"I'm calling my lawyer. As well as handling my business affairs, he happens to be an old and valued friend. Don't worry, this whole matter will be dealt with immediately!"

Ten minutes later, Mandy and James were dashing across the hospital parking lot to where Simon was waiting by his van.

"So it was a successful visit!" Simon guessed when Mandy and James skidded to a halt.

"Yes! Yes, it was! Mr. Samuels called his lawyer and he's changing Vera's lease," Mandy panted. "She can keep a dog there now."

"And Mr. Samuels's nephew will be getting a letter ordering him to stay away from Vera and her house," added James, shoving his glasses back into place.

"And . . . and first thing tomorrow Mr. Samuels and his lawyer will be calling the SPCA inspector who handles cases in the Kimbleton area," said Mandy. "They'll both explain what happened and Mr. Samuels will —"

"Vouch for Vera. That's the word he used," said James.

"The SPCA *will* agree to let Vera have Kimble back, won't they, Simon?" Mandy asked anxiously.

"I think so," Simon replied thoughtfully. "But they're bound to pay her a visit to check everything out."

The next three days passed slowly. Vera called every day to check on Kimble and the pups; she was becoming more and more anxious because she hadn't heard anything from the SPCA.

Then, on Thursday, when Mandy and James came home from school, Dr. Emily was parked outside in the Animal Ark Land Rover. "Throw your bikes in the back," she said. "We're going to Kimbleton. I've checked with your mother, James, and it's all right for you to come."

"But *why*?" asked Mandy. "Why are we going, Mom? What's happened?"

"Vera Morley's had a visit from the SPCA inspector," Dr. Emily told them. "She called Animal Ark to ask if you two could go to lend support. Now, Mandy, you've got to promise me that you'll accept whatever is said. No protest if the decision goes against Vera. Okay?"

"But, Mom . . ." began Mandy. Then she relented. She knew from the seriousness of her mother's expression that she meant exactly what she'd said. "Okay," she whispered. "I promise."

"Me, too," murmured James. "But it *will* be all right, won't it, Dr. Emily?"

"I don't know the answer to that, I'm afraid, James. We'll just have to hope it will be."

There was already a car there when they drove up to Vera's house. Mandy didn't know whether to be glad or not.

"If that's the inspector's car, at least we won't have to wait long before we know!" muttered James.

When Vera opened the front door, Mandy looked anxiously at her, trying to judge how things were going. Vera looked pale and worried and didn't speak. She just pointed silently toward the front room.

Dr. Emily introduced herself, Mandy, and James to the stern-faced inspector.

"I was about to impress upon Ms. Morley the possible consequences of abandoning an animal," he said. "It doesn't matter that she did her best to make sure the dog was unable to run off. It could have run off when the leash was unfastened. That could have caused an accident, even death, not only to the dog but to whoever was trying to help the dog. In other words, leaving a dog, even at the door of a veterinary practice, was a highly irresponsible act."

"I know that," Vera whispered. "I know I should have

taken Kimble and asked for help. But what if the answer had been no? What would I have done then?"

The clock ticked away as the inspector and Vera sat in silence. Then came a loud cock-a-doodle-doo and Vera rose to her feet. "I'm sorry," she said. "The hens need feeding and to be put in for the night. It's well past time."

"Tell us where everything is and James and I will take care of it," said Mandy. She didn't really know how she could bear to leave the room without any decision having been made. But the hens were hungry and their routine had been upset.

Before Vera could reply, the inspector turned to look at Dr. Emily. "Are the dog and her pups well enough to be moved?" the inspector asked Dr. Emily.

Moved to where? Mandy wanted to ask the question aloud but she knew she couldn't. She only vaguely heard her mother's confirmation; she was watching Vera stumbling back to her chair.

"Perhaps, Mandy, when you and James have fed the hens, you'd like to go back to Animal Ark in Ms. Morley's car," said the inspector. "I'm sure she'd like to get Kimble and the puppies and get them settled in their own home as soon as possible."

To Mandy's horror, Vera Morley said, "No, Inspector. I won't be going to Animal Ark. Not today," she added quickly, wiping away the tears. "Tomorrow morning, can I come tomorrow morning?" she asked Dr. Emily. "The waiting will be awful but I wouldn't dare bring them home in the dark. I'd be scared of having an accident."

"Come back with us now, Vera," said Dr. Emily. "You can stay the night. I'm sure Mandy will be delighted," she added, throwing a smiling glance at her daughter. "You can sleep in the spare room."

As they walked down the hallway to Animal Ark's kitchen, they heard anxious and excited whines and frantic scratching noises at the closed door.

"She's recognized my footsteps!" cried Vera, running forward. "I'm coming, Kimble. I'm here!"

The whines turned to yelps of joy when Vera opened the door. Kimble didn't jump up; she didn't need to. Vera knelt down and flung her arms around Kimble's neck. In between whining and yelping, Kimble licked Vera's face and neck and ears.

Mandy, James, and Dr. Emily stood in the hall, smiling as they watched the reunion.

"Oh, Kimble! Kimble," Vera murmured. The dog stayed still for a moment, her big golden head resting on Vera's shoulder.

Then Mandy drew a sobbing breath and whispered,

"Mom! Kimble's crying. I didn't know a dog could cry real tears."

"Oh, dear," said Emily Hope. "I think I need a tissue."

"Me, too," said James, taking off his glasses and blinking hard.

Then Kimble moved. She got hold of Vera's jacket in her mouth and started tugging. "I think she wants to show Vera her puppies," said James. "I don't want to miss this. Will it be okay if we go in, Dr. Emily?" Dr. Emily nodded.

Kimble's tail was wagging furiously as she led Vera to the box. Vera knelt down again, and after murmuring something to Kimble, she picked the puppies up. "They're beautiful, Kimble," she said as she petted and examined them.

Kimble lay down and put her head on Vera's knee. "What did you say you call the puppies, Mandy?" Vera asked over her shoulder. "Jake and Pippa?"

"Yes, but we won't mind if you want to rename them," Mandy replied.

"Oh, no!" said Vera. "We couldn't do that, could we, Kimble? Just move your head for a second, girl. I'll put your pups back, then I want another look at you. I've missed you so much."

Vera leaned forward and lay the puppies down.

"There you are, Jake," she said. "You snuggle close to Pippa."

As Vera waited to make sure the puppies were settling in, James glanced at Kimble. The dog's eyes were fixed adoringly on Vera.

James took a huge, long breath, then turned to Mandy and said, "I'm going now, Mandy. I think I want to get home and spend some time with Blackie." He gave a last, lingering look at Kimble, saying a silent but happy good-bye.

Vera didn't sleep in the spare room after all but on a cot in front of the stove in Animal Ark's kitchen. She just couldn't bear to be parted from Kimble. Kimble and the puppies slept on the cot, too. Vera apologized about that when Mandy crept into the kitchen early Friday morning.

"I tried to make Kimble keep Jake and Pippa in the box," she said. "But every time I moved them, she just picked them up and put them on the cot again."

"It's okay," said Mandy, smiling as she looked down at the contented family. Then she looked closer. "Vera," she whispered, "the puppies' eyes are starting to open! I'm sure they are. It must be because they know they're going home."

* * *

Three weeks later, Mandy heard a muffled thump coming from outside the front of the house. She opened the door to find Kimble standing here. But this time, the dog at the door wasn't tied to a flowerpot. She was holding a small card in her mouth.

Mandy bent down to cuddle Kimble, then, keeping one arm around the dog's neck, she removed the card and read it. *"Vera Morley and Kenneth Samuels request the pleasure of Mandy Hope's and James Hunter's company at their wedding . . ."*

Mandy stood up with a smile of delight as Vera and Mr. Samuels, each carrying a wriggling puppy, came from behind a bush. "You will accept, won't you, Mandy?" asked Vera, blushing a becoming shade of pink. "You and James *will* come to our wedding?"

"Of course we will!" said Mandy, moving forward to pet the puppies.

"And," Mandy said to James when she called him later, "I know just where we can go to buy Vera and Mr. Samuels a wedding present. A little old-fashioned apothecary in York!"

ANIMAL ARK®

Sheepdog in the Snow

Ben M. Baglio

Illustrations by Shelagh McNicholas

To the real Tess
And a special thanks to Jenny Oldfield.

One

Christmas was coming. Mandy Hope's school had been let out for the holidays. Brightly wrapped presents were stacked under the tree in the cozy kitchen at Animal Ark, and Mandy and her friend James Hunter were hunched over the table surrounded by invitation cards.

"Let's make a list," James suggested. He chewed the end of his pen. "In alphabetical order."

"What kind of list?" Mandy pushed her blond hair behind her ears and scribbled away. She was making out an invitation to Grandma and Grandpa Hope, and Smoky the cat. Each card was hand-designed by James and Mandy. They'd cut out squares of bright yellow poster board, drawn the black outline of a Christmas tree on each one, and written the words "PARTY TIME" across the top.

"A list of guests." James liked to be organized. He didn't want to leave anyone out. He thought Mandy was rushing into things too quickly. "Should we put pets or people first?"

"Pets," came the prompt reply. Mandy filled out her grandparents' card. "A Christmas Eve Party!" it read. "Pets, bring your owners to Welford Village Hall on Saturday, December 24, at 7:30 P.M. Music and Food!" It was signed with a miniature cat's paw print, from a stencil that James had made.

"Okay." James began his list. "Barney and Button . . . Blackie . . . Dorian . . . Eric . . . Houdini. . . ." He ran through the names of some of the pets they'd helped in the past. "Rosa won't be able to come because she's hibernating . . . but Sammy probably will, because squirrels only semihibernate, and —"

"Hang on a second; you left out Ruby and Prince." Mandy remembered the piglet and the pony as she tucked the invitation into an envelope.

"Hmm . . . Can we get a pony into the village hall?" James wondered.

Mandy thought carefully. "I suppose Susan could bring him and stay outside with him. Prince could stick his head through an open window and enjoy things from there."

"And what about pigs?"

She imagined friendly, adventurous Ruby trotting in and out of the trestle tables, rooting for food. She nodded. "Pigs are fine. We want everyone to come, remember. It's going to be the biggest, best Christmas party for pets anyone's ever seen!"

Mandy's blue eyes shone. Animals were the love of her life, and the idea of giving them a Christmas treat, where all the past patients of Animal Ark could get together with pets that Mandy and James had helped to rescue, and farm animals they'd managed to save, promised to make this a Christmas to remember.

She imagined everyone gathered there — cats and dogs, rabbits, hamsters, sheep, and pigs. She wanted to invite Ernie Bell and his squirrel, Sammy; Lydia Fawcett and her wonderful escaping goat, Houdini. She even wanted Pandora the Pekingese and Toby the mongrel, though this would mean having to invite their fussy owner, Mrs. Ponsonby. "I wonder if Pandora will come all dressed up?" Mandy smiled.

"No, but I bet Mrs. Ponsonby will." James pushed his glasses farther up his nose. He slotted Pandora's name into the list. "Hey, let's have a competition for the best party hat!" he suggested.

"And carols. And a Christmas procession down the village street." Mandy could picture the magic scene. For a few moments she stopped to daydream. She'd take along Mopsy, the tamest of her three rabbits, warmly zipped up inside the front of her jacket. They would have to make up a menu of food, from lettuce leaves for Mopsy to oats for Susan Collins's pony. It would be snowing outside, and they would carry candles down the street. They would crowd into the village hall, singing carols. Then the pets would be let loose on the party food. . . .

"Mandy?" James broke in.

"Hmm?"

"I said, do you want to invite Imogen with Button and Barney, or John Hardy?"

"Both," Mandy beamed. She was feeling generous. "You know, Imogen Parker Smythe isn't nearly so spoiled now that she has the two rabbits to look after. In fact, I'd even say she was quite nice!"

"And what about Claire?" James remembered his little, dark-haired next-door neighbor. She ran a hedgehog sanctuary in her garden. "Rosa, Guy, and everyone will be fast asleep for the winter in their nest-boxes."

Mandy's brow wrinkled. "Yes, we can't wake them up specially, just to come to a party. Claire will have to come by herself." She began to make out a fresh invitation. It was only five days until Christmas Eve, and they had lots to do.

In the background they could hear Adam Hope, Mandy's dad, puttering around the house. He went up and downstairs, in and out of the living room, humming and singing to himself. Then he put his bearded face around the kitchen door.

> *Christmas is coming,*
> *The goose is getting fat . . .*

he sang;

> *Please put a penny*
> *In the old man's hat.*
> *If you haven't got a penny,*
> *A halfpenny will do.*
> *If you haven't got a halfpenny,*
> *A farthing will do.*
> *If you haven't got a farthing . . .*

"God bless you!" Mandy and James chimed in, their faces wreathed in smiles.

"Busy?" Dr. Adam asked. He picked up an invitation card. "Good idea," he nodded. "Yes. Pets at a party, very good. A get-together, hmm. . . ." He wandered off again, grabbing his white coat from the back of a chair. Then he headed off to the Animal Ark office in the modern extension at the back of their old stone cottage. They heard him "pom-pom-pom"ing on an imaginary trombone as he went.

Mandy grinned at James. She loved her absent-minded, easygoing dad, and she thought his job as a vet in Animal Ark was the best there was. And when she grew up, she wanted to be a vet herself.

"What about Simon and Jean?" James thought of the veterinary assistant and receptionist. "They don't have anyone to bring. Pets, I mean."

"They can come anyway." Mandy watched James add them to the list. She jumped up from the table, uncurling her fingers and stretching her arms. "I have writer's cramp," she said. "How about going to ask Simon and Jean right now?"

James didn't need a second prompting. He liked the office, its reception area crowded during business hours with animal patients — hairy and sleek, big and tiny, noisy and silent. He was out of his seat and through the door before Mandy had finished stretching. He headed for the extension and its meowing, shuffling, snuffling patients.

James and Mandy rushed in to say hello to the people and pets they knew from the village and farms surrounding Welford. They noticed Jack Spiller, with his daughter, Jenny, and their old sheepdog. They worked on a small farm out of town. The dog had scratched her eye and it was infected, Jack said. He kept a close watch on Sam Western, who was also in the reception area with his new dog — a large German shepherd, mostly black, with a pale brown face and chest. He was a fine animal, but he seemed edgy. Sam Western didn't keep his dogs up at Upper Welford Hall as pets, but as guard dogs to chase off trespassers. Mandy bent to talk gently to the nervous animal. "What's his name?" she asked Mr. Western.

"Major." The reply was brisk. Mr. Western looked impatiently at his watch. "How much longer?" he asked Jean Knox.

The gray-haired receptionist checked the appointment book. "You're next, Mr. Western. It shouldn't be long now."

"They're running five minutes late in there," he complained. Sam Western was a busy and important man, and he liked everyone to know it.

Mandy smiled and stroked Major; then she and James approached the reception desk.

"What are you doing this Saturday, Jean?" Mandy leaned both elbows on the counter.

"Let's see, Saturday? Why, that's Christmas Eve, isn't

it?" Jean counted out the days on her fingers. "As a matter of fact, I don't have anything planned." She peered at them over her glasses.

"Would you like to come to a party at the village hall?" James asked. "It's for everyone from Animal Ark and their owners."

Jean took off her glasses and put her head to one side. "Shouldn't that be 'everyone and their *pets*'?"

"No, it's a *pets'* party," Mandy insisted. "But there'll be food and drink for people, too." She felt grateful that her mom and Mrs. Hunter, James's mom, had both agreed to contribute toward the cost. "We'd like everyone to come."

"Well, I suppose I could fit in making my mince pies earlier in the day. And I go to midnight mass, but that's much later, of course. Yes, I'd be delighted, thank you!" She beamed at them and began searching the counter. "Let me write that down!"

"Here's a pen." James handed her one. "It begins at seven-thirty."

Jean took the pen and looked helplessly for a spare scrap of paper.

"Here!" Mandy took one from her pocket. "And your glasses are around your neck." She was used to helping their receptionist find the things she'd lost.

Jean smiled again as she fixed them on her nose. "Ah, thank you, Mandy dear." She looked across the room as the door to the exam room opened. Walter Pickard emerged with his elderly cat, Tom. "Mr. Western, you can take Major in now."

Mandy went up to her old friend Walter, who lived in the row of small cottages beside the Fox and Goose tavern. "What's Tom been up to?" She tickled the cat's chin. "His ear's kind of a mess, isn't it?"

"He's been in a fight," the old man grumbled. "You'd think he'd know better."

Burly Tom looked as if he couldn't care less. Bitten ear or not, the next chance he got, he'd be tussling again. He purred proudly as Mandy inspected his chewed ear.

They stood to one side as Mr. Western pushed past toward the treatment room. He held Major on a short leash, but the dog managed to lift his head and growl at old Tom.

Simon stood at the door, waiting. When he spotted Mandy, he spoke rapidly. "Grab a white coat and give me a hand in here, would you? We're running behind." He smiled at Mr. Western and escorted him into the small, clean white room.

"Is that okay?" Mandy checked with James.

He nodded. "I'll go and do some more invitations. We'd better get up to High Cross later today to call on Lydia and on the Parker Smythes."

Mandy agreed. "I won't be long," she promised.

Inside the treatment room, Simon had already lifted the big German shepherd dog onto the table. Mr. Western stood against the wall. The dog's ears were laid flat, its teeth bared. But Simon dealt with him expertly and calmly, stroking his long back and encouraging him to stand still. "This is a magnificent animal you have here, Mr. Western," he said. "Where did you get him?"

"From a house in York. Small yard. Hopeless." Mr. Western didn't smile. He used words sparingly, as if they cost money.

"No good at all for a guy this size," Simon agreed. "You need plenty of space to run around in, don't you, boy?" He inspected the dog's ears and gently eased open his jaw. "He hasn't been ill-treated, at least."

Mr. Western grunted. "He just needs his injections. I don't want him keeling over on me, not after what I've just paid for him. And I don't want him infecting the other two dogs either."

Mandy frowned and went to a drawer to get rubber gloves and a syringe pack for Simon, while he took the drugs from a high, locked cupboard. Mr. Western owned a large estate nearby. He was a dairy farmer, using modern methods, but, strangely, he didn't seem to like animals. He was stocky and bad-tempered, and ran his place strictly. Mandy imagined a stern, open-air life for Major from now on, after his cooped-up existence in the city.

Simon spoke soothingly to the dog while Mandy stood at his head, holding his collar firmly. He jerked as Simon gave the injection, and his back legs shifted, but he gave no other sign. "That's it; good boy," Simon said. Mandy let him jump easily to the floor.

Quickly Mr. Western hooked the dog's leash back on. "That's it, you're finished?" he asked. Simon nodded. With a curt "thank-you," the farmer left the room. "Put this down on my account," he told Jean. Soon the outer doors were swinging behind him and his new guard dog.

"Simon!" Mandy found time for a quiet word before the next patient came in. She'd disposed of the gloves and syringe in a special sealed bin. "Are you doing anything on Christmas Eve?" She prayed he could come to their party. He could bring his music collection and be the disc jockey.

"Not much so far." When he heard Mandy's offer, he said he'd love to come.

She smiled. *So far, so good*, she thought.

Then it was time to get busy again, tending to a wounded rabbit's paw, inoculating another dog, binding up a kitten's sprained back leg.

Time flew. Before Mandy knew it, morning office hours were over and she was free to go back to James and the party preparations.

Two

By midday Mandy and James had gathered their pile of carefully addressed envelopes, put them into their coat pockets, and set off on their bikes for High Cross. It was a clear, sunny Monday as they biked down the driveway from Animal Ark, under the wooden sign swinging in the cold wind. As far as the eye could see, down the valley to the riverside, and up the steep, soaring hillsides to the Beacon and High Cross Farm, the air was crisp and bright. The trees stood gray and bare. The hills were a range of dull browns and sharp greens.

Mandy's breath clouded the freezing air. She pedaled hard to get warm. Soon she and James were riding through the village, up the main street, past the Fox and Goose, the church and the village hall, where their great event was to take place.

Their first stop was Bleakfell Hall, Mrs. Ponsonby's grand house just outside the village. "Might as well get this over with," Mandy sighed, knowing that Mrs. Ponsonby would go on and on about poor Pandora's latest mystery ailment. Even though Pandora was perfectly healthy, Mrs. Ponsonby seemed to bring the Pekingese to Animal Ark virtually every week. Mandy swung open the gate, and together she and James pedaled up the driveway.

The front door opened, and Pandora and Toby came flying out of the house to greet them, yapping and jumping up in pleasure.

"Down, Toby, down!" Mrs. Ponsonby scolded. She followed them out, wearing a pink flowered apron over her royal blue dress. Her round, plump face was set off by pink winged glasses with a sparkling rhinestone decoration. She ignored the fact that her beloved Pandora was gnawing at James's trouser leg, and bore down instead on poor Toby. "Bad boy! Down!"

Mandy smiled at the friendly mongrel and told him to sit. Toby obliged. His tail wagged to and fro against the gravel driveway. Mandy put down her bike, pulled out Mrs. Ponsonby's invitation, and handed it to her.

"What's this?" she exclaimed. She tore open the envelope in great excitement. "Oh, a party!" she read. Then her face changed. She frowned. "What's this? A party for pets? Oh, no; I don't think so, my dear." She shook her head.

"Why not?" Mandy looked in dismay at Pandora and Toby.

Mrs. Ponsonby creaked forward to scoop up a dog under each arm. "Pandora's not very strong, you see. A party would be too much for her. I'm afraid I will have to say no."

Pandora whined and wheezed.

"What about Toby?" James stood astride his bike, inspecting the small holes in the leg of his jeans.

"Toby can't go without his best friend, Pandora, can you, Toby-Woby?" Mrs. Ponsonby made squeaking noises with her lips. "That wouldn't be fair on Pandy-Wandy, now would it?" She glanced up at Mandy. "I'm afraid we shall have to decline your kind offer."

Mandy swallowed hard. It was a shame that the two pets would miss out. She knew for a fact that Pandora was as tough as the next dog; it was only Mrs. Ponsonby's fussy nature that made her see death and disaster around every corner. "I'm sorry you can't come." She picked up her bike and leaned forward to give the dogs a pat.

For a moment, Mrs. Ponsonby seemed to be about to change her mind. "I suppose your mother and father will be there to supervise?" She tried to sound casual. "And your grandparents?"

Mandy nodded. "I've already asked Grandma unofficially. She's promised to help with the food."

This seemed unwelcome news to Mrs. Ponsonby. She stepped back and sniffed. "Really? Has Dorothy asked for permission?"

Mandy remembered, too late, that bossy Mrs. Ponsonby and Grandma rarely saw eye to eye. They both loved to organize, but neither liked to take orders from the other. "What for?" she asked.

"To take food into the village hall. You must ask the pastor's permission, you know. It's a church hall, after all. In fact, Reverend Hadcroft is rather particular about it. He doesn't like a mess."

"Oh. I'll check," Mandy said flatly. She put it at the top of her list of things to do. "Let's go and ask Grandma about it," she said to James with a worried look. It was too late to change the party venue now, with Christmas Eve only five days away and the invitations already written out. . . .

"Take no notice of Mrs. Ponsonby," said Grandma.

Mandy and James had biked right over to Lilac Cottage. "She's only trying to throw a monkey wrench in the works." Her eyes sparkled and she spoke firmly. "It's because you asked *me* to help with the food, you see. Amelia Ponsonby can't bear anyone else to do the organizing. Now, if you'd asked *her*, my dear, I'm sure that she would have turned around and decided that Pandora was as fit as a fiddle after all, and she'd be down at the village hall right this minute, buttering mountains of sliced bread for sandwiches."

Mandy grinned with relief.

"No, don't worry. Reverend Hadcroft won't mind in the least little bit. And life will be quieter without Mrs. Ponsonby breathing down our necks!"

"It's too bad about Toby and Pandora, though," James said wistfully as they rode up the hill toward High Cross at last. "And all because Mrs. Ponsonby doesn't get to make the sandwiches."

They had to stop talking to concentrate on the steep climb. It made them hot and breathless, even on this crisp winter's day. When they reached the top and stopped beside some big iron gates, they saw the Parker Smythe mansion locked up, with no cars in the driveway. James went to slip Imogen's invitation into the mailbox. Then they were on their way again, past Sam Western's barking dogs on the grounds of his huge farm, on to the small stone farmhouse at the end of the path. It stood almost in the shadow of the ancient Celtic monument — Lydia Fawcett's goat farm, High Cross.

As she heard them approach, gentle, shy Lydia came out of the barn. She was dressed in her old brown work coat and boots. She smiled as she strode to meet them, leading high-stepping Houdini. The black-and-white goat had a wicked light in his eye and snickered a greeting. Mandy ran up and gave him a hug. "How would you like to come to a Christmas party, Houdini?" she asked.

"And you, too, Lydia." James handed her the invitation.

Lydia hemmed and hawed. She wasn't a party sort of person. She had her goats to look after. She didn't get down to the village much during these dark evenings.

"But it's Christmas Eve!" Mandy protested. She knew that Lydia didn't drive a car. "Listen, I'm sure I can get my dad to drive up in the jeep and get you and Houdini, and bring you safely back again. He wouldn't mind!"

Lydia blushed, and though she said she wouldn't dream of putting Dr. Adam out in that way, she gradually gave way to her friends' pleas. "Ernie will be there with Sammy," James promised. "You'll know tons of people. Please come, Lydia!"

Houdini nodded his head impatiently. They all laughed at him. "Very well," Lydia said at last. "Just so you know, I don't have any pretty party dresses."

"Come as you are," Mandy smiled. "Just as long as you come!"

They waved and rode off down the path, pleased with their success at persuading their shy friend and their favorite goat.

"Where to next?" James asked. They sped along the high hill road. The village nestled in the valley bottom. They could see for miles.

"Ernie and Sammy's?" Mandy suggested. "Since we've already told Lydia they'll be there!" It was a white lie, and all in a good cause.

James agreed. Ernie Bell had built the strong fences that kept Lydia's goats safely penned in. The two were good company for each other; Ernie was always less grumpy when Lydia was around, and Lydia was less shy. "Let's hope he says yes," he said. Besides, Sammy the squirrel was one of his favorite pets.

But they'd only pedaled a few more yards before a movement on the winding road ahead caught Mandy's eye. She braked and waited for the shape to reappear out of a hollow. It was heading slowly in their direction.

"What's wrong?" James slowed down beside her.

"I think there's an animal on the road." Mandy glanced around for traffic danger, but the exposed hill road was deserted. "There it is again, look!" She pointed. A black creature came up the hill.

"It's a dog." James saw it, too. "I think it's limping."

Quickly Mandy lay down her bike against the grass at the road's edge. "Don't scare it. Let's wait here." What was a dog doing in the middle of nowhere on a cold, raw day like this?

James and Mandy stood waiting for the dog to approach. It came with a halting step, its left front paw so sore that it could scarcely touch the ground.

"It looks like some kind of sheepdog," James whispered. "Do you think it's lost?"

Mandy shook her head. "I don't know. It's not from around here, though. At least, I don't recognize it."

The dog limped along. Its head hung low, its tongue lolled, its tail brushed the ground. The wind blew in its face as it mounted the hill, slowing it almost to a standstill.

"Poor thing!" Mandy's heart went out at once to the suffering creature. She saw it was female. "Look how thin she is!" She squatted down and called to the dog. "Here, girl, here!"

The dog lifted her dull head and caught sight of them at last. She halted, too weary to avoid them by heading off across the grass and over the low stone wall into the field beyond. She whined and hung her head.

"She must be starving!" James knelt down at Mandy's

side. "Here, girl. Look, she's not wearing a collar or a name tag. Who knows how far she's walked?"

Mandy sighed. "Who's left her here?" Again she scanned the countryside, but there was no sign of an owner, either in a car or on foot.

Eventually the dog seemed strong enough to resume her limping progress. She moved forward. From close up, they could see that her black coat was matted and the underside of her long tail was tangled with mud and thorns. Her front paws, speckled gray and white, were a dull, muddy brown. Worst of all, her thin sides heaved with the effort of hauling herself up the long hill. Through her coat they could see the shape of her rib cage and the lean, starved haunches.

"Poor thing!" Mandy gasped again. The dog came alongside, head down, trying to creep quietly by. But her injured paw hit against a small rock at the roadside. She yelped and staggered sideways toward them. Mandy and James ran forward to help.

The dog whined, her sides heaved, and she fell at their feet. She lay on her side, eyes and mouth open, tongue lolling. Gently Mandy put out a hand to stroke her head. The deep brown eyes stared back.

"There, girl, there." Mandy felt like crying for the wounded, starved animal. She looked up at James with tears in her eyes. "We have to get her back to Welford!" she whispered. "Let's get her to Animal Ark."

"She's nearly dead, poor thing!" James warned Mandy to be gentle.

The dog lay in the road. She made one sad attempt to wag her tail in greeting, as if she knew that these were her rescuers. She gave herself up to James and Mandy's care, closed her eyes, and slipped gently into unconsciousness.

Three

Quickly Mandy unzipped her warm woolen jacket and wrapped the dog inside it. "I'll leave my bike here," she told James. "Can you go ahead and tell Mom and Dad what's happening?" Ever so gently, she edged her arms under the limp body and lifted it from the cold ground.

"Are you sure you can carry her?" James stood astride his bike, his face pale and worried.

She nodded. "I'll manage. Get someone to bring the car out. Hurry, please!" Steadying herself, she began to carry the dog down the hill.

James set off, crouched over his handlebars, speeding into the dip, pedaling for all he was worth up the other side. He was soon out of sight.

Mandy trudged on. The dog didn't weigh much, even wrapped inside Mandy's coat. She was mostly skin and bone, but she heaved a sigh and her eyelids fluttered. Mandy spoke gently to her as she walked. "There, girl, there. We'll soon have you back safe and sound." Inside her head, another voice whispered, *Let's hope we're not too late!*

Several minutes passed. Still Mandy walked on toward Welford. Only one car passed her, traveling in

the other direction. Two curious faces looked out, but the car roared by.

Mandy's arms began to ache. The dog was a dead weight cradled against her chest.

At last she caught sight of the Animal Ark jeep speeding along the road toward her, her mom at the wheel. As the car pulled up, Mandy gave a gasp of relief. "Oh, Mom, thank heavens!"

Emily Hope and James leaped out. Dr. Emily hurried across and took a quick glance at the unconscious sheepdog. She ran back for her bag. "Bring her over here as quickly as you can," she told Mandy, flinging open the back door. "Lay her down. That's right. Now stand back and let me take a good look."

Mandy put the poor creature into the back of the car. She straightened up and peered anxiously over her mother's shoulder, knowing that if anyone could save the dog, Emily Hope could.

"She's badly dehydrated," Dr. Emily said after pinching the dog's skin. "Now, James, pass me that glucose solution. That's the one." She made sure the dog stayed warmly wrapped inside the jacket, then she lifted her head and offered a few drops of the sweet liquid by mouth, through a syringe feed. They saw the dog's throat constrict and swallow. Her pink tongue passed across her lips. Dr. Emily gave her a few drops more.

Soon her eyes opened and she was licking and swallowing greedily.

Mandy looked across at James. She sighed. Dr. Emily stroked the dog's throat to help her swallow. They saw the tip of her tail wag free of her makeshift blanket. "Is she going to make it?" Mandy asked.

Her mom stood up. "Let's hope so, thanks to you two!" She told them to hop into the car. "She was pretty far gone. Mandy, you sit here. Let the dog rest her head against your knees. Talk quietly to her and keep her calm while I drive back home."

Quickly Mandy climbed in and followed instructions.

James stood by the jeep, checking that Mandy and the dog were safely inside. "I'll go back for your bike and ride down," he told her as he closed the door.

Mandy and Dr. Emily agreed. Emily Hope backed up into a driveway, turned, and set off, roaring down the hillside. In the back of the car, Mandy softly stroked the dog's dark head, lying in her lap, staring up at her with her big, faithful brown eyes. "Please get better," Mandy whispered. She felt she'd never wanted anything more in her life than for this beautiful, gentle creature to return to health.

*   *   *

Simon ran out into the office yard as the jeep pulled up. He opened the back door and gathered the patient in his arms. Adam Hope stood waiting at the door.

Stiffly Mandy clambered out, following Simon and her mother. "I don't think there are any broken bones, just cuts and sores. She's badly dehydrated," Dr. Emily reported. "We need to remove something sharp from her left front pad and treat the infected area. Otherwise, it's a case of warmth, lots of liquid, and rest." She hurried into the treatment room.

Simon laid the dog on a treatment table, leaving the warm cover over her. She raised her head.

Mandy's father took a look. He felt gently with his fingertips, checking joints, listening for the heartbeat through his stethoscope. He looked up at Mandy. "She doesn't seem too bad," he said. "Very thin, though. It's a disgrace!" His voice was low and intense. "How can people let an animal get into this condition?"

Emily Hope put on some rubber gloves and took a pair of small tweezers from the sterile unit. She crouched down, talking gently to the dog as she took hold of the injured paw, swabbed the affected area, and deftly pulled a sharp object from the wound. She held it up to the light. "A splinter of glass," she reported.

The dog whined and tried to rise.

"Steady," Simon said. He stroked her neck.

"Look, she wants to get up!" Mandy said. The dog had struggled free of the jacket.

Adam Hope nodded. "Let her try. Let's see if she can make it. She looks very determined."

Simon eased the jacket away completely. They could all clearly see her starved, shaking body. Slowly she bent her back legs under her and eased herself up at the front. She straightened the back legs until at last she struggled up onto all fours.

Mandy came forward with a bowl of clean drinking water. She put it down within easy reach. Soon the dog lapped noisily, her flanks heaving, her tail wagging low and slow as she drank.

Dr. Adam smiled. "She's tough," he said admiringly. "I wonder where she came from."

"Is she lost?" Dr. Emily wondered. Satisfied with the treatment she began to clear away.

Simon folded his arms and watched the dog enjoy her drink. "This type of dog doesn't usually get lost. Their sense of direction is too good. She's more likely to have been abandoned, I'd say."

Mandy frowned. "You mean someone just dumped her?" She couldn't believe that anyone would do such a thing.

Her dad held up his hand. "Now, we're not sure. There may be a worried owner out there, searching high and low."

They all stood and considered this. "How can we find out?" Mandy noticed the dog wanting to jump down from the table, but she was too weak to attempt it. Checking first with her father, Mandy went to help. She lifted the dog and set her gently down on the floor.

"Hmm . . ." Dr. Adam stroked his beard. "Let me call around. Someone might have heard of a Border collie that's missing."

Mandy knew that her father was in close touch with all the vets in the area. His network of friends and colleagues might well turn up the owner. She nodded. "Do it now, please, Dad!"

He smiled at her earnest expression. "Right away."

"And you could try the SPCA and the Canine Defense League," Emily Hope suggested. At last she found time to take off her own jacket and scarf. Her long, wavy red hair hung free.

"Say it's an emergency," Mandy pleaded. "Say she has no collar, so we don't have a clue where she's from. Someone's probably frantic about her!"

Nodding, Dr. Adam went out into reception.

Dr. Emily came up to Mandy and put an arm around her shoulder. "Don't get your hopes too high," she warned.

"Yes, but . . ." Mandy began to protest.

"Look, maybe there's no frantic owner out there. Maybe the *last* thing that person wants is to get a phone call just before Christmas saying that we've found their dog. As we were saying, the collar's missing. And these sheepdogs are bred and trained to know their way around. They hardly ever get lost." She shook her head. "We'll do our best. But don't expect too much, Mandy. We'll just have to wait and see."

Mandy hung her head. She was glad when, five minutes later, they heard James come running into the office. It broke the anxious ticking of the clock. "The dog's fine," she told him, watching him crouch down and put an arm around her neck.

James stood up straight and gave her a high five.

"Dad's calling around now to see if we can trace where she came from."

They waited all evening for a return call — the news that a sheepdog had been reported missing from a farm on the other side of the county, or that a child in Leeds or York was pining over a missing pet. But the phone didn't ring. Night fell, and Mandy and James made the dog comfortable in a warm bed in a kennel in the residential unit at the back of the office.

Mandy gave her a small amount of ground food. The dog came and nuzzled gratefully against her, then sank into bed. Mandy smiled softly, turned off the light, and left the collie to sleep.

Four

The next morning, Mandy woke and looked out of her bedroom window to see a hard frost covering the ground. She ran downstairs, but before she could ask, her mother shook her head. "No. No news," she said. "But we know one thing for sure; if that poor animal had stayed out last night, there's no way she would have survived! She would have died of hypothermia, and that's a fact!"

Mandy sat down to breakfast, sipping slowly at her orange juice. "But you think she's been abandoned?" she asked.

"It's beginning to look that way."

Mandy shook her head. It was unbelievable; the beautiful dog was unloved, unwanted. And that left them with a problem; who would take her now?

In the middle of this puzzle, Mandy's grandparents stopped by. They were on their way to Walton, the nearest town, and Grandma was armed with a long list of food for the party: dog biscuits, apples, carrots, sugar cubes, and birdseed. Grandpa kept the human list safe in his pocket: rolls, cheese, pigs in blankets, potato chips, chocolate cookies.

They came into the kitchen to see Mandy brooding over her cornflakes. "A penny for your thoughts?" Grandpa said.

Mandy gave a wan smile.

"What's wrong, love?" Grandma came and sat at the table, her voice full of concern. "I can tell the party isn't uppermost in your mind, for a start." She put away the list that she'd intended to discuss with Mandy. "In fact, I can see you're not yourself at all."

Mandy let her empty spoon droop into the bowl. "We rescued a dog yesterday," she explained. "It was starving to death, up in the hills."

Grandma patted her hand. "Well done, dear. But what's the trouble?"

"She's gorgeous, Grandma. Absolutely beautiful. Her face is so trusting. You just have to look into her eyes and you can't help falling in love with her!" To Mandy, this wasn't just any old dog. She felt from the start that she'd rescued someone very special.

Grandma nodded. "So?"

"So how can anyone bear to part with her?" Mandy felt a lump rise in her throat. She was unable to go on.

Grandma got to her feet. "Why don't you show me and Grandpa this wonderful creature?" she suggested with a smile. "I'm sure we'd love to take a look."

Willingly Mandy obliged. She led her grandparents around the side of the house to the unit, through the door and down the row of kennels where the overnight patients stayed. A brown-and-black beagle sat, its head cocked to one side. A King Charles spaniel wagged its tail. At the end of the row, they came to the stray Border collie.

"Well!" Grandpa bent forward and peered through the wire mesh. "She looks happy to see you."

Mandy unbolted the door. The dog was still too weak to jump up, but she wagged her tail. "Come on, girl; let's take you for a little walk."

The dog trotted obediently after her.

"She's limping," Grandma pointed out.

Mandy explained about the splinter of glass. "The foot's already getting better, though."

"She's very thin." Grandpa watched her limp forward from the unit out onto the lawn. She began to sniff happily at a tree trunk, tramping through the frosty grass.

Mandy sighed. "How could anyone do this?"

Grandma and Grandpa stood watching the dog. "Do what, exactly?" Grandpa had his hands in his quilted vest pockets. He blew clouds of steam as he spoke.

"Dump her. Leave her to starve."

Grandma nodded. "It's a shame. Are you sure that's what happened?"

"It looks like it." Mandy had taken her mom's warning to heart. At first she'd been slow to believe that the dog had been abandoned, but why had no one come forward to claim her or put out a message to say that she was missing? How had she lost her collar and name tag unless someone had deliberately taken it off?"

The dog went and sniffed at the hedge bottom, then trotted toward them. She sat by Mandy's side once more.

"Good girl." Mandy bent down to pat her head.

"People do these things," Grandma said quietly. "Especially at Christmas. They go away for the holiday. The dog's a nuisance. They can't afford to put it in a kennel, so they drive into the middle of the countryside and abandon it."

Mandy felt her stomach turn. She bent to put her arms around the dog's neck.

"They should think harder before they get a dog in the first place," Grandpa put in. "But then, people don't. They like the look of them when they're puppies, and they buy them without stopping to consider what's involved in looking after a grown-up dog."

"Especially at this time of year," Grandma reminded them. "Remember. 'A dog is for life, not just for Christmas,'" she quoted the saying. "Not everyone keeps that in mind, I'm afraid."

Mandy looked up at them and sighed.

"I expect you'd love to keep her yourself?" Grandpa asked. He knew Mandy's habit of caring for all waifs and strays. "And I expect your mom and dad have had to say no?"

"I haven't asked." Mandy knew it was out of the question, not because her mom and dad were hard-hearted but because the house would be full to overflowing with stray donkeys, rabbits, hedgehogs, pigs, owls, and lambs, not to mention dogs and cats, if Mandy had her way.

"But you'd love to find a good home for this little lady if it turns out she's been abandoned?" Grandpa guessed.

Mandy nodded. "Look at her. How could anyone turn

her away?" she repeated. The dog had lifted one paw onto Mandy's knee and gazed into her face.

Grandma sighed. "You say Adam has sent out SOS messages to try to find out who owns her?"

"Yes, but no one's called back so far. Everyone we know is passing the word around."

"Hmm. . . ." Grandma stamped her feet to keep warm. She was muffled in a red woolen scarf and a red beret. "Have you thought about taking her to Betty Hilder down at the sanctuary?" Betty ran a home for stray animals in Welford. She would be sure to find room for the sheepdog.

Mandy stood up. "Not yet. I haven't thought that far ahead. I'd better talk to James about it first, since he helped to rescue her."

Grandma nodded. "Betty's might be worth a try."

Mandy turned toward the house. "Come on, girl!" The dog stuck like glue to her side. "I don't know, Grandma. Betty would take good care of her, I know, but she doesn't have all that much space. I'd like to think of this dog getting better and running around the hillsides, like she used to. I'm sure she'd make a good working dog on a farm somewhere." She could imagine the dog, sleek and fit, ranging across the fields, her long, bushy tail streaming in the wind.

"You're probably right," Grandpa agreed, "judging by how obedient she is. And nice natured, too." They went into the unit and Mandy took her down to her kennel.

"Good girl," she said as the dog went in and lay down. "You have a rest, get your strength back." It was probably her imagination, but she thought she could already see the dog gaining weight and recovering the gleam in her eyes, the shine on her coat. Her markings were lovely, now that she was cleaned up — black ears and eye patches with a white stripe down her muzzle, a white chest, and black hindquarters.

"Do I hear the phone?" Grandma asked as they emerged into the fresh air.

Mandy dashed ahead, just in time to pick up the receiver before the phone stopped ringing.

"Ah, you are there, Mandy dear!" Mrs. Ponsonby's rich tones rang out. "Do you have a moment to spare?"

"Yes, Mrs. Ponsonby." Mandy put one hand over the phone and rolled her eyes at Grandma and Grandpa as they followed her into the kitchen. "Just be a sec!" she mouthed. Then she turned back to the phone. "How can I help? Is Pandora all right?"

"Oh, there's nothing wrong. No, Pandora's fine, thank you very much. No, this is about your little idea for a pets' Christmas party."

"Ye-es?" Mandy waited to hear what came next. Had Mrs. Ponsonby taken it upon herself to call the pastor and get him to change his mind about the village hall?

"Well, I've been thinking. As you know, I was very much against the idea at first. I'm afraid the standard of behavior among pets these days leaves much to be desired."

"Yes." Mandy kept her voice level. So far, Mrs. Ponsonby hadn't dropped any bombshells.

"Many of them have no manners, but that's because their owners have none either, especially the young ones."

"Is that so, Mrs. Ponsonby?"

"Oh, I don't mean you, Mandy dear!" Mrs. Ponsonby's singsong voice rose an octave. "Well, anyway, I've been thinking it over. Perhaps I should let Pandora and Toby come to the party after all."

"Great!" Mandy jumped in. "I'm sure they'll enjoy themselves."

Mrs. Ponsonby ignored her and sailed on. "The point is, my dear, Pandora can come and set an example to all those other badly brought up animals. She'll raise the tone of the event, if you see what I mean."

Mandy managed not to laugh. "I'm sure she will. And Toby, too."

"Yes. Now, my dear, since my little darlings will be able to come, I'd like to offer my own services in the organizational side of things. I'm sure your grandma already has enough on her plate, and if there's any way I could possibly help get things ready beforehand . . ."

Mandy's jaw dropped at the idea of Grandma accepting help from Mrs. Ponsonby. She cleared her throat. "Actually, Grandma is here now," she said. "Would you like to talk to her?"

Grandma's eyes widened. As she came across the kitchen, Mandy dropped the phone into her hand as if it were a hot potato. Soon Grandma and Mrs. Ponsonby were deep into party planning.

Mandy slipped toward the door. She grabbed her jacket from the back of a chair. "I'm out of here!" she whispered to her grandfather. "I have to meet up with James. We're going to deliver more invitations."

"Wise move," Grandpa whispered back. He nodded toward his wife, who was talking animatedly into the phone. "I'm afraid this could take some time!"

So Mandy and James biked around, handing out invitations and getting in the mood for Saturday's party.

That evening Mandy sprawled on the rug in the warm kitchen at Animal Ark, one arm around the sheepdog's neck, trying to believe even now that the phone *would* ring, and a worried owner would be reunited with a faithful pet.

But no such luck. The phone stayed silent. Mandy's one comfort, as she went to bed on that Tuesday night, was that the dog was looking much better. She'd been fed and rested, brushed, pampered, and made to feel special. After another good night's sleep, she would be almost back to normal.

The next morning, Mandy arrived in the village just in time to see James being dropped off outside McFarlane's newsstand. His dad lifted his bike out of the back of their station wagon, closed the door, and climbed back into the driver's seat. He gave a wave and drove off in the direction of Walton, the nearest town to Welford.

"Only four days to go!" James greeted her. He took off his glasses to polish them. "We'd better get a move on with these last invitations. How's the sheepdog?" he asked, all in one breath.

"Much better." Mandy waited for him to mount his bike. "She's eating like a horse."

"Great. Hey, guess what, they've forecasted snow before the weekend!" James slung one leg over the seat.

"A white Christmas!" Mandy really liked this idea. It would add an extra something to their party.

"Just so long as it's not too deep for people to get through," James warned. He was thinking ahead as usual. "Where to first? Ernie's house?"

At last they were ready for another busy morning delivering cards.

Ernie Bell lived near Walter Pickard at the end of the small row of stone row houses by the side of the Fox and Goose. He came to the door and received his invitation straight-faced. "Eh, I don't know about that," he said slowly. Sammy, the gray squirrel, sat perched on his shoulder. "Parties aren't really my cup of tea." He rubbed his grizzled white head.

Sammy puffed out his cheeks and darted across his shoulders, chattering excitedly.

Mandy laughed. "Sammy doesn't agree, do you, Sammy?"

"He likes parties!" James said.

The squirrel chattered back.

"Lydia will be there," James added. "She's bringing Houdini."

"Is she now?" Ernie was weakening, they could see.

Just then another gray head popped out from the far end of the street. It was Walter, Ernie's pal. "He'll be there, don't worry, you two. I'll see that he puts on a clean shirt and tie."

James ran along to deliver Walter's own card. "No need for that," he explained. "You can make a party hat for the competition if you like. Otherwise, come dressed however you want."

Walter grunted. "We'll think about that, young man." He pocketed his invitation and went on badgering Ernie to accept.

Sammy joined in, hopping up and down Ernie's arm. "We'll see," he said at last.

"That means yes." Walter winked at James. The two old men shut their doors, and James and Mandy went on their way, across the parking lot to the pub to find John Hardy.

"Do you think he's home from boarding school?" Mandy asked, as they knocked at the back door of the pub.

James nodded. "I saw him the other day."

When John came downstairs in his neat cream cable-knit sweater, he was delighted with his invitation. He promised to bring along both Button and Barney. "Imogen's away for the whole vacation," he explained. "I'm looking after the rabbits for two weeks." Their arrangement to share the care of the twin brown rabbits was working out well.

"At least you won't have far to come to the party," Mandy told him. "We all plan to meet up here with lanterns and flashlights, and we'll walk in a procession down to the village hall. Will that be okay?"

"Great!" John's eyes lit up. "Thanks for asking me!" He waved them on their way.

Next came Susan Collins's invitation. They found her exercising her pony, Prince, in the frosty paddock at the back of her huge house, The Beeches. Rider and horse made a perfect combination, Susan erect in her saddle, Prince beautifully groomed and healthy. Mandy could tell that Susan was genuinely pleased not to be left out of their plans. She leaned from the saddle and took her invitation. "Party hats, huh?" she said thoughtfully. "Well, we'll see what we can do!"

James and Mandy left her to ponder and rode on to Greystones Farm along the valley bottom. "Hi!" they called to Ken Hudson, at work in a nearby field. He carried food to the hardy Saddleback pigs. "Have you seen Brandon?"

"In the barn with Ruby!" he yelled back.

They went on, and sure enough, they came across the tall, gangling figure of Brandon Gill, busy forking bales of hay onto a trailer, with round, rambunctious Ruby the pig squatting on her haunches, idly watching.

Ruby turned to the barn door and spotted them, gave a small squeal, and trotted up. James bent to scratch her pink-and-black back.

Mandy held out the card to Brandon. He blushed deep red and mumbled his thanks. The envelope was quickly shoved into the pocket of his denim jacket.

"Can you come?" Mandy asked.

He nodded.

"Seven-thirty. Bring Ruby," James reminded him.

"Just try and stop her!" Brandon laughed. "You know Ruby; she gets her nose into everything!"

Ruby grunted and snuffled at James's shoes. He took one of Blackie's dog biscuits from his pocket and held it

out to the pig. Ruby nibbled it delicately from his palm with her soft, velvety snout.

And then they were off again, heading on to the main road, pausing for breath at the village crossroads. "What about Claire?" James asked. "I guess she really can't bring the hedgehogs, but it would be more fun for her if she didn't have to come on her own."

Mandy thought about it. "It's a problem, I know." Little Claire McKay was devoted to her prickly winter lodgers in her hedgehog refuge, but even she would realize she couldn't disturb their hibernation to bring them to a party. For a while, Mandy was as stuck as James. "Wait, I have an idea," she said at last. "That is, if you wouldn't mind . . ."

James grinned. "Go on, Mandy. Spit it out!"

"Well, it's just a thought. Could you lend Blackie to Claire? They get along well, don't they? And that would still leave Eric for you to bring." She knew it was a big thing to ask James to trust Claire with his dog. But at least it would give him the chance to bring along his cat.

James hardly hesitated. "Fine!" he agreed.

"Oh, James, that's great! Why don't you go and tell Claire? See if she thinks it's a good idea. I'll just run over to Dorian's place and ask Andi if they can come along."

"Meet up at your place for lunch?" James asked.

She nodded. Even though preparations for the party were in full swing, there was still a lot to do. They biked off in different directions. As she headed for Manor Farm, Mandy hoped for great things; a get-together at the Fox and Goose, a Christmas card scene of snow, holly, and robins, a candlelit procession up the dark street, and mountains of food!

Five

Wednesday lunchtime arrived before Mandy knew it.
She hurried home after her visit to Manor Farm to meet
up with James and grab a bite to eat. To her surprise,
she found her dad playing with the Border collie in the
warmth of the kitchen.

"I just took her out of the unit to check her over," he
explained.

But Mandy knew better; he hadn't been able to resist
the dog's lovable face and trusting eyes.

"Adam, you're going soft in your old age!" Mandy's
mom stood at the stove, heating a large pot of vegetable

soup. She smiled as Mandy's dad rolled the dog onto her back and tickled her stomach.

"No way!" The good-natured game continued as the dog squirmed onto her feet and bounced up with her front paws against Dr. Adam's stomach. "Ouch! No, I'm just making sure she's recovered from her ordeal," he said.

"It looks as if she has." Mandy nodded and laughed. "It's great, isn't it? But have we had any word about where she came from yet?"

Dr. Adam shook his head. "A big negative on that one, I'm afraid."

Mandy sighed. "I wonder what she's called?" She went to stroke the dog's nose. "It seems wrong to just think of her as 'the dog' or 'the stray.' She must have a name that she would answer to."

"Why not give her one?" Dr. Emily suggested. She ladled hot soup into four bowls. "You and James. I think you're entitled to do that, since you were the ones who rescued her."

Mandy nodded and felt her face glow with pleasure. She waited impatiently until James arrived, then sat with him over the soup and crusty bread. The dog snoozed in a warm corner, tired out by the game, while Mandy and James made yet another list.

"Lassie . . . Jessie . . . Badger?" James suggested.

"Patch . . . Winnie . . . Sally?" Mandy tried out several names. None sounded quite right. They thought again.

"Flora?" Dr. Adam chipped in.

They shook their heads.

"Jemima, Ermintrude, Gwendolen," he suggested, rattling them off.

"Dad!" Mandy raised her eyebrows. "You can't call a dog Ermintrude!"

"Gwen wouldn't sound too bad," James added.

Mandy looked at the dog. She'd opened her eyes, head resting on her front paws, seeming to take some interest in this naming game. "Gwen?" Mandy experimented. There was no response. "How about Tess? Tess, here, girl!" she called softly.

The dog stood up and walked smartly toward her.

"Sit, Tess!"

She sat.

Mandy looked at the others in pleased surprise.

"Tess it is!" said Dr. Emily.

Everyone was delighted. "Do you think that really is her name?" James asked.

Adam Hope shrugged. "Who knows? All I can tell is, she seemed to like the idea."

"Tess suits her, doesn't it?" Mandy felt it was a good name for a working dog — short, sharp, and sturdy.

"Tess thinks so," James laughed. "You'd better watch it, Mandy. You're already her best friend." He watched the dog licking Mandy's hand and putting her head on her lap.

"Seriously," Dr. Emily agreed. "We mustn't let her get too attached. Remember, we can't keep her." She looked kindly at Mandy before she cleaned up the lunch things.

Mandy stood with a sigh. "Down, Tess," she ordered. "And we still have so much to do for the party, so I'd better get you back to the unit. That's a good dog." Quickly she led her outside through the yard to the residential unit. "Good girl," she whispered as she locked the door.

Leaving her there was hard. Try as she might to toughen up and be sensible over Tess, Mandy had to admit that the dog had touched her. In fact, she was head over heels in love with the gentle, affectionate creature.

James peered at Mandy as they pocketed the last of their invitations and set off on their bikes once more. "Are you sure you're okay?" he asked.

She nodded. "Yes, thanks. Where to now?" Her head was still in a whirl over Tess, and her heart wasn't in the task for the afternoon.

"The Spillers'," he suggested. They biked in silence toward the field, where Jack Spiller and his family worked their small plot of land. James carried an invitation for six-year-old Jenny Spiller and her pet sheep, who was also named Blackie. James seemed to be thinking long and hard. "Mandy," he said, "you don't think Jack Spiller might . . . I mean, he keeps a few sheep. . . . He might . . . want to take Tess!" At last he managed to get the words out, holding his breath for Mandy's reaction.

Mandy felt her heart give a little jolt at the new idea. She caught her own breath and pedaled silently along a flat stretch of road. The Spillers were nice people. They already had a working dog on the farm. She tried to think it through. If Tess had to go somewhere, she realized the Spillers would make good owners for her. "Let's ask," she agreed. It was better than Betty Hilder's sanctuary, and that was the only other idea they'd come up with so far.

As they arrived at the house, Jenny Spiller came running to meet them, with Blackie close on her heels. He'd already grown into a sturdy young sheep.

"And everywhere that Jenny went . . ." James laughed at the sight of the inseparable pair.

Soon Jack Spiller appeared at the door. "What brings you two up here?" he called.

James explained about the party. Jenny jumped up and down in excitement. "Can I go, Dad? Please!"

Jack Spiller readily agreed. "Thanks for asking her. I'll drive her down. Half-past seven on Christmas Eve, you say?"

Mandy stood by while James and Mr. Spiller made the arrangements. She felt her stomach turning nervously. Finally, as Mr. Spiller looked at his watch and took Jenny by the hand, she plucked up the courage to speak.

"Mr. Spiller, would you by any chance be able to take an extra dog?" she asked straight out. There seemed to be no point sidling into the issue. "We've rescued a stray, and so far no one has come forward to claim her. We need to find her a good home. James thought you might be able to do with the extra help?" She gripped her handlebars tightly and waited for the answer. The icy feel of cold metal seeped through her gloved hands.

Jack Spiller halted and turned. "A working dog?"

Mandy nodded. "A Border collie. A female. She's so gentle. We've called her Tess." She found it hard to keep her voice steady, but she was determined to do her best to find the dog a good home.

"Female?" Jack Spiller slowly began to shake his head. "That would mean we'd have two female dogs around the place," he said. "That wouldn't work, I'm afraid. They wouldn't get along. Now, if it had been a male, we might have found room for him!" He smiled at Mandy. "It's a no go, I'm afraid."

"Thanks anyway, it was just an idea," she said. Suddenly she realized how much hope she'd pinned on Mr. Spiller saying yes. Tess would have loved it up here, working for her keep.

"Sorry. Better luck next time," Jack Spiller said. He led Jenny back to the house, with Blackie trudging along behind.

Mandy sighed and looked at James. He shrugged. "Nearly," he said.

"So near and yet so far," she agreed. They set off down the hill.

"Right!" James set his jaw and sounded determined. "We're not going to let this problem ruin our Christmas, are we?"

Mandy took up the challenge. "We are not!"

"We are going to get Tess settled in a terrific new home before the party!" he insisted. He let go of his brakes on a straight downhill stretch.

Mandy followed, feeling the wind in her hair. "We are!" She began to smile as they swooped down into the valley.

"We will work this one out!"

"We sure will!"

"We will not give in!" he shouted over his shoulder. "Never!"

By the time they'd reached the bottom of the hill, Mandy had shaken off her regrets about parting with Tess. She knew they owed it to everyone to do their very best to find a home for the dog before Christmas.

Mandy's gaze swept along the road by the riverside. "Do we have time to stop by Greystones?" she asked suddenly.

"Of course. Why?" James was catching his breath after the downhill charge.

"Wait and see. It's my turn to have an idea!" she grinned. She biked ahead.

"But we gave Brandon and Ruby their invitations yesterday." James gasped to keep up. They sped between bare hawthorn hedges, still white with frost. Soon the gray square building came into view.

"I'm not looking for Brandon." Mandy put on her brakes and squealed to a halt. She came level with the field where the Gills kept their pigs. "I'm looking for Ken!"

Ken Hudson was the pigman at the farm. He was small and wiry, a no-nonsense sort of man who'd recently moved to live with his sister on her upland farm. He still worked here in the valley at Greystones Farm. James spied him now, crossing the field between the arched shelters where the black-and-white pigs lived and fed. He carried two buckets of food and whistled as he walked. "There he is!" James pointed to him emptying the buckets into a metal trough.

Mandy spotted him, too. She laid down her bike and jumped over the wall into the field. Several pigs came running toward her, including Napoleon, the huge, friendly boar. "Hi, Ken!" She waved both arms, glad to see him put down his empty buckets and stride downhill. James joined her, and together they scratched the backs of the pigs and let them root around their feet.

"Now, then, what can I do for you?" A smile wrinkled up Ken's thin face. He shifted Napoleon out of the way with a hefty shove and stood with hands on hips, his cap tilted back on his head.

Merry Christmas, Ken!" Mandy grinned. She liked Ken. His looks reminded her of a wizened jockey, skinny and bowlegged in his black rubber boots.

"No, you haven't come all this way just to wish me Merry Christmas," he countered. He looked quizzically at Mandy.

"We came to see how your move went," Mandy continued. "Didn't we, James?"

"Yes!" He gave her a sideways look.

"It went like clockwork." Ken scratched his forehead. "I didn't have much stuff to move. Got it all up to the farm in one trip and settled in just great. Dora's been fattening me up since I went to live with her."

"That's good." Mandy shifted from one foot to the other.

"And?"

"And what?" She opened her eyes wide.

"And what else can I do for you?" Ken half-smiled. "You can't fool me; you're up to something, Mandy Hope!" He turned to James. "She is, isn't she?"

"Search me." James tried to look innocent. But he gave Mandy a quick shove.

"You like dogs, don't you, Ken?" Mandy had decided the best tactic this time was to go slow and easy.

"I like everything that goes on four legs," he answered. Napoleon nudged against him, sniffing at his pocket. Without thinking, Ken dipped in his hand and offered the boar a wrinkled windfall apple.

"You'd like Tess, then." Mandy gazed up at the frosty hillside, a plaid scarf knotted around her neck, her green jacket zipped tight.

"Who's Tess?" Ken filled the pause.

"Tess is a great dog, isn't she, James? Super friendly. And she does everything you tell her. She's a black-and-white Border collie with big brown eyes. I'm sure she could be a champion dog!"

"Whose dog is she, then?" Ken sounded interested.

"Ah!" Mandy held the suspense.

"I haven't heard of a new dog around here," he insisted. "She sounds like she might be something special!"

"She is! Would you like to see her?" Mandy felt him grab the bait. She knew Ken wouldn't be able to resist the build-up she'd given the dog.

"Maybe." He considered it, his head to one side.

"Why don't I bring her over?" Mandy offered.

But Ken shook his head. "Not here. I'm heading home now, up to Dora's place. I've finished work for the day."

"Well, we could bring her up. In fact, we'd love to. We could put her through her paces for you, if you like. She's great to watch."

"She is, is she?" Ken looked suspiciously at Mandy. "A wonder dog?"

At last Mandy decided to come clean. "The fact is, she needs a new home. I thought you might take her." Again she held her breath.

"You did?" As usual, Ken answered with a question.

Mandy nodded.

Ken tugged at the peak of his cap. He looked down at his boots. "A new home?" he repeated.

"Tess is a stray. James and I rescued her. She really is a fantastic dog, Ken! I'm sure you'd love her!"

Ken studied Mandy's eager face. "A Border collie? A champion?"

"I'm sure she could be! You could train Tess to do anything. What she needs is a place where she could be put to work rounding up sheep. You have to take a look at her and see!"

"Maybe there's room for another dog alongside Whistler," Ken admitted. "Now, I don't know what Dora would say, but . . ."

"We can bring Tess up to show you!" Mandy couldn't contain her excitement. She ran up to Ken, her face shining.

He nodded. "Why not?"

James whooped and jumped up.

"Bring her up first thing tomorrow. Let's have a look at this marvelous sheepdog," he told Mandy. "After all, I can't see any harm in taking a look, can you?"

Six

To the outsider, Dora Janeki's sheep farm was a miserable place, cut off by steep hills and bare expanses of brown, wintry grass. But it was sheep farm country, wild and unwalled, where sheep grazed in the distance and the dogs ran far and wide.

Tess sat in the back of the Animal Ark jeep with Mandy and James at her side. Dr. Adam had offered to drive them up to meet Ken Hudson early on Thursday morning, before he began his rounds. "I'll pick you up on the way back," he said as he came to open the back door. Tess jumped down and sniffed the grass, her tail curving up in an elegant arc. It had a white tip that seemed to float among the low brown tufts. "Don't expect her to do too much," he warned them. "She's still building up her strength, remember."

Mandy nodded. "Thanks, Dad. See you later."

She and James jumped down after Tess. The weather had turned cloudy, with a strong, cold wind. It was one of those winter days when it seems it will never get fully light. Mandy pulled her plaid scarf around her chin and whistled Tess to heel.

"Good luck!" Adam Hope jumped back into the driver's seat and leaned out. "I'll keep my fingers crossed!"

They waved him off, then turned to tramp up a bridle path to Syke Farm. Sensing the freedom of the open spaces, alert and eager, Tess loped beside them until they reached the bare farmyard. Then James went ahead to knock at the faded red door of the house.

Mandy kept Tess back as she watched Dora Janeki come to the door. She spotted Whistler, the farm dog, peering out of his kennel at the far side of the yard. He was a tall, rangy animal, with a long gray coat. He was speckled all over with small patches of black, and his left ear was black, too. His eyes were a strange pale gray color, almost white. Now she saw his hackles rise, and he growled as he spotted Tess.

"Yes?" Mrs. Janeki looked suspiciously at James. Small and skinny like her brother, but without Ken's friendly smile, she was a short-tempered woman with sharp, poker-straight features. Mandy knew her reputation as a worrier and a skinflint, and realized now that she certainly didn't welcome visitors.

"Hello, I'm James Hunter. We've come to see Ken," James explained.

Dora grunted. "That's the first I've heard of it. Are you sure?" She quieted Whistler with a sharp word and frowned at the newcomers.

"He asked us to bring Tess up to see him." Mandy put Tess on a lead and walked forward. "He said he'd like to take a look at her."

"Did he, now?" The frown deepened. "I can't think why. Wait here."

She closed the door abruptly and vanished. Mandy felt her hopes dive as they stood in the cold, wintry yard.

But they revived when Ken emerged, wrapped up against the weather in a high-necked thick green sweater and a big blue duffel coat, wearing his cap low on his forehead. He closed the door behind him and stamped his feet. "You've come at a good time," he said, glancing at Tess. "So, this is her." He began to walk around her in a slow, wide circle.

"Sit, Tess!" Mandy felt the dog stir uneasily. A few yards off, Whistler kept up his low growl. "Stay, girl," she said quietly, praying that Tess would submit to Ken's inspection.

Ken walked full circle, then came up to them. "Thin as a rake," he commented, still staring down at Tess.

"You'd be, too, if you'd been through what Tess has just been through." Hurriedly Mandy described the dog's long, cruel walk; how they'd found her weary, starved, and footsore, on the very point of collapse. Through the story, Tess sat quiet, one eye on Whistler, waiting for the next command.

"She's not strong, then?" Ken bent to run his hand down Tess's long black-and-white coat.

"She soon will be," Mandy promised. "She's getting the best treatment. We're building her up on food and vitamins. And she's tough. You'd be amazed at how quickly she was back on her feet"

"Hmm." Ken crouched down. The dog looked back at him curiously. "And she'll do anything you tell her?"

"Yes. Do you want to see?"

Ken gave her a brief nod.

"Stay, Tess!" Mandy gave the clear order. Then she and James moved off across the yard. Tess sat still as a statue, with Ken looking on. "Here, Tess!" Mandy called. Tess bounded forward and joined them in a flash.

"Let's try something else," Ken suggested. He scouted

around for a piece of broken branch from the bare horse chestnut tree that overhung the yard.

"Good girl, Tess!" Mandy breathed. She held up crossed fingers to show James.

"Great," James agreed. He patted the dog and stood up to see what the next test would be.

Ken came across with a stick. "See if she'll fetch this when you tell her."

Mandy took the stick and showed it to Tess. The dog sniffed and frisked up at it. Then Mandy turned away from the house and threw the stick toward the field with all her might. "Fetch, Tess!" she called.

And the dog was gone, streaking through the grass as the stick arched through the air. She bounded out of sight. The stick landed. Tess reappeared with it clamped between her jaws. Quickly she ran back to Mandy and dropped it at her feet. Then she sat, front paws neatly together, head up, panting, her tongue lolling out.

"Good girl." Mandy smiled with relief. She turned to Ken.

He nodded. "Not bad. Now let's take her up on to the hill and see how she gets along with the sheep, shall we?" He led the trek across country toward four or five distant white specks.

James and Mandy struggled to match the tough little farmer's pace, but Tess loped easily, seeming to know exactly what was expected of her now.

"I only hope she can do this!" James whispered to Mandy. "You don't think we're expecting too much?"

Mandy's own heart was in her mouth, as eventually they came to a stretch of short, firm grassland. The sheep were now in the near distance, a couple of hundred yards up the slope.

"Right," Ken said. "Step aside, you two. Let's see what she can really do." He gave a low, short whistle. Tess pricked up her ears and glanced at Mandy. Then she trotted to Ken and sat, waiting.

Ken gave a second whistle, higher and longer. Tess leaped to her feet and ran straight as an arrow toward the group of grazing animals. He whistled again, a piercing sound that rose high at the end. Tess's track curved to the right, around the back of the sheep. Ken gave a blast of short, sharp whistles. She circled around and around, drawing the sheep into a tight cluster.

"Wow!" James stared openmouthed. "She's good!"

Then Ken's call altered. The note was lower. He was calling Tess back. She hustled and darted, heading off the front sheep, slowing turning the bunch toward Ken and driving them downhill. She brought them back without faltering once.

Wild-eyed, the sheep clustered around Ken. He called to Tess to heel. The sheep scrambled away, free to take up their grazing farther down the hillside. Mandy and James ran up to Ken and Tess. "Well?" they said, impatient for his verdict.

At his feet, Tess crouched low. Her sides heaved like bellows; her pink tongue lolled sideways. "Too much like hard work, huh?" Ken muttered.

"Well?" Mandy couldn't restrain herself a moment longer. "What do you think?"

Ken looked up. "It's not so much what *I* think. It's what the boss thinks." He gave a wry nod toward the house. "Dora has the final say around here."

"But what do *you* think?" Mandy insisted. She felt the wind blow from behind. Flakes of snow began to drift from the dark sky.

Ken paused. He bent to reward Tess with a firm pat against her side. "Champion," he confirmed. "If it were up to me, I'd take her like a shot!"

Tess wagged her tail. Mandy grinned at James.

"What will your sister say?" James asked. "Will she agree?"

Ken shrugged and looked down toward the house. "Here she comes now. Why not ask her yourselves?"

They turned in surprise to see Dora Janeki striding toward them in a long blue overcoat, wearing a checked brown scarf tied firmly around her head. She didn't smile as she approached, hands in pockets, shoulders hunched. "Can't you see it's snowing?" she complained. "Do you want me to call out the snowplows to get you two back home?"

Mandy swallowed. James frowned. Ken grinned. "You watched that, didn't you?" He went down to meet her. "I saw you looking out of the bedroom window as I was putting her through her paces. I knew you couldn't keep your nose out of it for long!"

Dora sniffed. "I don't know what you mean."

"What did you think?" Ken insisted.

"About what?"

"Oh, pull the other one, Dora!" Ken enjoyed teasing her. "You saw Tess at work, all right. Mandy and James here want to know what you thought of her."

Dora looked up at the snow clouds, she frowned at Mandy, she told her brother off for going behind her back, she grumbled about the cost of taking on another dog. But in the end, she gave in. "She's all right, I suppose," she admitted grudgingly. "Considering we don't know a thing about her."

"All right!" Ken retorted. "She's wonderful!" Again he patted and fondled Tess.

"And you'll keep her?" Mandy could hardly believe it.

"That depends on how much you want for her," Dora said with narrowed eyes.

"Nothing."

"Nothing?" It was Dora's turn not to believe her ears.

"We just want you to give her a home," Mandy assured her.

"And something useful to do," James added.

"In that case," Dora said, speaking in a rush before they could change their minds, "we'll have her, thank you very much!"

"She can stay?" James and Mandy asked together.

Dora Janeki nodded once and turned on her heel. Ken Hudson slapped his thigh and grinned. Mandy grabbed James's arm and danced around in a circle. Tess jumped up and joined in.

"I won't tell you again — it's snowing!" Dora yelled at them. "Don't expect me to get up a rescue party!"

Ken laughed. "Come on, she's right. We'd better get you back down." Together they went to the farm to wait for Dr. Adam. "My sister's bark is worse than her bite," he whispered as they walked. "She's really taken to Tess, only she doesn't like to show it."

Mandy nodded. They had what they wanted. Tess had a home. She would be out on the hillsides where she belonged. Ken was the best; he would be firm and kind, and look after her for the rest of her life. Tess would never again be found abandoned and starving.

But as she stood in the farmyard, watching the jeep wind its way through the flurry of snowflakes and wind, Mandy's heart felt torn in two. Yes, she wanted Tess to stay up on the wild hill with Ken Hudson. But deep inside, it hurt to leave her. As she bent to give Tess one last hug, the dog's soft black nose nuzzled against her cheek. She put her paw on Mandy's lap and growled softly.

"Come and see her whenever you like," Ken said quietly.

Mandy stood up with a lump in her throat, feeling the snowflakes settle and melt on her cheeks. Wondering which were tears and which was snow, she nodded quickly, turned, and walked away.

Seven

"Well done!" Adam Hope said as he stopped to pick up Mandy and James on the lonely road by Syke Farm. Tess was nowhere to be seen. Snowflakes whirled around and settled on them, then melted into glittering drops on their hair and jackets as they climbed into the warm car. "I take it Ken said yes?"

Mandy nodded. She didn't trust herself to say anything as they set off, the jeep's thick, wide tires firmly gripping the snowy surface. The wipers worked hard to keep the windshield clear.

"I hope this weather doesn't set in." Dr. Adam glanced at Mandy. "Snow may be pretty to look at and all that, but it makes a vet's job twice as difficult, and the animals don't like it much either."

"The forecast says it'll clear later in the day," James reported.

From the flat conversation, Mandy could tell that they, too, were feeling the absence of Tess's friendly face in the back of the car.

They drove on for a while in silence. Then, as Welford village came within sight and Dr. Adam turned to go down their street, he remembered a message for Mandy. "Oh, Grandma asks if you two can go and meet her at the village hall as soon as you get back. She wants to talk to you about decorations or something like that."

Mandy nodded.

Her dad braked and stopped. "Should I drop you here to save you a walk?" He looked closely at her. "It's best to keep busy," he advised. "It'll help keep your mind off Tess."

She smiled. Her dad always had a knack of knowing what was on her mind. "Thanks, Dad. Good idea. We'll see you later."

"Could you call my mom and tell her where I am, please?" James jumped out into the cold air. Already the snow seemed to be lighter, the sky clearer.

Dr. Adam said he would, so together James and Mandy jogged back into the village, heading for the hall.

When they arrived, they stamped the snow off their boots and opened up the big oak door. Inside, Grandma greeted them cheerily from halfway up a stepladder. Rolls of colored paper streamers, glittering gold stars, and packages of balloons lay scattered over the floor. Grandpa was busy wedging a six-foot-high Christmas tree into a wooden barrel in the far corner of the big room, while Ernie Bell stood offering advice. "Left a bit, now right a bit; right, right, left a bit!" he barked, until at last the tree stood perfectly straight.

"See those balloons?" Grandma asked. She pointed to the packages on the floor. "Your young lungs are stronger than ours. See how many you can blow up, while I try hanging these streamers."

Mandy and James set to work, blowing with all their might. Soon their cheeks ached and they ran out of breath. One balloon burst with a hollow bang. But the floor came alive with floating red, yellow, blue, orange, and white balloons of all shapes and sizes.

Meanwhile, Grandma fought the streamers. She straightened out the tangles and pinned thumbtacks into hard, wooden rafters. Then she came down the ladder and draped the streamers across the room, from corner to corner, with James's help. Grandpa and Ernie were by now busy with tinsel and lights, decorating the beautiful tree.

At last Mandy blew up the final balloon. James had collapsed on the floor, head propped against the wall, surrounded by the multicolored sea of balloons.

"Let's gather them up and attach them to pieces of string," Mandy gasped. She began to crawl on her hands and knees, chasing after them as they floated out of reach.

"That's the idea!" Grandma said. "We can hang them up around the walls."

But just then the outer door opened and a gust of wind whirled in and scattered the balloons. Mrs. Ponsonby's voice "whoo-hoo"ed through the hall. Grandpa and Ernie cringed and carried on with their tree. Pandora came in, yapping excitedly. Toby stood at the door and growled in confusion. Soon both dogs pounced into the midst of the whirling balloons.

"Hello!" Mrs. Ponsonby slammed the door shut. "Dorothy? Mandy? Is anyone there?" She peered through her steamed-up glasses, putting a pointed heel firmly through a red balloon. It popped and the dogs ran in circles, barking loudly. "Oh!" Mrs. Ponsonby's hand flew to her ample chest. "Oh, my!" Pandora yapped and charged at the balloons.

"Here I am!" Grandma called from the top of her ladder. Mandy could tell she was gritting her teeth. "What can I do for you?"

"Oh, no, no! What can *I* do for *you*?" Mrs. Ponsonby swept off her heavy tweed coat and scattered more balloons. She flung it across the back of a wooden chair, then rolled up her sleeves. Then she spied Grandpa and Ernie hard at work on their tree. "Ah," she said, "it looks as if I arrived just in the nick of time!" She bustled across the room. "I always say men have no idea how to decorate a Christmas tree! They fling the tinsel on any old how. It has to be *arranged*, just so!" She pushed Ernie to one side and grabbed a piece of silver tinsel from Grandpa. "And these lights!" she said scornfully. "Just thrown on! Look, you have two pink ones together, and *three* blue ones! You need to *rearrange* them!"

Ernie and Grandpa looked at each other and retired, hurt. "Let her get on with it, if she's so eager to," Ernie grumbled. He took his cap from his pocket and went off in a huff to the Fox and Goose.

Grandpa coughed and made his excuses. "I have to slip down to McFarlane's for a roll of tape." He, too, shuffled off.

Mrs. Ponsonby nodded. "Men!" she said. She went on happily dismantling their tree.

While Dr. Emily stayed up her ladder, well out of reach, and James went on chasing stray balloons, Pandora fought on. Another balloon popped. Mandy lay flat on the floor, chin in her hands, staring Toby in the face. The scruffy mongrel had resigned himself to a long wait for his mistress. He stared back at Mandy, his mouth stretched wide in a patient, long-suffering smile. She giggled. Balloons drifted past. "Merry Christmas, Toby!" she laughed.

The dog lifted his head and gave one sharp bark.

"Ah, there you are, Mandy, my dear!" Mrs. Ponsonby sang out. "Yes, and a Merry Christmas to you, too. Oh, it's so lucky that I came to help when I did. How would you ever have gotten everything ready for the party without me?"

By Thursday lunchtime, James had managed to escape to his house. "See you later," he told Mandy. Mrs. Ponsonby was still going strong, helping to *arrange* clusters of balloons along the walls. "I told my mom I'd be back by one. She wants me to go Christmas shopping with her in Walton."

"Lucky!" Mandy whispered back. She held up an armful of balloons to Mrs. Ponsonby. "I still have to stay here for a while."

It wasn't until one-thirty that Mrs. Ponsonby was finally satisfied with the decoration of the hall. Mandy, her grandmother, and Mrs. Ponsonby stood back to admire their work, then Grandma showed them out and was able to lock the door and drive Mandy back to Animal Ark. "Don't say a word!" she warned her granddaughter. "If you even mention that dreadful woman's name, I shall explode like . . . Mount Vesuvius!"

Mandy sat beside her and laughed out loud. "But the hall does look great," she pointed out. "Looks really Christmassy!" She felt a flutter of excitement as the day for the party approached.

"Only two days to go!" Grandma said as she stopped the car and dropped her off.

Mandy nodded and dashed into the house in high spirits. She was starving and wanted to tell her mom and dad of the progress they'd made at the hall. "The party is going to be great!" she promised. She stopped in her tracks. "Hey, I just remembered — I've never given you an invitation!" She stood, poised over the cups of tea she'd just poured. "You will be able to come, won't you?"

Her parents sat and laughed at her. "Try and stop us!" they chorused.

Mandy gave them their tea, smiling happily.

* * *

In spite of Christmas, business went on as usual that afternoon at Animal Ark. First, Emily Hope was called out by the Canine Defense League. One of their men needed help with a dog who had been left at home alone by its owners. Neighbors had called to help the animal, but it was too distressed for one person to handle. Willingly, she volunteered to go lend a hand.

Adam Hope shook his head. "Sometimes I think they should ban Christmas for owners like that," he said angrily. They listened as Dr. Emily drove off in her four-wheel-drive.

It made Mandy think of Tess. "I wonder how she's doing with Ken?" she said out loud.

"Who, Tess?"

She nodded. "I hope she settles in okay."

"She will," Dad assured her. "I'd trust Ken with any animal of mine. He knows everything there is to know. And sometimes I think he prefers them to people."

Mandy sighed. "You're right. Can I come and help you this afternoon?" She followed him from the kitchen into the empty reception area.

"I was about to ask if you had time," he confirmed. "Grab a white coat. Let's help Simon clean out the residential unit before we start office hours. We only have half an hour. Let's go!"

So Mandy went and said hello to Simon. She got engrossed in her favorite work, lifting cats out of their cages and putting them gently into baskets while she cleared trays and put in food, milk, and clean newspaper. Then there were dogs to exercise and groom, the floors to sweep and disinfect. They finished work with five minutes to spare before Jean was due in reception. The phone was ringing, and Mandy headed quickly back into the office.

She picked up the phone, ready to slip in an appointment or arrange visits. She hardly expected the bad news that was about to break.

"Animal Ark. How can I help?" she said brightly.

"This is Dora Janeki here," the voice snapped back. "I need you to send someone up double-quick!"

"Yes, Mrs. Janeki." Mandy took up a pen, ready to scribble down the details.

"This is an emergency. I have a sheep here who's in a bad way. There's not a scratch on her as far as I can see. Only something's scared her and she won't let us near. She's one of my pregnant ewes. I don't like the look of it."

"Okay." Mandy jotted it down. "Do you want me to send someone straight to the house?"

"No. I'll be up on the hill, waiting. She's gone down just by the wall, past High Cross. Her legs have given way, and she may not last much longer. Can you come quickly?" Dora slammed down the phone.

Mandy thought quickly. She was just about to dial her mother's car phone when she heard the car pull up in the yard. Mandy ran out and told Emily Hope the news face-to-face.

Dr. Emily leaned out of the window. She looked serious. "Want to hop in?" she asked Mandy as she revved the engine and turned the car around the way she'd just come.

Mandy jumped right in beside her mother. They were off again, headlights glaring, speeding up the narrow roads to Dora Janeki's isolated farm.

"A pregnant ewe?" Dr. Emily swung the steering wheel to take a sharp bend. Mandy clung to the hand-hold.

"Yes. That's bad, isn't it?"

Her mom nodded. "It can be. It depends. If the shock's great enough, it can cause the sheep to go into premature labor."

"So she'll have the lamb too early?"

"Yes, and that can give problems to the mother, too. Internal hemorrhaging. In other words, she could bleed to death."

Mandy gripped the handle and swung from side to side. She searched the hillside for Dora Janeki. "There!" She spotted an old red four-wheel-drive van in the distance. Dr. Emily swung her car off the road, across a rough, open path toward the van.

As she saw them approach, Dora Janeki ran across the hill to meet them.

Dr. Emily and Mandy jumped down. "How bad is it?" Emily Hope asked.

"Come and see for yourself." Dora shook her head. She led them twenty yards uphill to a low, crumbling stone wall. In its lee, out of the harsh wind, lay a matted gray shape. It had a swollen belly and sticklike legs. It was lying there too weak to stand.

"Can you do anything for her?" Dora turned anxiously to Dr. Emily.

"I'm not sure yet. Let's see if we can get her back on her feet, for a start."

The three of them gently tried to ease the ewe into a standing position. But her legs buckled, and her neck and head sank against the ground. They gave up and stood by to let Dr. Emily continue her work.

"It's premature labor, all right." She swiftly examined the swollen abdomen. Then she opened her bag and worked quickly to help with the delivery. Mandy watched. She could see that the sheep was already too feeble to help herself. It was with a heavy heart that she watched her mom deliver the tiny, dead lamb.

"Stillborn," Dr. Emily murmured. "And it doesn't look too good for the mother either." She used a stethoscope to listen for the heartbeat. It confirmed that the sheep was suffering from heart failure and probably from internal bleeding. Soon Dr. Emily packed away her instruments and stood up. The animal lay completely still. "I'm sorry, Dora," she said. "There was nothing I could do."

Mandy stared at her mom. They stood helpless on this bleak hillside, and she felt weighed down by their failure.

Dora Janeki nodded. "Thank you for coming. I knew from the start we'd be lucky to save her."

Emily Hope zipped up her bag. "We gave it a try. What happened to her, do you know?" She was walking Dora back to her van.

"I can't say for sure. I brought Whistler up with me to drop off some winter feed. He was the one who found her. Something had terrified the poor beast. But by the time I got here, whatever it was was long gone."

"And do you know how long she'd been there?"

"Not really. Not overnight; I know that for sure. We were up here yesterday, rounding them up, and Whistler would've spotted her then." Dora opened the back door of her four-wheel-drive and let the dog jump down. "Wouldn't you, boy?" Dora's voice softened, and then she straightened up. "Well, that's that, I suppose." She shook Dr. Emily's hand and arranged to send a check for the bill.

"I really am sorry," Mandy's mom frowned. "I know you could do without this just before Christmas. And it's bound to set everyone else wondering."

Dora nodded. "There'll be a scare now," she admitted. "And who can blame them? Something frightened this sheep to death, and no farmer around here will rest easy until we find out what did it!"

"I'll keep my ears open," Dr. Emily promised.

She and Mandy watched Dora start up the engine. "Ken will come back up with me when he gets home," Dora said. "He'll help me tidy things up." She sighed. "Let's hope it's a one-time thing. We don't want any more of these in the days before Christmas!"

There was nothing they could say. She eased away over the farm track, leaving them to walk back to their own car.

"Well, that's that, as Dora says," Emily Hope said sadly. She glanced once more up the hillside.

Mandy knew that her mom hated to admit defeat. "Would it have made any difference if we'd gotten here sooner?"

"Who knows? But it didn't look to me as if that sheep would have survived the shock in any case. Her heart was affected. And the lamb was too little to have any chance at all. No, I don't think anything could have saved them."

Mandy felt cold and shaky as she climbed into the car. "But what could have done this?" she asked. "What sort of thing could it be?"

"A dog, most probably. That's the usual thing. That's why the farmers will all be up in arms. They'll say it's a dog from the village, or even from Walton. They'll blame someone from town for not keeping his dog under control. When word gets around, I wouldn't be surprised if they're all out with their guns, scouring the countryside for the culprit."

"A dog?" Mandy found it hard to believe that a tame pet could do this amount of damage.

"Yes." Dr. Emily slung her bag into the back and set off down the hill. The car bumped and swayed. "It doesn't even have to be a very big dog to worry a sheep to death."

Mandy sighed. "Let's hope it doesn't happen again, then."

"It's Dora Janeki I feel sorry for. She can't afford to lose livestock like this. She has a struggle to make ends meet as it is."

Mandy sat in silence. In her mind, she saw a picture of men with shotguns fanning out across the wintry hillside, scouring the fields and rocky outcrops for the rogue dog that had killed Dora Janeki's ewe. She went to bed that night with the image still clear. She dreamed of a dark shape hurtling at the defenseless sheep, fangs bared, springing out of nowhere. When she woke up in the morning, the telephone was ringing and she feared the worst.

Sure enough, there was another possible incident. Adam Hope had taken the call and hung up before Mandy had clambered into her robe and raced downstairs.

"That was Ken Hudson on the phone," he reported. His face looked worried. "He says a sheep from Jack Spiller's farm has just been brought in suffering from shock. Like before, there was no visible damage, but the poor thing was scared half to death. Jack managed to revive it by himself, and the sheep's out of danger. But the word's out. There's not a farm in the area that's not on alert."

"But why did Ken call you?" Mandy asked. "If it wasn't one of their sheep?"

Dr. Adam shook his head. "Can you take some bad news, love?" He led Mandy to a chair by the kitchen table. "Now sit down and listen to this."

"What is it, Dad?" Mandy felt her throat go dry. She looked up into his face. "Tell me, quick!"

"Ken called me because in a way he's involved. Or at least he thinks he might be, and he thought we should know." He paused. "The fact is, Dora has been putting two and two together. She's worked out that this sheep-worrying only began yesterday when Ken agreed to keep Tess at the farm. She's come to the conclusion that the dog might not be reliable; they know nothing about where it came from or how it might have been mistreated in the past. She says a dog like Tess could easily turn."

Mandy shook her head. She looked up in disbelief. "Not Tess!" she said. She just knew in her heart that Tess couldn't possibly be responsible.

"No, but you can see how Dora might see it that way," Dr. Adam pointed out. "Ken himself doesn't know what to think. He just called us to warn us what was going on."

"It can't be Tess! It can't be!" Mandy would not believe it. "Tess wouldn't do that!"

Adam Hope sighed. "It's not me you have to convince, honey!" He went slowly off to tell his wife the latest development.

"I have to talk to Dora!" Mandy said to herself as soon as he'd gone. She jumped up. "Dora has to understand that Tess would never do this! She has to stop spreading rumors about her!"

She ran upstairs to scramble into her clothes. She called James and met him in the village. By nine o'clock they were on their bikes and pedaling toward the farm. The mission was to save Tess from the farmers and their guns!

Eight

There was no sign of Dora Janeki's red four-wheel-drive in the farmyard when Mandy and James arrived. Whistler's kennel was empty, too.

"They must be up on the hill," James said. "Let's head on up there and try to find her."

But Mandy leaned one arm on the gate and stood to catch her breath. "Do you think she's taken Tess with her?" She longed for a glimpse of the dog, to make sure she was still safe and well.

James looked at Mandy. "I suppose you want to check?"

She nodded. Quickly they vaulted the steel bars of the gate and ran across the yard, "Let's try the house first," Mandy suggested. She went and knocked loudly at the faded door.

As they waited, they felt a cold north wind bite through their jackets. There was no reply. James shook his head. "She must have taken both dogs."

"Shh!" Mandy warned. She strained to listen, convinced she could hear a faint whining sound. It came not from the house but from the stone barn next door. She beckoned James toward the tall, windowless building. "I think Tess might be in here!" she whispered.

James caught the sound. "There's definitely something in there!" He pushed at the huge wooden door. It was locked. The whining grew louder.

"That's Tess. I know it is!" With a thumping heart, Mandy searched the length of the barn for a way in. Gradually the whining grew into a series of small yelps as the dog heard their footsteps and their search for another door.

"Here's one!" James had investigated the far side of the barn and found a narrow entrance, a kind of shed door. He pressed down the latch. The door swung open. "This way, Mandy!" he called.

She ran to join him, and together they entered the

dusty gloom. They heard a chain rattle on the stone floor, a dog barking out a welcome. Tess had recognized them and strained on her metal leash to greet them.

"Tess!" Mandy ran forward and dropped to her knees. She flung both arms around the dog's neck. Tess leaned against her, furiously wagging her tail.

"At least she's still okay," James breathed. He crouched to their level to look Tess over.

Mandy nodded. "But they've chained her up, poor thing. Why did they have to do that?" She examined the length of heavy, rusty chain ten or twelve feet long, attached to the wall at one end by a sturdy ring. Mandy saw that Tess wore a new leather collar and that the other end of the chain was attached to this by a strong steel clip. Steadily she stroked the dog until Tess grew calm.

"It's not hurting her." James tried to keep a clear head. "I bet it's to stop the other farmers from finding her. If they knew where she was, or if they found her roaming around, who knows what they'd do to her?"

"But look at her. Who would she attack? Poor Tess wouldn't harm a fly!" Softly Mandy stroked the gentle dog's head. Her black nose pushed against Mandy's chest and nuzzled up to her warm scarf. The white tip of her tail waved to and fro. "It's all right, Tess," Mandy whispered. "Let me take this horrible thing off!" Carefully she unclipped the chain and let it drop to the floor.

Tess shook herself all over and trotted in a pleased fashion up and down the empty barn. She sniffed here and there into hidden corners. James ran to check that the door was closed.

But as he tried to push the latch down firmly, he felt someone resist from the other side. Shocked, he stepped back. He squinted against the flood of daylight as the door was flung open. A figure blocked the doorway.

"What the heck's going on here?" a voice demanded.

"Ken!" Mandy recognized him. She ran to the door. "It's us, Mandy and James! We came to check that Tess was okay! We're sorry. We tried to ask permission, but no one came to the door."

Ken stepped in, holding the door half open. He kept a careful eye on Tess. "You took her off the chain," he said with a frown, as his eyes got used to the dark.

"Just for a few minutes!" Mandy pleaded. "To let her stretch her legs."

Ken nodded. "All right then. I bet Dora's up on the hill with a vanload of food. You'd better not be here when she gets back," he warned. "I came back up from Greystones myself to try and calm her down over this sheep-worrying business. She's up in arms about it, I can tell you!"

"She's really mad?" James asked. He wrinkled his nose and pushed on his glasses more firmly.

Ken nodded. "I was afraid she might do something rash, so I fed the pigs, then I came up to have a word." His warning sent tingles of fear down Mandy's spine. "What will she do?"

He shook his head and scratched the back of his neck. "I don't know yet. She hasn't made up her mind. But she's fixed on Tess here as the culprit." Tess had gone over to James and poked her face against him.

"And once Dora has made up her mind, nothing can change it."

Mandy let out an exasperated cry. "But just look at Tess, Ken! She's gentle as anything. How could anyone think she frightens sheep?"

He sighed and blew the air out through his thin cheeks. "They can fool you. They might look completely harmless, like Tess does now. But you turn your back for a minute, and something comes over them. They get it into their heads to go after the sheep. It's a kind of mad streak that gets into a dog."

Mandy went and stood by James and Tess. "But not into Tess!" she insisted. "Dora's wrong, I know she is!"

Ken looked anxiously at the trio, Mandy, James, and Tess. "But there *is* the fact that we don't know anything about her," he pointed out. "She could have a whole history of being unreliable that we don't know about. Maybe that's why the last owners got rid of her."

Mandy heard the words, but she wouldn't let them sink in. "No!" She blocked her ears with both hands. Still Ken's muffled voice came through.

"Then there's the fact that no sheep was attacked before she came. Now we've had two in twenty-four hours. That's what makes it look bad. *And*," he said, grinding to a decisive halt, "the fact is, Tess disappeared yesterday, when all this was going on."

His words dropped into silence.

"Disappeared?" James stood up straight. "How come?"

Ken explained. "I wasn't here, you know. But Dora says she left Tess with food and water here in the barn, to let her get used to the place. She didn't tie her up, and she went down into the village with Whistler. When she got back, the dog was missing — probably slipped off through the side door. It was swinging open when she walked in. At any rate, Tess didn't come back till well after dark. And she looked tired out, wet and cold as if she'd been outside all that time. She just curled up in a corner and fell right asleep. That's when Dora began to have her doubts."

James stared at Mandy, who shook her head. "It doesn't prove anything!" she protested.

"But on the other hand, it doesn't look good." Ken put his hands in his duffel coat pockets and sighed.

"What will Dora do?" James asked.

"I don't know yet. But I know she won't keep her on after what's happened."

Lost for words, Mandy stared helplessly at James, then at Tess. The dog seemed to have picked up the worried mood. She sat quietly in their midst, waiting patiently.

"But what actual proof does Dora have?" James found his voice. "Just because of the things you've said, it doesn't mean Tess is guilty!"

Ken shrugged. "But think about it; would *you* take the risk, with what we know?"

"Yes, I would!" Mandy cried. "Because we don't know anything! All Dora is doing is guessing." She felt like crying; the success of finding the ideal home for Tess had crumbled away to nothing. Now there was even the chance that Dora Janeki would insist on having the dog put to sleep, as a danger to livestock. Or she might let the other angry farmers of the district decide for her.

As they stood in silence, Tess let out a sharp, single bark. It echoed through the empty barn. She trotted up to the closed side door. She barked again.

"I think she wants to go out," James said. "But don't let her!"

Tess came back to them. She barked and trotted back to the door, then bounced up against the simple latch.

"Down, Tess!" Mandy ordered. The door rattled and the latch lifted slightly. Mandy went over. "Stay down, that's a good girl."

But Tess jumped and whirled, barking loudly. She ignored Mandy. Instead she lunged at the latch and released it. The door swung open. Tess bounded into the open air. She turned to wait for Mandy, then ran a few steps ahead, barked and waited.

"Stop her!" James yelled. He began to run for the door.

"Stay, Tess!" Mandy put out one arm to stop James from careering ahead. "I think she's trying to tell us something! Look, she wants us to follow!"

Tess's bark rose impatiently. She ran to the gate and stopped again, obviously meaning them to come after.

Ken emerged from the barn and shook his head. "I don't know about this. I don't think we should," he said.

"What is it, Tess?" Mandy ran ahead once more, sure that the dog had something important to show them. She turned in a tight, excited circle as Mandy approached, then slipped out between the metal bars of the gate. "What is it, girl?" Mandy said, low and tense. She glanced over her shoulder at the other two. "We have to see what she wants, at least!" she pleaded.

At last Ken gave a tight little cough and a nod. "Fair enough," he said.

Mandy swung open the gate and they followed Tess through.

Before long, Tess had led them clear of the farm buildings and up toward the hill, her black shape streaking ahead. Mandy strode after her. She realized that the day was turning gray and cold. A freezing mist descended down the hillside, and it was hard to keep Tess within sight. Even Ken's urgent whistle didn't stop her from forging ahead.

"Tess!" Mandy shouted, as a thicker cloud of mist seemed to swallow the dog from view. "Why won't she do as she's told?" She turned to Ken with a feeling of panic. Tess was so set on getting them to follow that she seemed to have lost her usual obedience and common sense. "Where are you, Tess?" she called.

They began to run up into the mist.

"Stick together," Ken insisted. "Whatever you do, don't split up. I don't want anyone getting lost!"

They called and ran until they came through the billowing mist and out the other side. The view cleared, and there was Tess, sitting on a black boulder, waiting for them to catch up.

"Good girl!" Mandy cried out in relief.

Tess put up her head and sniffed the air. Suddenly her ears pricked up. "She bounded from the rock and began to streak across the hill, once more ignoring Ken's expert call.

"Let's go!" James said. He began to race after her.

"Would you believe it, she's heading for those sheep!" Ken pointed to a few distant gray specks, grazing in the shelter of a big, rocky outcrop on the horizon.

Mandy's heart sank. She knew it was no good calling Tess back now. This is what she'd wanted to show them all along, whatever it was. Mandy chased over the rough ground after James, with Ken bringing up the rear.

They ran through another band of mist, their feet crunching over narrow, iced-up streams, the wind whipping down on them. Now Tess seemed to have forgotten they were even there, racing up the hillside; she was a low, lean, dark shape, heading straight and fast toward the unsuspecting sheep.

"No, Tess!" Mandy gave a last, desperate call. Her heart was in her mouth. She pushed herself faster and faster, unable to believe what she was seeing with her own eyes — her beautiful, gentle Tess about to attack!

But she saw the startled sheep raise their heads and skitter sideways. They bunched together as Tess approached, looking wildly in all directions. Mandy saw Tess streak up behind them, and up the almost sheer slope onto a narrow ledge of rock. The sheep trampled into one another in their alarm, bleating loudly. One went down on its front knees and skidded several yards down the hill. The others scattered for the protection of boulders, bushes, any cover they could find.

Tess towered above them on the rock. She snarled, teeth bared.

"No!" Mandy came nearer still, a hundred yards away, begging Tess to hold back.

Tess leaped. She was on the ground among the sheep, charging through them. Mandy heard a ferocious growling and snapping, bodies hurtling through bushes. She saw a sheep's terrified eyes.

Then a sharp shot rang out. Everything froze. A mist billowed across the scene, and Dora Janeki emerged, a shotgun raised to her shoulder. Whistler crouched at her heel.

Mandy caught a glimpse of Tess, lying low, but ears up, poised ready for more action.

She ran toward the woman farmer. "Oh, don't!" she pleaded.

Then the hillside seemed to come alive with men running. Two or three followed Dora's small, stern figure, shotguns at the ready. Mandy recognized Jack Spiller and Dennis Saville, the foreman at Sam Western's farm. From lower down the hill, James and Ken ran to the spot where Mandy faced Dora. Meanwhile the frightened sheep had scattered in all directions, and both Whistler and Tess lay quiet, warily eyeing the scene.

Dora stormed at her brother. "What did I say?" she shouted. "You saw that with your own eyes! I knew it was that dog right from the start!" She waved the barrel of her gun at Tess. "But you wouldn't listen!" she accused. "And I was dumb enough to hang back from doing what I knew I should do in the first place! What a fool I am!"

Ken sighed and shook his head at Mandy. "What can I do?" he muttered. "You saw it, as clear as daylight. There's the proof you were looking for!"

With the sound of the gun, Mandy had felt something snap inside her. She'd believed in Tess. Yet she'd seen her leap, teeth bared, from the rock into the midst of the sheep. The shot had rung out. It was like a nightmare. With tears in her eyes, cold and trembling, Mandy gazed silently at James.

Dora pushed them to one side and strode past, heading for Tess. Jack Spiller and Dennis Saville went to back her up. They raised their guns.

"Oh, no!" Mandy put her hands to her face.

James gripped her wrist. "Look, Mandy!' He pulled her hands away

Tess had spotted the three shapes coming menacingly toward her. She sprang to her feet and turned. Then she was off, darting up the hill into the shadow of the rocks. Three shots rang out. Still Tess fled. She vanished behind the rocks. Moments later they saw her again, making her way along the ridge. The farmers raised their guns.

Tess paused for a second, turned her head toward them, and gave a low whine. Then, with a whisk of her white-tipped tail, she vanished out of sight.

Nine

All day Friday a light snow fell. By evening, Welford lay under a crisp, white covering that sparkled in the clear moonlight. Snowplows came out to clear the roads, but the fields and hillsides lay under three or four inches of even snow.

Mandy felt numb. She'd seen Tess attack the sheep with her own eyes, and knew that Dora Janeki, Jack Spiller, and Dennis Saville would still be out on the snowy hillside with their guns. But she and James had set off for home before the snow set in, too disappointed to talk.

Ken had called Animal Ark to tell Adam Hope what had happened. Mandy's mom and dad came out to meet them. Grandma and Grandpa rallied around. They took James back to his house and persuaded Mandy to come shopping for last-minute party food. Mandy spent the afternoon and evening at Lilac Cottage, baking cakes and pastries for the party the next day.

Christmas Eve dawned bright and clear. At eight o'clock Mandy opened her bedroom curtains to a pale blue sky and a sweep of white hillsides. The bare trees were coated in thick frost, and the walls and roofs sparkled in the sunlight.

"It's a lovely day!" Emily Hope called upstairs. "Breakfast's ready!"

Mandy pulled on some jeans and a thick blue sweater, then went down for her winter breakfast of oatmeal, honey, and milk.

"It looks good for the party tonight." Dr. Emily brought a pot of tea to the table. "As long as it stays clear, there won't be any problem about getting there."

Mandy nodded. She knew there were still dozens of things to do.

"How do you feel?" Her mom put a warm hand over hers. "Do you think you'll be able to cope?" She pushed a stray strand of hair back from Mandy's face and gave her cheek a light kiss.

Mandy took a deep breath. "I'll be okay, Mom. I keep thinking of Tess, that's all."

"I know. You must be very upset."

"I never thought for a second she would do what I saw her do. In fact, I still can't believe it." Mandy shook her head. "I thought I knew her!"

"It's hard," Dr. Emily agreed. "But I think the party will help keep your mind off things, don't you?"

"Oh, yes. I don't want to let anybody down." Mandy finished her breakfast and got up from the table. "Everyone's looking forward to it. The hall's all ready, except for last-minute things. I have to stop by Simon's to help him bring the music system over and set it up. Then Grandma and Mrs. Ponsonby will start bringing the food. In fact, I'd better get going!" She reached for her jacket and scarf.

"Good for you!" Dr. Emily smiled at her. "We have a busy day in the office ourselves. See you later."

Mandy and her mom went their separate ways. Soon Mandy had met up with Simon and they were driving to the village hall in his battered white van, with the music system safely stacked in the back. They lifted it out and carried it through the open door to find Grandpa and

Ernie already putting up tables, and Grandma and Mrs. Ponsonby standing by with piles of white tablecloths.

"Wow!" Simon put down the CD player and took a look around. He saw the tree lights twinkling, the balloons, and the streamers. "This should get us all into the Christmas mood, all right!"

He plugged in wires and arranged speakers, then went off to work. James and Mr. Hunter arrived with armloads of holly from a tree in their garden. James said, "Dad thought this would look nice along the windowsills." He peered out from behind a mountain of shiny green leaves and red berries.

Mrs. Ponsonby swooped down on him and took the holly. "Perfect!" she cried. "I'll *arrange* them, just so!" She began to place the twigs and to order Mr. Hunter around. "Put those down there, would you? And the rest on that empty table, out of reach. We wouldn't want Pandora to hurt herself on those nasty prickles, would we?"

Pandora snuffled up to Mandy, who picked her up and petted her. Then she set to work helping her grandmother cover the tables with clean white cloths.

During the early part of the morning other visitors dropped by. Susan Collins offered boxes of Christmas cookies that her mom had sent. "She says there should be enough for everyone!" Susan piled the gold and silver treats into the middle of the table. "There are party hats inside for those people who don't bother to make one for the competition."

James stopped in his tracks. He put down a pile of plates with a clatter. "Uh-oh, the competition!" He suddenly remembered.

"Yes, I've already made a hat for Prince," Susan told him. "But I'm keeping it a secret."

James turned to Mandy. "I've just thought of something — we don't have anyone to judge it yet!"

"Shh!" Mandy nudged him. But it was too late.

"What's that I hear?" Mrs. Ponsonby cried. "You need someone to judge the party-hat competition? Why, I'd be glad to do it for you!" She climbed down from a chair with an armful of holly. "No need to worry about that, my dear. Let me take one more thing off your mind. Leave it to me. I'll *organize* your little competition. In fact, let me donate the prize!"

Mandy graciously accepted the offer. "I planned to ask Grandma to be the judge," she whispered to James with a grin.

"Oops, too late now!" He picked up the plates and began to set them out on the tables.

As Susan went out, John Hardy came in. "My dad wondered if you could use these," he said to Mandy. He carried a giant cardboard box full of bags of potato chips. "And there's a box of peanuts to follow." For half an hour he trooped across the street from the Fox and Goose with boxes of snacks and cans of soft drinks.

Claire McKay came next. She brought Blackie, James's Labrador, to see what was going on. She peeped around the door, her dark bangs framing her face, her brown eyes staring in delight at the preparations. Blackie ran ahead, wagging his tail at James.

"Hi, Claire!" Mandy called. "Do you want to give me a hand with these paper napkins? We have to fold them up into little hat-shaped things so they stand up, *just so!*" She grinned at James as she imitated Mrs. Ponsonby, who had just slipped out with Pandora and Toby on their "walkies."

Claire nodded and came in. She soon learned how to fold the napkins. Grandpa and Ernie finished setting up tables. Grandma was happy with their preparations. "Coffee, everybody?" she asked. She took a huge thermos flask from her shopping bag, then plastic cups, and homemade ginger cookies. "It's time for a break!"

Only now, when she had time to think, did Mandy's mind swing back to sad thoughts. As she munched her cookie, she pictured Tess, cold and miserable, cowering behind rocks, leaving telltale footprints in the new snow. Dora Janeki would be up there, too, tracking her down. She imagined a final scene — Tess shivering, her brown eyes staring down the barrel of a farmer's gun. . . .

Mandy broke out of the circle of chattering helpers. She reached for her jacket.

"Where are you off to, love?" Grandpa asked.

"Can you manage without me for an hour or so?" she asked. "There's something I'd like to do."

Grandpa looked at Grandma. They nodded. "Of course we can. We'll carry on here until you get back," he said.

"I'll come!" James jumped up. He guessed what was on her mind.

Mandy nodded. She heard him follow her out of the hall. "I'm going up to the hill," she told him quietly.

He nodded. "That's why I said I'd come." He joined her in the yard. "We'll have to walk."

"Or run." They set off at a jog up the village street. "We might not be able to save Tess," Mandy explained. "Not if the farmers have their way. But there's no need for her to suffer and die that way, not if we get to her first."

James kept pace with her. They'd cut across fields, out of the village. On the horizon, the black Celtic cross landmark showed up sharp and clear. "What are we going to do?" he asked.

Mandy ran on with her head down. Their feet crunched over untrodden snow, sinking through the frozen crust into a powdery layer below. "We're going to find her and take her back to Animal Ark before the farmers get her," she promised.

"Then what?"

Mandy stopped to stare up the hillside. "If Tess has to die because of the sheep, I'll ask my mom and dad to do it," she said. "If she's not going to be allowed to live anymore, we'll put her to sleep at Animal Ark!"

She wouldn't let Tess feel the pain of the gunshot. She wouldn't let her end her days as a hated, hunted fugitive.

They reached the tall hedges of Upper Welford Hall and had to pause again for breath. Running uphill through soft snow was hard work. They stood gasping as Sam Western's dogs barked out a warning. Then they ran on, past High Cross Farm, along the ridge where Dora Janeki's sheep usually grazed. Today it was empty, a white wonderland.

"She must have rounded them up and taken them into the barn." James gazed all around. There was no sign of life.

"Because of the snow," Mandy agreed. "But Tess is still out here somewhere. Come on!" She forged ahead through drifts of snow that had collected in hollows, searching for a dog's prints, heading for the wild rocks and hills.

"She could have frozen to death by now!" James pulled his own legs clear of a drift. He scanned the landscape.

"No!" Mandy refused to believe it. They plunged on, knee-deep in snow.

Way up in the hills, beyond Syke Farm, they stopped to look down on the scattered houses. So far they'd found no sign of Tess. But now James and Mandy thought they spotted a small group of people tramping across fields with a dog, each armed with a shotgun. It was too far away to see clearly, but they knew what it meant. The farmers' search for the rogue dog was still on.

"This way!" James dodged behind some rocks, out of sight. Mandy followed. They slid down a flat slope, over the ridge, and down the far side.

Here the snow was less deep. There was a blown scattering of powdery flakes. A strong wind had swept the hillside clean. Some sheep remained in the shelter of high rocks, still nibbling at patches of exposed grass. In this new valley, the sun had partly melted the snow and crept up the frozen slopes toward the sheep. Mandy and James slid to a halt, still deep in shadow, trying not to disturb the nervous animals.

But something else seemed to attract the sheep's attention, a sound or a smell. They glanced along the hillside, then bent to nibble the grass. Mandy held James's arm. "Wait a minute," she whispered.

She spotted a dark shape crouching low behind a far rock. It was about twenty yards from the sheep, downwind of them and creeping nearer.

Mandy longed to spring up and wave her arms in warning. She wanted to get the sheep away from the prowler. But something kept her fixed to the spot. She and James crouched and stared. The shadowy shape was a dog, and every second it crept closer to the sheep.

Nearer and nearer. The dog's back was black. Its ears and nose were pointed. It had a strong, bushy tail. But the tip wasn't white. And they could see that the belly of the dog, as it crept forward, was tan-colored. It bared its teeth, ready to pounce.

"That's not Tess!" James whispered. "It's too big!"

"It's Major!" Mandy said, her eyes wide with surprise. "It's the new dog at Upper Welford Hall!"

The German shepherd froze in its crouching position, waiting for a sheep to break from the group before he sprang.

But before anyone had time to move, Mandy felt another shape hurtle past from behind. A thin, black dog curved across the hillside between Major and the sheep, working them into a tight circle. They stopped grazing and shuffled into a tight knot. The new dog hustled them and moved them off, darting at strays, rounding them up and out of danger.

"Tess!" Mandy leaped to her feet. "She's protecting the sheep! She's trying to save them from Major!"

The rogue dog bared his teeth and snarled. He advanced on Tess from behind.

Then James ran toward the sheep, shooing them downhill toward the sunlit valley. Once on the move they ran quickly, alert and well out of reach of their attacker.

"Tess, watch out!" Mandy warned. She saw that the Border collie was in danger herself now. Major snarled again and charged at her. Tess turned to defend herself.

Major leaped at Tess. The two bodies crashed and hurtled together. They rolled down the hillside before Tess twisted free. Mandy ran at them, shouting Tess's name. Major attacked a second time. There was a yelp, more snarls and growls. "Major, get back!" she cried. Mandy stood by, helpless, as Tess struggled to defend herself.

At last the terrifying fight came to an end. Tess broke free of Major's snapping jaws, whirled on the spot, and raced away. The other dog snapped at nothing and backed off as Mandy and James moved in. A deep growl rattled in his throat. He crouched low. Then he turned tail, away from the sheep, sloping off along the side of the valley.

"Tess!" Mandy turned back up the hillside in time to see the Border collie reach the ridge and pause. "Here!"

But Tess had looked down the barrel of a gun, and she trusted no one now. She gave a quick, sharp bark, held her head high, and panted for breath. Mandy thought she met her gaze, and Tess's dark brown eyes told her that she was innocent after all.

Then she ran on out of sight, into snowy Welford valley, back toward the farmers with their guns.

Ten

Mandy knew they had to act quickly. She ran on to the crest of the hill, too late to spot where Tess had gone. But she saw her tracks running along the ridge, up the valley into the wild, hilly countryside.

James grinned as he scrambled up the slope behind her. "It isn't Tess!" he shouted. "It's a different dog!" He dipped his hands into the snow and scooped it into the air.

"She was trying to *save* the sheep! Yesterday, when we saw her in the mist and it looked like she was attacking them, she was really fighting Major, trying to keep him off. She was *protecting* them!" Mandy joined in James's celebration. "Isn't she fabulous? And the best part is that she's innocent!"

She went yelling down the slope toward Sam Western's house, half sliding, half running. "We have to tell Mr. Western about Major!" she cried. "He'll have to let the others know that it's his dog, not Tess!"

By the time they arrived at the big gates of Upper Welford Hall, Mandy and James were breathless and covered in snow. Two sturdy bulldogs came barking through the grounds toward them. A side door was flung open and Sam Western strode out.

He was dressed in a patterned sweater and brown trousers, his graying hair combed neatly to one side. He came like a true lord of the manor down his snow-covered drive.

The two bulldogs leaped at the gate, snarls on their squat faces. Mandy and James stepped back.

"What's going on?" Mr. Western looked down his nose at them. "Oh, it's you," he said coldly. "The vets' girl, isn't it?"

Mandy nodded. "And this is James. James Hunter."

"What do you want?" Mr. Western ordered the bulldogs to be quiet. "This isn't some Christmas prank, is it?" He seemed annoyed at the disturbance.

"Oh, no!" Mandy wanted to make everything clear all at once. But how did you tell someone that his dog was a sheep killer? She hesitated.

"I hope you're not carol singers. Because I don't pay carol singers, so you can pack up and be off," he warned.

"No, Mr. Western. It's about your dog Major."

A deeper frown set in. "What about Major?"

"First of all, do you know where he is right now?" James asked. He looked around the grounds, past the frozen ornamental pond, across the lawns toward the fine old house. There was no sign anywhere of the German shepherd.

Western grunted. "If you must know, he's out with my farm manager." He raised one eyebrow, ready to send them packing. "Not that it's any of your business."

"But it is!" Mandy protested. "Major must have broken free from Mr. Saville. We've just spotted him over the ridge in the next valley."

Western was caught off guard. "Darn dog," he muttered. "Why didn't you get hold of him and bring him down with you?"

"We couldn't." Mandy looked to James again for help.

"He was attacking the sheep, Mr. Western!" James came straight out with it.

The farmer let out a hard little laugh. "Nonsense!" he

began. Then he paused. "Look, I know there's a sheep attacker on the loose," he admitted. "Dora Janeki told Dennis all about it. As a matter of fact, he's out there now, helping to track it down."

Mandy and James watched Mr. Western grow red in the face. They saw a puzzled look develop.

"Major went with him, as it happens. But Major's not the villain. That's ridiculous!" He tried to bluster his way through.

Mandy looked him straight in the eye. "Where was Major on Thursday, when the first sheep were attacked?"

There was a long pause. "Now, look!" Sam Western shot her an angry glance.

Mandy stood firm. "Where was he, Mr. Western?"

"Well, he was missing for part of that day," he admitted. "Dennis had to go out in the late afternoon and round him up. But that doesn't prove anything!" He lifted his chin defiantly.

Mandy and James waited for a few moments. The two bulldogs had calmed down and began to tramp through the snow, snapping up mouthfuls and sniffing in the hedge. "But Major's on the loose again now," James said calmly. "And we've just seen some sheep being attacked. Don't you think you'd better come and check?"

Mr. Western looked sternly through the bars of the iron gates. "Wait here!" he ordered. He called to the dogs and strode off up the drive. He disappeared through the side door and closed it with a slam. Five minutes later he reappeared, dressed in green boots and a heavy jacket. His collar was turned up, and he wore a tweed hat with a curled brim, pulled well down. In one hand he carried a mobile phone, which he stuffed into his pocket.

"We'll have to be quick," Mandy said, as he came out through the gate. "The sooner we find Mr. Saville and ask him about Major, the better."

The three of them set off together along the path past High Cross Farm. They cut through a small grove of trees at the back of the empty goat field. Mandy caught a glimpse of Lydia Fawcett emerging from her barn. "Lydia, have you seen Mr. Saville?" She cupped her hands to her mouth and yelled.

"Heading up to Syke Farm!" Lydia called back.

"Thanks!" Mandy waved.

Sam Western frowned and strode ahead. "I hope this doesn't turn out to be one of your tricks," he muttered. "You'd better be telling me the absolute truth, or else!"

"We are," James promised. "You have to talk to Mr. Saville and stop him from shooting the wrong dog."

Western glanced sideways. "The wrong dog?" he repeated. He swung up to the right, heading for Dora Janeki's bleak farm.

"Tess," Mandy explained. "She's the stray Border collie we found. Dora took her in. But now she thinks Tess is the sheep worrier."

Western grimaced. "And you two say it's *my* dog, is that it?" He stopped.

Mandy's heart missed a beat. "We *saw* Major attacking the sheep, Mr. Western! It was Tess who tried to save them!"

"Hmmm." Sam Western seemed to be thinking of his warm fireside and slippers. He glanced back toward his house. "You could be trying to shift the blame here. I wouldn't put it past you."

"No, honestly!"

He sniffed. "Better not risk it, I suppose." Reluctantly he trudged on through the snow. "Isn't that Dora Janeki right over there?" He pointed to the hillside, where three tiny figures were coming down the slope toward them. He raised a hand and gave a loud shout.

While Sam Western rested and waited by a low wall, Mandy and James jumped over it and ran to meet the group. They recognized Whistler by his mottled gray coat and stooped to give him a welcoming pat. "Good boy," Mandy breathed. She looked up to see Dora, Dennis Saville, and another boy from Sam Western's farm approaching.

"It's the boss," the boy said to Dennis. He hung back to let the estate manager deal with what looked like trouble.

Dora came down frowning at Mandy. "We just spotted that stray dog and took a couple of shots at it. We haven't had any luck so far, but we will before the day's out!"

"But it's not Tess's fault," Mandy began. She felt James hold her back.

"Mandy, come over here!" He drew her away to listen to the conversation between Dennis Saville and Mr. Western.

"Where's the dog?" The farmer didn't bother with explanations. "Come on, Dennis, where's the darn thing gone?"

Dennis shuffled his feet. "Didn't he come back to the Hall?"

Western glowered but said nothing.

"He cut back home just after I brought him out. I saw him skirting back through the side gate. I figured he was headed straight home." Dennis Saville stood with his gun slung through the crook of his elbow. "Didn't he get there?"

"He did not." Sam Western sighed and took the phone from his pocket. "Let me call and check that he hasn't turned up there now." He pushed buttons to dial the number.

"What's all this about?" Dora demanded. "Whatever it is we'd better sort it out and get a move on. Have you seen those big, dark clouds? I don't like the look of them."

On the horizon, a bank of heavy snow clouds gathered. The sun had sunk behind them, leaving a golden rim of bright light.

Sam Western spoke into the phone. "What's that? No sign of Major, eh?" He listened. His frown deepened further. "Say that again!" he demanded.

Mandy and James held their breaths. They stamped their feet and looked worried. Sam Western seemed to have gone pale as he clicked a button and put the phone back in his pocket.

"Well?" Dora was anxious to press on.

"That was a message from my secretary," he said quietly. "She's just had a phone call from the Spillers' place. Word's going around that another sheep has been attacked about half an hour ago. Jack Spiller's on the scene right now. No one actually saw what happened, but the sheep's in a bad way. She's losing blood. They've just sent for the vet from Animal Ark. Spiller wants the dog caught before it does any more damage. Every farmer this side of Walton is out after it!"

"See!" Mandy cried. "You have to believe us! Major is a menace to every sheep around. Not Tess — Major!"

Her pleas fell on deaf ears.

"What's it matter which one it is?" Dora said. "We know there are two dogs on the loose up there. And there are more sheep being savaged. Let's go!" She marched across the hill, followed by Sam Western, Dennis Saville, and young Dean, Western's farmhand.

Mandy wanted to cry out in protest. Instead she turned to James. "Why won't they believe us?"

"Because they're not thinking straight, that's why. So *we'll* have to. Listen, Mandy, Mr. Western said that Jack Spiller called Animal Ark. Someone will be on his way right this minute. Let's run down to the road and try to head him off. That way we'll get to Spillers' first and explain about Major. There's a better chance that your mom or dad can make people believe what's happening than we can!"

Mandy agreed. Without another moment's hesitation, they sped off in the opposite direction to the gang with the guns, downhill toward the winding road, scanning the valley for a glimpse of the Animal Ark jeep.

"There!" Mandy cried. There was a gleam of windshield lower down the valley, the faint sound of an engine, before a blast of wind drowned it out and a flurry of snowflakes began to fall. They ran on toward the road.

When the jeep climbed into view again, Mandy and James stood in the midst of a sudden blizzard. They waved their arms and shouted. Dr. Adam skidded to a halt.

"Mandy! James!" He flung open the passenger door and told them to get in quickly.

"Are you going up to the Spillers'?" Mandy sank back against the seat, with James beside her.

Dr. Adam revved the engine. He turned the high beams on. "Yes, if we make it," he warned. "How did you know?"

Mandy explained in a rush how Mr. Western and his dog Major were suddenly involved; how it was Major who attacked Jack Spiller's sheep. "We have to stop the farmers from going after Tess!" she pleaded. "Can you tell them that she isn't to blame?"

Adam Hope frowned and nodded. "I'll do my best." The jeep edged forward up the slippery hill. "But remember, my most important job is to save Jack Spiller's sheep!"

Mandy nodded and hung on as the car skidded and bumped along.

At last they arrived at the small farm. Snow still fell thick and fast. Mrs. Spiller came out to the gate and directed them off the road, along a rough track between two stone walls, already hidden by snowdrifts. "You'll have to drive about three hundred yards up the tractor track!" she yelled. "Jack's stayed up there with the sheep!"

They drove on. The car lurched and swayed. Soon they spotted a dark figure bending over the injured sheep. Dr. Adam stopped the car and ran across, knee-deep in snow. Mandy and James ran to help.

Jack had covered the sheep with a piece of sacking to keep off the worst of the snow. There was a wound low down on its neck, and a stain of blood on the white ground. Mandy winced as her father went down onto his knees, opened up the bag she gave him, and injected the shoulder with a shot of anesthetic. He waited for it to take effect while he cleaned the wound. "It doesn't look as if she's lost too much blood," he assured the farmer. "And at least this one isn't pregnant."

Jack Spiller nodded. "Are you going to put in a couple of stitches to stop the bleeding?"

Adam Hope worked fast. "That's what I'm doing now. There. Now, Jack, you'll have to help me lift her into the back of the jeep. That's right."

Mandy and James picked up the sacking and walked behind her dad, Jack Spiller, and the sheep. She handed her father his bag as he climbed up into his seat.

"Hop in the back with the patient," he told them.

But Jack interrupted. "There's more bad news, I'm afraid. Dennis Saville came down this way with a boy and a dog, just before you showed up. He asked me to tell you there's another one up the hill, not far off." His face looked drawn and worried as he pointed across the snow-swept hillside.

"Another injured sheep?" Dr. Adam roared the engine into life, grabbed his bag, and jumped to the ground again. "Has this dog gone crazy?" He pulled Jack Spiller toward the car. "Here, Jack; you'll have to drive your sheep down to the house in the jeep. Mandy and James, you stay with him. I'll have to go and take a look!"

Mandy began to protest as Jack Spiller climbed into the driver's seat.

"No, get the sheep down into the warmth as quickly as you can!" Dr. Adam ordered. He zipped his jacket to the chin, ready to set off across country.

"Dad!" Mandy said. "Wait for me. I want to come!"

But her dad insisted. "Stay in the car, Mandy. That's right. You'll have to help Jack at the other end. Carry the sheep inside with him. Keep her warm. Now go on, I won't be long!"

Mandy and James did as they were told. The snow gusted against the car, the wipers whined, the engine stuttered.

"Let's go," Jack Spiller said. "If we're not quick, the poor thing will die of cold!"

So Mandy and James clung to the bar as the jeep rattled back down to the cottage. The last Mandy saw of her father was a small, dim figure heading into the blizzard to save another life.

Eleven

The snow fell fast and furious. At Jack Spiller's house, Mandy and James helped carry the injured sheep into the small barn, where they settled her into a bed of straw and left Jenny and Maggie Spiller to take care of her.

"Sam Western's waiting in the house," Mrs. Spiller said. "He wants to have a word with you, Jack."

They went ahead and found the small kitchen swarming with people who had taken refuge from the sudden storm. Dora Janeki sat at the table with Dennis Saville and Dean. They huddled over cups of tea, guns resting against a nearby wall. Everyone avoided meeting

Mandy's and James's eyes as they came in. Dennis shuffled his feet in embarrassment.

Mr. Western himself stood by the window, clearing his throat. He took a step forward. "Er, Jack, I need to have a quiet word." He looked uncomfortable as he beckoned Jack across.

Mandy glanced at James. Mr. Western was not his usual confident self. She listened hard, trying to overhear the conversation.

"Dennis saw it all . . . yes, the second sheep . . . he was there . . . I'm afraid it was . . . yes, Major, my new dog . . . most awfully sorry!" Sam Western muttered.

Mandy caught disjointed phrases. She held her breath as she saw Jack Spiller frown and nod. Then she couldn't bear to be in the dark any longer. She went up to Dennis Saville. "What happened?" she asked.

"Well, we caught Major in the act," he confessed, glancing at Dora's stern face. "We came along the ridge looking for the Border collie, and found Major attacking another of Jack's sheep. Dean here managed to grab him from behind, and we brought him straight down. We put him in the shed outside until the snow stops and we decide what to do with him."

Mandy's eyes filled up with relief. At last they knew

the truth. She turned to Dora. "Does that mean that you won't go after Tess anymore?"

Dora nodded. "I owe you and James an apology," she said gently. "I was a bit hasty. I'm sorry."

James came up with a smile. "What will happen to Major now?" He stood next to Mandy in a pool of melting snow.

"That depends." Dennis Saville kept one eye on his boss, still deep in conversation with Jack Spiller. "We want to hear what Jack has to say. After all, it's his sheep and Dora's here that have been attacked. I think Mr. Western still wants to keep him on and have him properly trained as a guard dog."

Mandy agreed that this was a good idea. "There's no need to have him put to sleep, is there?" Even though Major was the one who had caused all the trouble, she would never want to see a healthy animal put to death. "If he's treated well, I'm sure he'll improve!" She kept her fingers crossed for the poor dog, who didn't know how to use his freedom on the hillsides, after a life cooped up in a city yard.

At last Jack and Mr. Western came to an agreement. "I'll pay your vets' fees, and Mrs. Janeki's, too," Western announced. "I'll cover all the expenses that this trouble has caused. And I promise to keep Major well under control in the future. He's a fine animal, really, and I intend to look after him well."

Jack nodded. "If you stick to your promise and there's no more trouble from Major, I think we'd all agree with that."

Dora Janeki, too, came around. She sniffed and grumbled for a while, but in the end she didn't object. It ended in handshakes, relief, and smiles.

But outside the snow still fell. It whirled through the door in a great gust as Maggie Spiller and Jenny came in to report that the injured sheep was recovering well in the barn.

"Is Dad back yet?" Mandy asked. Through the window she could see the snow drifting up to three feet deep against the farmyard walls. It was more than half an hour since Adam Hope had set off after the second injured animal.

"No. I thought he might be in here," Mrs. Spiller looked anxiously around the room. "Shouldn't he be back by now?"

Mandy peered again through the window. She could hardly see beyond the tiny yard; the hillside was lost in the snowstorm. Dark clouds swept down, and the wind gusted. There was no sign at all of her brave father.

"Dennis, you know the spot where the sheep was." Mr. Western took charge. "How far is it from here?"

"About half a mile. I couldn't be sure, exactly. We were busy keeping Major under control." Dennis Saville looked at his watch. "Let's give him about ten more minutes before we start to worry."

They agreed. The minutes dragged by. Mandy sat with her face at the window staring out, praying for the snow to ease. And still Dr. Adam didn't show up.

"All right!" Mr. Western broke the edgy silence. "Let's make up a search party. We can't wait any longer. This is an emergency."

Mandy felt a jolt of fear pass through her. She watched the others put on their boots again and zip up their jackets. "Can I call my mom?" she asked Mrs. Spiller.

"Of course." She pointed to the phone.

Quickly Mandy went and dialed the number, urging her mother to hurry and pick up the phone. "Mom, it's me. I'm at the Spillers'. Dad's missing in the snow. We're sending out a search party." She spoke in a rush, then stopped short. There was a long pause. "Mom, are you there?"

"Yes, Mandy. I got all that. I'll run down to Grandpa at the village hall and get him to drive me straight up. Don't worry, we'll find him. Your dad knows what to do in these situations. We'll soon have him back safe and sound." Emily Hope hung up.

Mandy put down the phone. She felt less afraid. Her mom's calm voice was a huge help. Now she passed on the message to Mrs. Spiller. "Mom will try to get up here with Grandpa. Can you watch out for them, please?" She rushed to the door to follow Mr. Western's search party.

"Don't split up," he was telling the group as they emerged into the freezing white air. "Stick together. Dennis will have to lead the way. Come on!" Together they tramped out onto the tractor track, heads down, forming a tight bunch as they set off up the hill.

Mandy settled into the pace, steady but slow through the soft snow. She wore her scarf wrapped high around her face, but still the freezing wind tore through her and the snowflakes blinded her. Beside her, James struggled to lift his legs clear of the snow with each wearying step.

Up ahead, Dennis came to a halt. "I think it's this way now." They cut off to the left like Arctic explorers, into a wilderness that no one recognized.

For a few more minutes they trekked over the uneven ground. Mandy stepped into a snow-covered hollow up to her waist.

James hauled her out. "We must be nearly there!" he gasped.

But Dennis had hesitated a second time. "I was sure it was this way!" He searched all around for landmarks, but covered in snow, the terrain was strange and unfamiliar. The group scanned the hillside without seeing any sign of Adam Hope and the sheep.

"Try shouting!" Sam Western suggested.

The call went up in every direction. They cupped gloved hands to their mouths and shouted for the vet. But the snow deadened their cries, and there was no reply.

Dennis Saville shook his head. He turned to Dean. "Which way now?"

"It all looks different. I couldn't say."

"And how long has he been out in this now?" Dora Janeki asked. She looked grim, as if she knew there was a limit to what a person lost in the snow could stand.

"About an hour and a half," Jack Spiller said.

Mandy scoured the snowy slopes for signs of her father — footsteps, a half-covered trail. But the snow drifted as it landed, and wiped away all tracks. She felt a hopelessness settle on them. "Dad!" she called out. The hillside threw back a dead, muffled silence. She looked desperately at James.

"Well, this is no good. I suggest we go back to the house," Sam Western decided. "We've gone wrong somehow. It's no one's fault. Conditions up here are terrible. We'd better get on the phone to the rescue service and get them up here as fast as we can."

He turned and led them down the hill, using his mobile phone to call for paramedics and the police. They had to guess their way back to Jack Spiller's place, arriving weary and downhearted as Mrs. Spiller threw open the door to greet them.

"We can't find him!" Mandy ran the last few yards and dashed into the kitchen. "Is Mom here yet?"

"No. No one's gotten through so far." Mrs. Spiller had hot tea waiting.

Jack told his wife that the police were sending a rescue vehicle from Walton. The police realized it was an emergency — a man missing on the hill in this weather. They would pull out all the stops.

But the waiting was dreadful for Mandy. She stood with James out on the porch, straining to hear the sound of a car engine, longing for her mom to arrive. She looked for headlights in the snow, imagining them and then feeling her hopes die. At last she caught a sound and struggled out into the snow, across the yard to the gate. Sure enough, her grandfather's camper came crawling up the hill, skidding sideways, its back wheels sliding and kicking up snow.

Mandy ran down the hill. Her mom jumped out of the van, dressed in a heavy blue jacket and boots. Grandpa braked into the side of the road and turned off the lights. He ran to join them.

"Oh, Mom, hurry!" Mandy cried. "We can't find him. The snow's too bad. He's lost!"

Emily Hope nodded. "Okay, keep calm. Which way?" She turned to her father-in-law. "Let's take another look."

"This way! We went up with the first search party, but we all got lost." She waded into a drift, toward the two stone walls that showed the line of the tractor track. They were still just visible under the snow. She wondered how her mom could stay so calm.

They all set their faces against a head wind and struggled on. "Here!" James came to the end of the tractor track. "This is where we found the first sheep, remember!" This time he felt they were on the right track. "And Dr. Adam headed up that way to the second sheep!"

Mandy nodded. She felt a flicker of hope. But as they sank waist-deep into more drifts, she grew desperate again. She heard Grandpa begin to shout out his son's name. Snow whirled down without end. Still they pressed on.

Then Mandy stopped. She thought she heard a low whine. She told herself that it was impossible, but she peered through the storm. "Wait a minute, Grandpa! Did you hear that?"

There was another whine, coming nearer, and a bark.

"Tess!" Mandy would have recognized the sound anywhere. "Here, girl!" They stood fixed to the spot, waiting for her to appear.

A shape scrambled down the hill. It was Tess. Her dark coat was matted with frozen snow, but her brown eyes were alert, her tail carried high. She bounded toward Mandy, who fell to the ground to hug her.

Grandpa, James, and Emily Hope came crowding around. "Good girl!" James told her. "At least we can take you back with us this time!" He told Dr. Emily the story of who had really attacked the sheep.

"Hold on a minute; it looks like she wants us to follow, not the other way around!" Grandpa pulled Mandy to her feet and stood looking at Tess. The dog barked and ran up the hill a little way. Then she came back and barked again. She looked up at Mandy, darted away, and came back.

"She does!" Mandy could see she wanted to show them something.

Right away they set off after Tess, treading deep into new snow, only waiting when Tess stopped to listen, ears pricked up. Then she dashed forward again, impatient for them to follow.

"Is she up to what I think she's up to?" Grandpa asked. "Is she trying to show us where Adam is?"

Mandy looked at her mom and grandfather and nodded. "I'm sure that's what she's doing!" She plowed ahead, with James at her side.

"What do you think?" Mandy's grandfather asked Emily Hope.

"I think we should trust her."

Mandy heard them hurry to catch up. "Go on, Tess! Show us the way. Good girl!" Still the dog struggled shoulder-deep through the snow, looking, listening. She answered a signal with a sharp bark and a swift change of direction.

"What was that? I didn't hear anything!" James said.

"No, but Tess did. Come on!" Mandy would have trusted her to the ends of the earth.

At last, after what seemed like forever, Tess came to a steep dip. It ran twenty yards to a row of beech trees beside a frozen stream. Tess waited for them, then bounded down the slope.

"Listen!" Mandy said. "I heard a whistle!"

James nodded. They ran after Tess, half-tumbling, skidding and sliding down the hill. "Where, Tess? Where is he? Show us, girl!"

Snow had drifted against the trees in white mounds that came shoulder-high. Tess was light, able to leap from mound to mound. The whistle grew louder.

"Dad!" Mandy called. She strained to see through the snowflakes. "Dad, where are you?"

There was a faint sound. "Here!"

Mandy shouted back. "Oh, Dad, thank heavens!" She turned to her mom and grandfather. "He's alive!" They came running down the hill. "Hang on, Dad! Tess is trying to find you. Whistle again!" She watched as Tess began to scrape with her front paws at the side of the farthest drift.

"Here!" Mandy heard her dad's muffled voice again. She and James scrambled to the far side of the drift and dropped onto their knees. They saw a deep tunnel scooped into the snow. Mandy leaned inside. She found the huddled shape of their father waiting patiently for rescue.

Tess bounded up the slope and barked out their success. The others came running. Emily Hope fell to the ground and wriggled into the snow hole to check Adam's condition. There were tears in her eyes as she crawled back out. "Let's lift him out," she said. "I think he's going to be all right, but we'll have to go carefully."

Gently they lifted Mandy's father out of the shelter he'd dug into the snow. He was stiff and numb. Snow had frozen into his beard, he couldn't feel his feet, and his legs could scarcely stand.

"Don't forget the sheep," he told them. "Try and pull her out as well."

Grandpa and James dug deep into the tunnel. They scraped the snow out until they found the animal. She was still alive.

"We'll have to carry her down to Jack's place," Adam Hope insisted. He staggered and tried to stand.

"*You* won't be carrying anyone," Emily Hope told him. She watched as Mandy helped to steady him and slung his arm around her shoulder. "You'll have enough trouble carrying yourself down. Here, let me help."

Mandy looked up at her dad, tears in her eyes. "Can you walk?" she whispered.

He nodded and found his balance.

"We'll bring the sheep," James said. He and Mandy's grandfather began to work out how they should carry her. Emily Hope took her husband's hand and began to lead him up the slope.

Mandy stayed behind for a moment with Tess, by the snow hole that had stopped her father from freezing to death. "You saved his life," she whispered in the dog's soft ear. She tried to wipe the snow from Tess's back. "You're a wonderful dog, and now everyone knows it!" She spoke gently. "There's no danger now, Tess. You can come back with us." She got to her feet and walked a couple of paces up the hill. "Come on, girl!"

But Tess had completed her task. She'd saved Adam Hope's life. Now she turned away from Mandy and began to tread lightly up the opposite slope.

"Tess, here, girl!"

The dog didn't falter. She walked on, up the hill toward High Cross, without looking back.

Mandy watched her go. How could Tess know that it was safe to come back? She wished she could make her understand. She wished dogs knew human words. She longed to take her home.

But Mandy watched in silence as Tess reached the top of the ridge. The clouds lifted now; the snow began to clear. Mandy could follow Tess's lonely shape along the white horizon. She didn't call again.

With a sad heart she turned to follow her father, her mother, Grandpa, and James. The dog who'd saved many lives was a stray again. She was homeless on Christmas Eve, wandering the snowy hills.

Twelve

"Tess certainly saved us a hard job!" the paramedic told Mandy. They'd arrived just in time to see Adam Hope being brought off the hillside by members of his own family. All the rescue team needed to do was to check that he wouldn't suffer any long-term effects from his afternoon in the snow. "That dog of yours must be some kind of heroine!"

Mandy had told him all about Tess, how her sharp hearing had picked up Dr. Adam's whistle, how she'd come to find them and show them the way. She stood by as the rescue team led her dad into the ambulance and insisted on seeing him safely home.

Sam Western and his group of rescuers stood at the Spillers' gate, watching them go. All had ended well. Both sheep would recover, thanks to Adam Hope. And Mr. Western had taken the blame squarely on his own shoulders.

Dora Janeki came forward to tell Mandy how she felt: "I'd take Tess back right now if I could." They watched Emily Hope climb up into the ambulance and the doors close. "We'd have to go a long way to find another dog like that!"

Mandy nodded. But she said nothing. The truth had come out too late to save Tess.

"I really am sorry." Dora patted Mandy's shoulder and walked away.

"Come on, you two!" Grandpa came and told James and Mandy to jump into the camper. "Let's follow the ambulance. We can go and tell your grandmother that everyone's safe."

So they left the hillside, still deep in snow. The storm had died as quickly as it had come, and the skies were clear. The afternoon was ending in pale sunlight that sparkled along the hilltop.

They went home to Welford. Mrs. Hunter met James in the village and took him back to their house. Grandma stood waiting anxiously outside the village hall. She watched the ambulance drive past with Adam and Emily safe inside. Grandpa stopped the van for her to climb in. "Don't worry, everyone's fine!" he told her.

Grandma took a deep breath. "Of course everyone's fine!" she said. "I warned you not to make a fuss. Adam knows what he's doing." She turned to smile at Mandy. "We Hopes are a tough lot!"

Mandy was secretly glad that Grandma hadn't been out in that blizzard. No matter how tough the Hopes were, she knew her dad wouldn't have survived much longer.

"And . . ." Grandma announced proudly as they followed the ambulance up the driveway to Animal Ark ". . . everything's ready for the party! We went ahead and brought the food over to the hall. It's all set out, ready and waiting!"

"Grandma, are you sure?" Mandy slid open the side door and jumped down into a foot and a half of crunchy snow. "I thought we might have to cancel it after all this!"

Grandma stepped down and stood, hands on hips. "Cancel! Just because of a little snowstorm?" She made it sound like a ridiculous idea. "Whoever heard of a drop of snow stopping us from enjoying ourselves at Christmas?"

Slowly Mandy's face broke into a smile. She went up and hugged her grandmother, letting a quiet tear fall for Tess, who wouldn't be there to join in the fun.

"There, that's better," Grandma said gently. "Now dry your eyes and get yourself into the party spirit. In spite of everything, I have a feeling that this is going to be the best Christmas Eve you can ever remember!"

The snowplows drove out from Walton to clear the main roads. Farmers brought out their tractors and cleared a way through from the high farms down to the village. Snow lay heaped against the walls in white banks that dwarfed the cars as they came down to the village for the candlelit gathering at the Fox and Goose.

Mandy arrived just before half past seven. Mrs. Ponsonby was already there with Pandora and Toby. Pandora was decked out in a Christmas ribbon tied around her neck in an enormous bow. John Hardy came out with Button and Barney warmly snuggled inside a spare cat carrier. He wore a pirate's hat and an eye patch, to the amusement of little Claire McKay, who had just turned up with James's Blackie. She wore a cardboard crown covered in gold foil, with rubies and diamonds made of shiny hard candies stuck on around the rim. Everyone laughed and chattered. Grandma arrived with a tray of candles stuck into oranges, decorated with spices, candies, and red ribbon. She began to light them and hand them around. The party was about to begin.

Mandy took a peek insider her jacket at Mopsy, the favorite of her three pet rabbits, curled up safe and warm inside a specially made sling. Her ears twitched. Her sleepy eyes blinked back at Mandy.

"Hi, Brandon!" Claire and Blackie ran to meet the latest arrivals. Mrs. Gill had dropped Brandon and Ruby the pig in the pub parking lot. Ruby was wearing the party hat, a battered straw number decorated with plastic sunflowers. Brandon picked her up as she made a beeline for Pandora's shiny bow. "Behave yourself," he warned, red with embarrassment.

Mandy knew that Grandpa had driven the van up onto the hill again to fetch Lydia and Houdini. He brought them now, with young Jenny Spiller and her sheep. The door opened and they tumbled out into the snowy yard, noisy and excited. Houdini kicked up his heels, ready to make a break. "Steady, boy!" Lydia warned. She held him back. "I guess he's looking for something to eat," she explained.

Soon Walter Pickard came out of the pub with old Tom, his chewed ear ragged but nicely healed. Ernie Bell followed with Sammy, proudly producing his cap from his pocket and pinning a sprig of mistletoe to the side. He put it on his gray, stubbly head. "You never know your luck!" he grinned. He and Lydia got ready to join the procession together.

"Where's James?" Mandy looked around the glowing group. She took a candle from her grandma. "He should be here by now."

Grandma looked mysterious. "I expect Eric is acting up. Maybe James has had to stop and look for him."

"Oh, but hadn't we better wait for them?" Mandy didn't want to start without James.

"We could go ahead," Grandma said. "I'm sure he wouldn't mind!"

Mandy frowned. It wasn't like James to be late for something so important.

Next Andi Greenaway turned up from Manor Farm. She led Dorian along the main street. The old donkey stepped sturdily through the snow, his large, flat feet plodding softly, his nose poking over all the garden gates as he came along. Andi was dressed in an old striped blanket, with a dish towel tied around her head, carrying a shepherd's crook in her hand. "I'm a Christmas shepherd," she told Brandon and John. "Anyone can see that!"

But the star was Susan Collins with Prince. She arrived five minutes later, riding tall in a red sombrero. Her wide brim was laden with fake oranges, bananas, pineapples, and grapes. Prince wore one to match, with holes cut in the crown for his ears, the brim tilted at a jaunty angle. Susan wore a Spanish guitar slung across her shoulder, and a silvery shirt covered in frills and ruffles.

"Oh, my!" Mrs. Ponsonby cried, as Pandora ran yapping toward the late arrivals.

Dorian and Ruby wandered across to investigate the fruit. The little pig snorted and snuffled. Dorian backed off, disappointed to find that the pineapples were plastic. Susan laughed. "Sorry I'm late!" she called.

"Ready?" Mrs. Ponsonby scooped Pandora into her arms and called Toby to her. She formed them into a procession and struck up the first carol.

> *Good King Wenceslas looked out*
> *On the Feast of Stephen . . .*

She stood at the head of the line, hitting a lively rhythm. Soon the others joined in.

"Don't worry about James," Grandma winked at Mandy. "He'll soon catch up!"

The procession was on the move. Mandy stood holding her candle, waiting until the last minute. She gazed down the road for any sign of her best friend.

"Come on, Mandy!" Mrs. Ponsonby urged from up front.

So Mandy joined them, breaking into song.

> *. . . Brightly shone the moon that night,*
> *Though the frost was cruel,*
> *When a poor man came in sight,*
> *Gathering winter fu-u-el!*

It was a lovely sight, the long, candlelit procession trailing down the snow-covered street. The sound of music rang out; the stars shone down from a clear sky. People came to their doors to smile and join in the Christmas spirit. The guests slowly made their way, pets and owners, all shapes and sizes, ages, colors; all part of the magical event.

Mrs. Ponsonby drew them to a halt outside the porch of the village hall. Everyone stood around in a semicircle to finish their song.

"Come on, Mandy," Grandma whispered, taking her by the arm and leading her forward.

"What's going on?" Mandy found herself surrounded by smiling faces lit by soft yellow candlelight. She was gently drawn to the front. Sammy the squirrel darted onto her shoulder and ran chattering up and down

her arm. Then he sat perched, his tail brushing her cheek.

"Go ahead." Mrs. Ponsonby stepped aside with a gracious gesture. "This is *your* party, Mandy. Without you, none of this would have happened!"

Many took a deep, deep breath. She delved inside her jacket to take Mopsy out of the sling she'd made to cradle him. Sammy still sat jauntily on her shoulder. She handed her candle to Ernie and kicked the snow off her boots. Then she stepped onto the porch and opened the door.

Inside the brilliantly lit hall, her mom and dad stood waiting to greet her. Mom's red hair was swept onto the top of her head. She wore her best blue party dress and smiled happily. Dad, showered and spruced up, and none the worse for his ordeal, stood with his arm around his wife's waist.

Beyond them, all Mandy could see through her happy tears was a riot of colored balloons, streamers, holly, Christmas lights, and the tall green tree. She smelled spicy fruit punch, heard festive music drifting from the loudspeakers. The lights seemed to float and swim. The whole room was alive.

Then she saw James walking toward her, carrying Eric. She felt the other guests jostle her forward. She heard Grandma whisper in her ear. "Look, Mandy. Look who James has brought!"

James grinned as he gave a command. "Sit, girl! Tess, sit!"

Mandy stared down at his feet.

Tess sat looking back at her with her liquid brown eyes. Someone had brushed her coat to a smooth, glossy shine. Her white chest and the white stripe down her muzzle gleamed. At the sight of Mandy, her tail swept the floor, back and forth.

"Tess!" Mandy felt Sammy jump from her shoulder in surprise. She handed Mopsy to her grandmother. Then she went forward to touch the dog, to make it real, so that she wouldn't wake up and find this all a dream. She ran her hand down Tess's neck and patted her shoulder. "Is it really you?" she breathed.

Tess growled softly. Then Ruby came in and broke them apart with her little hard hooves and soft snout. She buffeted Tess out of the way, heading straight for the nearest food.

"Where . . . ? How . . . ? When?" The questions tumbled out as the party began.

James explained everything. He'd persuaded his mother to take him back up to High Cross before it got dark. Ken Hudson had spotted him and agreed to help find Tess. They knew which way she'd headed after the rescue. They had found Tess's trail by the Celtic cross and began to call her name. Lydia came out of her house and said she'd seen a dog in the woods at the back of the farm. James and Ken ran to find her curled up in an exhausted sleep in the shelter of a tumbledown wall. Ken had put her on a leash and they took her back to Dora's, who soon set her right with food and good care. Ken had brought Tess down to the village in time for James to bring her to the party in secret.

"I wanted it to be a surprise for you!" he said.

"It was!" Mandy felt her heart swell. "It's perfect! It's everything I ever wished! Thank you, James. Oh, thank you!"

"So Tess is the guest of honor?" Grandpa stepped carefully between cats and dogs to come and speak to them. "I'm glad everything's worked out fine."

Mandy smiled. She sat with Tess at her feet as Mrs. Ponsonby organized the competition. She awarded the party-hat prize to Prince and Susan just before Houdini snatched a bite at the pony's felt sombrero. Then Simon played more music, the pets got their party food, and the people were fed, too. Grandma brought hot mince pies from the small kitchen, and Pandora disgraced herself over the pigs in blankets.

All in all, the party was a great success. Everyone agreed that the pets behaved perfectly — even Mrs. Ponsonby said so!

"Of course!" Mandy said to James. She still sat with one arm around Tess's neck.

He smiled at her. She smiled back. They'd made it. Everyone was safe, Tess had a home, the pets were at their party. "Merry Christmas, James!" she said. "A very, very merry Christmas!"